TheirStory

The Beginning

ISBN 0984702466

EAN-13 9780984702466

LCCN 2013937278

TheirStory
The Beginning

a novel by

Paulette Jones

Editor

Paula Tromp

Your Time Publishing, LLC P.O. Box 872365 New Orleans Louisiana, 70187

ALSO WRITTEN BY PAULETTE JONES

Fiction

HerStory; Revelations

Hidden Emotions; Family Ties, Family Lies

Nonfiction

Katrina; One Set of Footprints

Children Books

Girls' Day Out; The Adventure

ABC On the Streets Of New Orleans

Her First Sleepover

Collaborations

The Brass Band Gig

Paulette Jones

TheirStory
The Beginning

Your Time Publishing, LLC P.O. Box 872365 New Orleans Louisiana, 70187

TheirStory

A special thanks to my friends and family for their constant support.

TheirStory

ONE

Viola hailed from a remarkable lineage of strong women, and it's no wonder they embodied resilience through unimaginable challenges. The harsh realities of life may have been daunting, yet their unwavering spirit shone brightly amidst the darkness. The stories of their endurance carry a powerful energy that can inspire anyone who hears them. Rather than robbing people of their humanity, such experiences often cultivate a profound strength and compassion within them.

When Paul arrived at the plantation, Viola had already welcomed her eldest child, Isza, into the world. The moment she gracefully walked past him; her confidence was captivating; he found it impossible to look away as she made her way around the corner of the big house. Even as her figure disappeared from sight, he felt an exhilarating urge to rush after her, yearning to confirm that this radiant vision was indeed real. In that enchanting moment, his heartbeat echoed the rhythm of the drums that filled the air during planned escapes. Lost in the magic of her presence, the harsh realities of bondage faded away, and an undeniable sense of goodness enveloped him.

Just days earlier, Paul had been wrestling with thoughts of fleeing, acutely aware that the journey to freedom was fraught with danger and despair. Separated from everything he knew, he had even contemplated that perhaps death seemed a gentler fate. But in that fleeting moment of joy, with Viola in his line of sight, a bright spark of hope ignited within him. Her presence reminded him that life, even against the odds, can still offer glimpses of beauty and possibility.

All day, Paul couldn't help but smile as he thought about the woman who had gracefully strolled by him. She was everything he admired, radiant chocolate skin, an enchanting curvy silhouette, long legs, and a determined yet warm expression. Paul firmly believed that the eyes are the windows to the soul, revealing a person's true compassion. After three exciting weeks, he finally had the chance to look into her captivating hazel eyes. Just as he had hoped, her gaze reflected her genuine and kind-hearted nature. In that moment, Paul felt a spark of confidence that she might be the one for him. He envisioned a beautiful future together, filled with love and the promise of jumping the broom someday. Excitement filled him as he considered what wonderful adventures awaited them both.

Viola had a unique way of expressing her feelings towards Paul, sometimes appearing to blame him for the hardships around them. Yet, Paul had a keen sense for what lay beneath her tough demeanor. He caught glimpses of admiration in her eyes, especially when she thought no one was watching. This motivated him to show her that he was genuinely kind and that they could make a wonderful pair.

He discovered that a charming smile alone wouldn't win her heart. Viola believed that a slave's smile shouldn't shine when in the presence of white folks, and his cheerful demeanor sometimes made her feel frustrated, like she wanted to shake him awake to the realities they faced. Paul would share his feelings with anyone who would listen, hoping to rally support for his quest to see Viola open up to him.

It became clear to Paul that Viola preferred sincerity over smiles. She seemed to appreciate a more somber expression, one that resonated with the weight of their circumstances. This realization was a bit disheartening for Paul, who had often relied on his charm, but it also sparked a new level of respect for Viola's spirit. He admired her resilience, realizing it was rare for a woman in her position to maintain such strength and defiance.

Instead of feeling disheartened, Paul decided to focus on being a true friend to Viola. He was committed to understanding her better and supporting her in any way he could. By embracing her spirit and acknowledging their shared struggles, he believed he could gradually convince her of the deep connection they could share. Together, they could navigate their circumstances with hope and strength, creating something beautiful from their bond.

When Viola heard Paul confidently share that one day she would be his wife, a wave of emotion surged within her, and she felt an overwhelming urge to walk over and passionately confront him. Instead, she mustered the toughest glare she could manage. As she passed by, Paul couldn't help but chuckle at her fierce determination to assert herself. However, in that moment when their eyes met, he caught a glimpse of the incredible woman inside her, yearning to break free. He truly believed that the beautiful spirit within her would eventually shine through.

Paul understood that giving up was not an option; they needed each other. With this realization, he decided to take a more thoughtful approach. He began surprising Viola with delightful treats from the farm, fresh vegetables, eggs from the hens, and creamy milk. As the way Viola perceived him began to shift and soften, he noted that she still held back the warmth he longed for, but he felt a hopeful change in the air.

Then, he learned about Sitter, who crafted cherished dolls for the white children on the plantation. With Christmas approaching, Paul envisioned a lovely gift; a doll made especially for Isza. He was convinced that this heartfelt gesture would surely touch Viola's heart. It dawned on him, though, that asking Sitter for such a favor was a big deal, given the prevailing attitudes of the time. It was believed that a talented person like her shouldn't waste her skills on toys for a Negro child. Yet, Paul wanted to challenge that narrative and create something special for Isza.

The only doll a Negro child might possess was a simple makeshift toy crafted from a sack filled with cotton, with a rope forming its head, the rest left to imagination. Paul envisioned a beautifully crafted Negro doll that could inspire joy and hope. When he approached Sitter about making a doll for Isza, he learned she hadn't even made one for her own daughter out of concern for potential repercussions. Paul felt hopeful she would recognize the significance of his request and its potential to win Viola's affection.

While he understood the weight of this request and the risks it posed for Sitter and her family, he was inspired by the idea of creating something extraordinary. It showed how small acts of kindness could challenge perceptions and pave the way for a brighter future. With determination and hope in his heart, Paul set forth on this mission, believing that together they could make a difference.

Everyone would fondly remember the inspiring story of George, a talented craftsman who created beautiful toys for his master's children. When he welcomed the birth of his only son among thirteen daughters, he poured his heart into crafting a remarkable little wagon, a true replica of the master's own. Unfortunately, the overseer learned of this cherished creation, and rumors circulated that George's children were taken away because he valued his son so dearly. This tragic turn of events led to heartache for George, resulting in the loss of his beloved wife. Yet, even amidst this sorrow, George demonstrated unyielding love for his son.

Amidst the laughter and play of the overseer's children with that exquisite wagon, George felt deep pain but also a flicker of hope. One day, overwhelmed by the weight of his heartache, George made a bold decision. He approached the wagon, a symbol of his struggles, and in a moment of cathartic release, he smashed it against the barn. This act, while born from despair, ignited a spark within him; George chose to pursue freedom. Though he was never seen again, the community cherished the hope that he journeyed towards a brighter future.

Inspired by this very spirit, Sitter embarked on an adventure of her own by creating the very first Negro doll. Excitement mingled with nervousness in her heart, but she knew that this was her true calling. With the support of her community rallying behind Paul to win over Viola, Sitter's life transformed after crafting that first beautiful doll. In a clever and imaginative turn, she inspired little white girls by introducing the idea of their dolls having their own slave doll, this resonated with families across the South and beyond.

This marked the dawn of Sitter's remarkable legacy. Through her innovative spirit, she ultimately garnered the resources to liberate herself and her family, all sparked by Paul simple desire to impress Viola. Those dolls found their way into general stores far and wide, creating connections that spanned generations and empowered countless lives. Sitter's journey became a powerful testament to the resilience and creativity found in the pursuit of dreams.

When Paul handed the adorable little Negro doll to Isza, she immediately named it Angel and hugged it tightly, gently rocking it back and forth just like she had seen other mothers do with their children. Isza was captivated by the doll's beautiful brown skin, sparkling eyes, lovely painted white teeth, and the elegant white gown paired with a matching bonnet. A tear of happiness rolled down Viola's cheek as she watched Isza's joy, never having witnessed such pure delight before in her child.

In this moment, Paul noticed something remarkable; Viola looked directly at him and, he caught a glimpse of her smile. It was a moment that held so much promise, a tiny window into the future they all wished for.

As their conversation unfolded, Viola opened up about the challenges they faced. She belonged to the Master's oldest son, Tommy, and she explained how precarious their situation was. If Tommy suspected anything between them, the consequences could be dire, Isza could be sold away, or even worse. While Viola's feelings for Paul were strong, she understood that, for his own safety, he would need to move on and forget their connection.

However, after months of grappling with her emotions, Viola decided to embrace the possibility of a relationship with Paul. They became imaginative in their efforts to find secret moments together, and the community rallied around them, helping to keep their bond discreet. Paul, whose work as a blacksmith often took him out at night, found it easy to sneak away during the day, he had the relatively simple tasks of cleaning the barn and caring for the horses. Meanwhile, Viola would cherish her time with Isza, often seen strolling the grounds with her little one. Because no one paid them much mind, they recognized this as an ideal opportunity to connect.

Sometimes, they cleverly used a decoy who resembled Viola from a distance, walking alongside Isza so that no one would notice. They coordinated lookouts who kept watch for approaching threats, ready with a signal whenever someone was nearby. At a cue, the decoy would move to a designated spot where Viola was waiting for the exchange. Though this secretive strategy was no small feat, they persevered and enjoyed their moments together for quite some time.

Each encounter deepened their bond and hope for the future, reminding them that love, even in the most difficult circumstances, can flourish with creativity and support. The road ahead was challenging, but their commitment to each other was unwavering, and they faced it together with courage and optimism.

When Tommy tragically lost his life in a hunting accident, Viola discovered a surprising sense of liberation from the constraints of her previous life. Although his family struggled in their grief and distanced themselves from her, as if to place blame, Viola embraced a new chapter. She joined her fellow workers in the fields, where she experienced the unfamiliar task of picking cotton for the first time. With her hands not yet accustomed to the tough labor, she often bled, with a few wounds reaching deep, but she remained undeterred. The joy of cotton picking filled her heart; she felt a profound sense of freedom shared with her fellow laborers, taking pride in their collective resilience.

When Isza was four, Viola and Paul joyfully celebrated their union by jumping the broom, honoring a beloved tradition within their community. Over the next seven years, their family flourished as they welcomed seven beautiful daughters; May, Hilda, Teacee, Viola, Picola, Clara, and Baby. Each daughter was a radiant star, bringing love and laughter into their lives.

Raising daughters in their circumstances brought unique challenges, as they were often seen as potential slave makers. Understanding this, Paul cherished every moment with his daughters, although he knew their time together might be limited. His greatest hope was that slavery would come to an end, allowing them the freedom they so deserved.

Every night, Viola voiced her prayers for her daughters, wishing to shield them from the heart-wrenching realities that could tear families apart. In the dark of night, young girls could be taken away, leaving parents in despair; after all, enslaved individuals had no ownership of their children or their belongings. To protect her daughters, she nestled close to them in sleep, ensuring that they remained connected, ready to feel any change in their security.

As time went on, tensions arose between Isza and Viola, particularly when May turned six. Isza watched her mother take May to the Master's house in the evenings, only to be left wondering when she would return. She was told that May was keeping the Master's daughter, Sally, company, and when Isza expressed her desire to join, Viola's sharp glance held an unmistakable message; this was not a conversation to continue. Understanding the unspoken boundaries, Isza began to seek out truths elsewhere.

After months of witnessing unusual events, Isza felt a spark of curiosity and decided it was time to uncover the truth for herself. Whispers among the plantation workers about something called "The Gift" piqued her interest, and one night, she quietly slipped out of the house to follow the hushed conversations. As she observed May entering the

Master's bedroom, a sense of urgency washed over her, and she began to see that her mother's reassurances about May being a companion for Sally were not quite accurate.

Determined to understand the situation, Isza approached Viola to discuss what she had witnessed and to seek the truth. In a surprising twist of emotions, Viola, unable to process the discussion, reacted in anger and struck Isza across the face. It was an unexpected moment that left them both in stunned silence; it was a first for Isza to experience such an outburst from her mother. As tears filled her eyes, Viola emphasized that their family's matters were private. Isza began to grasp the profound challenges and fears families faced when it came to their children and their futures.

Refusing to remain in the dark, Isza resolved to confront May about her experiences in the big house. May generously opened up, sharing that she slept on the floor of the master's room, ready to assist the master or mistress with anything they might need during the night. As Isza learned more about May's situation, she realized that May was being prepared for a role referred to as "The Gift." While many viewed this position as the most challenging, Isza understood that in many circumstances, remaining with family was a blessing compared to the heart-wrenching possibility of being sold away.

Years later, the opportunity finally arose for Isza and Viola to share a heartfelt conversation about, The Gift. Viola's story was one of resilience; at just six years old, she had also faced the training to become The Gift, a fate that culminated in her being presented to the Master's son, Tommy, on his thirteenth birthday. The lack of control over one's children's futures weighed heavily on her heart, but Viola found solace in the idea that staying on the same plantation meant a chance, however slim, to remain with family. Her own experience, at the tender age of six, had led to the devastating separation from her parents.

TheirStory

TWO

aul and Viola were incredibly devoted to protecting their daughters from the harsh realities surrounding them. They raised their girls with a dream of freedom on the horizon, fully aware that, in their world, they were considered the property of their owners, always at risk of being separated. The pressure to conform to the expectations of their circumstances was immense, and even the youngest children faced challenges simply due to their natural curiosity. Unfortunately, some believed that the ways of slavery came instinctively to those born into it. Parents had the difficult task of teaching their children to navigate this rigid society, and they often had to start imparting these lessons very early on.

Despite the intense pressures they faced, Paul and Viola instilled a spirit of resilience in their daughters. By the time children reached the age of three or four, many began to understand the subtle dynamics of their environment. Compliance could sometimes lead to small rewards, as the

Master preferred to see cheerful faces surrounding him. Children quickly learned to adopt bright smiles, knowing that, when skilled at this performance, they might be treated to a piece of candy or another small delight.

This challenging situation encouraged many to create a second persona geared toward their owners, forming a unique bond among the slaves as they navigated their daily lives. Paul's childhood experiences equipped him to sense and understand the difficulties faced by his peers. His parents taught him how to express himself in front of those with power, fostering a sense of awareness of their expectations.

In a world where resilience and composure were crucial, young males learned that displaying strength or confidence could evoke fear among their owners. This instinct pushed them to temper their natural spirit. The expectations were clear; the owners preferred to see submissive body language and joyful smiles, creating a façade that masked their true feelings. By the time young people reached their teenage years, they had often mastered this delicate balance of behavior, understanding that adapting to their environment was essential for survival.

Yet, amidst these trials, there was an unwavering hope. At home, every smile, every act of resilience, and every spark of resistance in Paul and Viola's daughters was a step toward something greater. Their spirits shone brightly, and they embodied the possibility of a brighter future, showing that, even in the toughest circumstances, they could dream and strive for freedom and dignity.

Paul and Viola were dedicated to raising their daughters with an understanding of their environment, believing that by learning to navigate their world thoughtfully, the girls could keep their family close and safe. They emphasized the importance of moving gracefully and together, teaching them to walk in single file when in the presence of others. When meeting white individuals, they encouraged the girls to wear warm smiles and to speak only when addressed, responding slowly and respectfully. At home, they creatively practiced these social skills, playfully allowing one of the children to take on the role of a white adult, fostering both awareness and resilience.

The cotton fields presented a significant challenge, as picking cotton required both skill and endurance. Initially, the girls instinctively tried to grasp the cotton bolls with their whole hands, but through guidance, they learned the art of using just three fingers. With practice, they discovered that the right technique allowed them to easily and efficiently collect the cotton, making the task less daunting and more manageable.

They worked hard in the fields, dreaming of the exciting outings when their father would choose one of them to accompany him to town to gather supplies for the master. For the girls, one of the most thrilling moments was when their father selected one of them for this special trip.

Sundays were especially vibrant in their household, with neighbors from the plantation gathering for a hearty meal made possible by Paul's extra provisions from the master. While many in their community lacked access to meat, Paul and Viola delighted in sharing generous portions of ham, roast, or game with their friends and family. Their home became a joyful hub of connection, where stories were shared about life on the plantation, who had left and who had arrived.

Visitors from the North shared inspiring tales of change, expressing how more enslaved individuals were finding their freedom or acquiring the means to do so. This news sparked hope in Viola and Paul, igniting their dreams of a brighter future where their family might one day experience the joys of freedom together. With each conversation, they nurtured a spirit of optimism and determination, believing wholeheartedly in a time when they could truly be free.

As the end of slavery drew nearer, hope filled the air, even though the exact moment remained uncertain. Paul and Viola were deeply committed to ensuring that their daughters would be ready for the bright, new world ahead of them. They envisioned a future where their children could thrive, thinking independently and embracing the changes that would come. While Paul and Viola felt a mix of apprehension about their own journey to freedom, they nurtured a vision of hope and anticipation for their girls.

They instilled in their daughters the understanding that slavery was merely a circumstance and not who they truly were. With unwavering belief, they taught the girls that a brighter future awaited them. As time passed, Paul and Viola recognized the importance of preparing their children for any situation, whether that meant embracing freedom or facing challenges with resilience. Above all, the girls needed to remember their heritage, the love and strength they carried as the daughters of Paul and Viola.

Paul emphasized the importance of living without fear, reassuring his daughters that even in separation, they were never alone; God would always be with them. He encouraged them to hold on to their lessons and to be the teachers of their own dreams, instilling hope for future generations to come.

In their home, no matter what challenges the day held, a spirit of learning and growth thrived, with each family member uplifted to reach their fullest potential. Paul believed deeply that they could achieve anything they set their hearts on.

Paul and Viola envisioned a brighter future for their children, where they could boldly step away from oppression and embrace their freedom. They wanted their children to feel empowered, knowing they were not trapped by the plantation that had been their home but were instead poised to embark on a transformative journey. While honoring their past, they aimed to equip their children with the essential lessons that would help them thrive in a new life. Yet, as time passed, Paul and Viola often found themselves wondering if the world would truly change for the better.

Despite the uncertainty, Isza, felt a special connection to her parents' message about freedom. She sensed that it was particularly meant for her, fostering a determination within her to be a catalyst for change. In her dreams, she sometimes found herself navigating a daring escape, with her father leading the family through the enchanting woods. With each twist and turn, he seemed to instinctively know every path and hidden spot, guiding them through the dark.

However, as their adventure unfolded in her dreams, ominous sounds of dogs barking in the distance. In those moments, Paul would encourage Viola to follow the route they had planned, taking a separate path to divert the dogs away. Yet, Viola's heart was steadfast in keeping the family together, believing in the strength of unity. Despite her father's persuasive arguments, her resolve was unwavering, illustrating the deep bond they shared. Although her dream was vivid and haunting, Isza found comfort in sharing them with her mother. Viola reassured her that she would have supported Paul's plan, reminding Isza, that even one escape could spark hope.

As whispers of change swirled around them, the atmosphere became charged with anticipation. The signs of a new dawn were evident, as the slave owners sensed the end of slavery was near. Although fear manifested in hostility and increased restrictions, the spirit of the enslaved individuals remained unyielding. They faced these challenges with resilience, their identities undiminished. While the owners may have attempted to choke out their humanity, the truth remained, humanity is a light that cannot be extinguished; it can only be illuminated.

In the hearts of the enslaved, a flicker of hope grew brighter with each passing day. As they stood on the cusp of freedom, their spirits soared with the possibility of a new beginning. United in their resolve, they were ready to grasp their destiny and step toward a world filled with promise, leaving behind the chains that once bound them. This hope became their driving force, and together, they looked toward a future where joy and liberation awaited.

Three

Isza began to seriously contemplate her dreams of freedom when troubling news circulated about the plantation owners having a list of slaves scheduled for sale, with whispers that her parents were among those listed. With an auction set to take place in town in the coming weeks, the urgency of her thoughts intensified. After discussing the idea of running away with her parents, it became increasingly clear that time was running out. People flocked to the plantation, eyes set on purchasing, and the woods offered little safety for a fleeing runaway. Meanwhile, the festive atmosphere on the farms painted a stark contrast to their reality, as guests reveled with food, drinks, music, and dancing throughout the night.

On the day of the auction, Isza was filled with relief when she learned that her parents had been spared. Although her sisters celebrated their parents' safety, Paul and Viola remained grounded in their knowledge that this was not the end. It was entirely possible for someone to be purchased before the official auction began, and once the new owner arrived to collect their acquisitions, the future could change in an instant. Despite the uncertainty looming over them, they decided to let their daughters enjoy this time together. In the days that followed, the girls delighted in the music that swirled around them, sharing songs that spoke of families, journeys, and destinations, each melody revealing the stories of those around the plantation.

Months passed after the auction, and one morning the girls awoke to an unsettling truth; their parents were gone. They were told that their mother and father had left in the night and would be back soon. However, if this were truly an escape, the girls would have faced harsh consequences. Isza sensed something deeper was happening when she heard the mournful refrains of the children's sorrowful song. Singing was their lifeline, a means to communicate vital news even when words failed. As days unfolded, the truth about their parents' departure surfaced, and Isza understood it was now her responsibility to care for her sisters and strive to keep their family united.

Ever since their birth, Paul and Viola had prepared their daughters for the harsh reality ahead, the threat of being sold. The unsettling truth was that the plantation owner only held onto slaves who could bear children, and after Viola had her final child, the midwife gently warned her and Paul that it would be her last. They both recognized it was only a matter of time before one or both of them would be sold. Following their parents' mysterious exit, there were fears that the girls might likewise be sold, yet, against all odds, they remained together on that Mississippi plantation, hopeful for the day when freedom would embrace them.

Isza, was resolute that their fates would not mirror their parents'.

Though their parents had met when Isza was just four years old, Paul had always been her father in her heart. She was often recognized as the Master's granddaughter, for she bore a striking resemblance to him, perhaps even more so than his own children. During childhood trips to town with her family, Isza noted the different ways people looked at her; she seemed to be perceived as part of the Master's family, a privilege that felt both empowering and disorienting. This sense of detachment from those who knew her allowed Isza the freedom to imagine a life unshackled by societal boundaries. It was from this realization that the spark of escape ignited, and now all that remained was uncovering a path to make those dreams a reality. Together with her sisters, Isza was determined to find their way to freedom and rewrite their own story.

The moment they had all been anticipating had arrived; the Master had decided to separate the sisters. As they approached breeding age, the potential for financial gain through sale loomed large. It was quite uncommon to have eight sisters living together on one plantation, much less under the same roof. Isza took it upon herself to prepare her sisters for the changes ahead, drawing on the wisdom their parents had shared about embracing individuality, an unshakeable part of who they were.

Isza was transitioned to the big house alongside May, allowing her to stay close to the Master's children, while May would be nearer to the Master's grandson, the one she was being groomed for. Despite the circumstances being less than ideal for May, Isza understood that her priority was now her sisters' wellbeing. With their parents gone, she embraced the responsibility wholeheartedly, determined to do whatever it took to protect her beloved siblings.

Recognizing the importance of community, Isza reached out to Momma Pearl, the wise elder, asking her to keep a watchful eye on the girls. Their visits became a cherished beacon of hope, though they grew fewer, often stretching into long days without a sight of one another. Then came the day when Momma Pearl informed Isza that Baby was unwell and in distress. The sorrow in her tone struck Isza to her core, igniting a feeling of urgency within her. She would take action.

Isza cleverly convinced the children that having Baby join them would be an incredible adventure, a charming companion for playtime. When Baby recovered, her laughter filled the air, capturing the essence of what freedom should represent for a child; joy and innocence. Yet, one day, Isza noticed a white man watching Baby with a disturbing gaze. Her instinct told her that something had to change.

For some time, Isza had been secretly plotting their escape, fully aware of the risks involved. The Master's informants were everywhere, and discretion was paramount. She hadn't even shared her plans with her sisters; they would be blissfully unaware of the intentions that would soon transform their lives in ways they couldn't yet imagine. Isza use to spend her days with Mathew, someone she cared for deeply, but she had to keep her distance from him. Revealing her plans could endanger him and jeopardize everything.

Leaving Mathew was a challenge that weighed heavily on her heart. From their first encounter, his gentle demeanor reminded her of her beloved father. There was an immediate connection, a spark that felt like love at first sight. Yet, in that time, practicality prevailed; she knew Mathew was not part of the future she envisioned.

Isza was resolute. She would protect her sisters and forge a new path for them, no matter the cost. Changes were on the horizon, and she would face them with courage and an unwavering spirit. This journey required strength and tenacity, but Isza believed in their freedom, an unyielding truth that would guide them toward a future. Together, they would navigate the twists and turns ahead, and she would not rest until they were safe. Hope shone bright in her heart, lighting the way forward.

To achieve her dream of freedom, Isza knew she had to navigate her surroundings with keen caution to avoid any unwanted attention to the plantation. She understood that even a mere whispered rumor about plans for an escape could lead to disaster. Memories flooded back of an incident from her childhood when a young boy innocently asked his mother about runaway slaves. An informant overheard that conversation and swiftly reported it to the Master, who imposed severe consequences not only on the boy but also on his entire family. That tragic event left a deep impression on everyone, creating a chilling atmosphere that deterred any thoughts of leaving the plantation. The Master took pride in maintaining this control, a façade of security and domination.

In a clever twist, Isza planted a rumor, expertly disguising its origin. She skillfully guided an informant to think he had stumbled upon the escape plan on his own. When he brought the news to the Master, he lacked any specifics, details on who was involved, when, where, or how. This caused panic to ripple through the slave quarters. In his haste to regain control, the Master hastily locked down the plantation, securing doors and windows, restricting movement unless for work. As a desperate measure to quash any potential escape, the Master sold off a group of men, including the informant's own family, believing this would dispel any threat. He reveled in the illusion that he had successfully curtailed all attempts at escape, never suspecting the cunning mind behind the unfolding events.

With tension eventually calming, Isza knew it was time to plant another seed of rumor. This time, silence surrounded the plantation, signaling the absence of informants. The Master had mistakenly thought that ridding them of the men would solve the problem, yet what remained hidden was Isza's skillful orchestration of the entire situation. One of the strengths the slaves possessed was their owners' underestimation of their intelligence, a perspective shaped by the early brutalities of slavery, which left many enslaved individuals struggling with language and cultural barriers. This misconception allowed for the crucial human connections necessary for survival and escape plans, as anything discussed within the confines of the big house eventually filtered down to the appropriate ears.

The path to escape was incredibly challenging without collaboration from other slaves, especially for those ensconced deep in the South.

Feeling empowered, Isza set her plan into motion, making stealthy visits to neighboring slave quarters to spark connections and enlist support. Initially, gaining trust was difficult; everyone was acutely aware of the dangers associated with aiding a runaway. To bridge that gap, Isza began bringing small gifts during her nighttime visits, slowly earning the trust of the local enslaved community. After introductions and a few engagements on nearby plantations, she connected with someone who not only believed in her mission but also had the resources to assist. She shared her vision, and excitement began to stir, setting the wheels of her plan in motion.

The second part of her plan loomed large, especially considering the critical need to be perceived as a white woman for her and her sisters' safety. During the annual town meeting, a gathering that drew people from various regions, Isza recognized the opportunity to test her ability to blend in seamlessly. That evening, she carefully borrowed clothing and toiletries from the Misses and made her way off the plantation. Spending hours wandering the town, she marveled at the newfound freedom of anonymity, as no one, not even her grandfather, recognized her at all.

With hope ignited and connections solidified, Isza began to understand that the steps she was taking weren't just for her own freedom; they were for something much larger. Together with those she connected with, the vision of a brighter future was beginning to take shape. Every day brought her closer to realizing a dream that was worth pursuing, one filled with courage, resilience, and the possibility of a life beyond the confines of the plantation.

When Isza overheard the Master talking about selling her beloved sister, Baby, to a cruel and notorious owner, a spark ignited within her, it was time to set her plan in motion. With only five days ahead, she felt a sense of urgency but also a flicker of hope. Day one would be devoted to creating a misleading trail, planting evidence that suggested they were headed north. On day two, she would take the opportunity to visit nearby plantations and scout out potential safe havens. Day three would be crucial for assessing their escape route to ensure it was clear. Then, on day four, she would gather information by listening closely to the locals, and finally, on the evening of day five, just as night fell, their bold journey would begin.

Under the shroud of darkness, they traveled along the northern trail all night long. As dawn began to break, they arrived at the nearest plantation in search of a brief rest. Isza crafted a story that she had just acquired them and was eager to return home. Having dealt with neighboring plantations before, she felt confident that her con might work, as long as they avoided anyone who might recognize them and kept their stay brief, after all, it was only a matter of time before the hounds were on their heels.

As night fell once more, Isza and her sisters returned to the road, their senses heightened by the atmosphere of impending danger. To lift their spirits, the children sang "Shoo Fly, Don't Bother Me," a small act of defiance that reassured them they were still free for the moment. But soon, the unmistakable sounds of barking dogs reached their ears. In the swampy terrain, Isza knew it would take time for the dogs and overseers to track them. At a critical turning point, her sister May, the second oldest, urged Isza and the others to press on with their plan. May, brave and selfless, decided to venture north, hoping to lead the dogs away from the rest of the family. "If I can throw them off my scent, perhaps I'll find refuge in the first Free State," she reasoned, her eyes alight with determination. She told Isza to come looking for her when freedom was finally theirs.

Though it pained Isza to separate, she remembered a foreboding dream that gnawed at her heart. She embraced May tightly and whispered promises of reunion, urging her to be safe. May set off toward the north while Isza and her sisters headed south toward Louisiana, with New Orleans as their goal. Isza had heard whispers about the city; tales of free Negro individuals and even some who owned property filled her with hope. Her idea was to secure a hiding place for her sisters and gradually present them as if she had purchased them.

That night, after May departed, Isza was haunted by a vivid dream. In it, the dogs swiftly picked up May's scent, and she was running through water when a gunshot echoed in the distance. Yet, in this sorrowful vision, May wore a smile, knowing her sacrifice might ensure her sisters' safety. Awakening in tears, Isza decided to shield her sisters from the weight of her fears, instead sharing a message of resilience, that they were free now. Who could have imagined that a group of determined sisters would orchestrate one of the most talked-about escapes in history? It was said that the Master could never truly recover from their escape, his relentless search continuing even after freedom was within reach.

After several days of travel, Isza and her sisters discovered a secluded cabin nestled in the woods that appeared abandoned. With cautious optimism, Isza entered to confirm its emptiness. For the first few days, their nerves ran high with uncertainty as they adapted to their new surroundings. One afternoon, while peering through a window, Isza thought she glimpsed someone outside and warned her sisters to stay quiet. Fear gripped the girls as they worried for Isza's safety, anxious that someone might discover them and drag them back to captivity.

When Isza finally opened the door to investigate, she was greeted by an older Negro woman standing a distance away. The woman's reassuring presence brought a wave of relief. "You have nothing to fear here; this place is safe," she said, her voice gentle. Just as mysteriously as she appeared, the woman melted away into the swamp.

Isza stood there momentarily bewildered, scanning the area for the woman, but she seemed to have vanished without a trace. Returning to the cabin, Isza shared her thoughts on how they could strategically make their way to New Orleans. Over the next few days, she felt a growing sense of security; the old woman's words rang true as they experienced no disturbances. Each morning, Isza ventured out to gather berries, pears, and peaches that grew abundantly around them. Occasionally, she returned with meat or fish, skillfully making the most of their new surroundings. Each day brought new hope, and with every stolen moment of peace, Isza knew they were one step closer to their dreams of freedom.

Isza was wholeheartedly committed to keeping the vibrant legacy of her parents alive by sharing the cherished stories she recalled from her childhood, moments spent nestled at their feet. These tales would provide a solid foundation for embracing their newfound freedom and navigating the world that lay ahead. She often gathered her sisters to discuss the profound meaning of freedom, the significant distinction between being a slave and a free individual. Isza knew that it was essential for them to understand that they were no longer bound by the oppressive grip of a master, no longer subject to fear or the threat of being torn apart from each other.

In those early morning hours, when the world was still cloaked in slumber, Isza would slip into the woods. Standing beneath the vast sky, she'd lift her voice in exultation, shouting, "Momma, Daddy, we're free. We are free. " Each time she voiced those words; they filled her heart with unparalleled strength. In that moment, she felt a profound connection to her parents, knowing they would be at peace, watching over her and celebrating the dreams they fought so hard to achieve.

With every opportunity she had, Isza instilled in her sisters a sense of pride in their remarkable accomplishments. She encouraged them to look forward to the endless possibilities and knowledge they had been denied during their time in slavery. The most crucial lesson was to shed the fears that had overshadowed their lives for so long. They would be able to tell their children that they were the first generation in their family to break free from bondage. Just the thought of this noble heritage filled their hearts with serenity, as if the weight of their newfound freedom enveloped them all at once.

As time went on, the sisters ventured into the enchanting woods, eager to explore their beautiful surroundings while remaining cautious not to wander too far. The landscape was breathtaking; the trees formed intriguing silhouettes, and the gently swaying moss seemed to embrace them in a comforting cocoon. Everywhere they roamed, the delightful aroma of ripe fruit danced in the air. After a fresh rain, Isza relished the chance to stand outside, inhaling the diverse scents that filled her senses. She would twirl joyfully, just as she had in her childhood, her arms outstretched and her face turned toward the sun. Yet, amidst the joy, there were moments of bittersweet sadness as she longed for her mother, imagining how much she would have adored this home, the stunning surroundings, and, above all, the sweet embrace of freedom.

Four

When Clara and her sisters first stepped into the cabin the woods, Clara felt a mix of hope and anxiety. The night was filled with imagined sounds of barking dogs and distant voices, conjuring fears that any moment, someone might force their way in and take them away. Terrifying stories about runaway slaves played in her mind, and the idea of witnessing such horrors happen to her beloved sisters was almost too much to bear.

One bright early morning, Clara awoke from a nightmare, convinced that men and dogs were lurking outside. Her sisters huddled together in the corner, their eyes wide with fear, anticipating the worst. Isza, summoning her courage, peeked out the window, but the dark morning kept her vision cloudy; the beautiful moss hanging from the trees remained hidden from view. With determination, Isza told everyone to be quiet, asserting that if there was danger outside, they needed to confront it with bravery rather than give in to fear. They were finally free, and there was no reason to let anxiety control them. Clara implored Isza not to venture out, sharing the heart-wrenching fate of David's family when his father was captured. However, when Isza opened the door, she stood firmly at the threshold, bracing for anything. In that moment of uncertainty, nothing happened. Assuring her sisters that all was well, she encouraged them to find rest.

At breakfast the next morning, Clara's thoughts wandered to her time on the plantation. On weekends, her father, would venture to other farms to work with horses and engage in blacksmithing. At the Smith Homestead, where Clara often accompanied him, she had formed a close bond with a boy named David. As a little girl, she would watch her father work, and David would often sit nearby, eager to learn. Master Smith didn't mind their friendship, believing David was picking up the trade. Over time, David blossomed into a talented blacksmith. Paul noticed their strong connection and felt it was beneficial for Clara to have someone reliable in her life while also allowing their families to connect.

One evening, during a visit to the Smiths with her father, Clara learned that she couldn't see David because he and his family were in the barn. Clara instantly understood what that meant; someone was in trouble. Later, she discovered that it was David's father who was on the run. This memory remained vivid in Clara's mind, a haunting reminder that would never fade.

David's mother had faced brutal consequences because the master and overseer believed she had information about the escape. One harrowing night, David's sister was ripped from their mother's arms, only to return the next day, battered and broken. Although David himself was physically unharmed, living through such torment was unbearable. His heart became a storm of emotions, anger, fear, revulsion, and despair. He felt genuinely crushed, wishing that he could take on the pain himself rather than witness the suffering of his family. The longer his father remained missing, the more hopeless their situation appeared.

In the following week, Clara remained hopeful as she sought information about David, but ultimately, she couldn't bear the thought of what could happen if it drew unwanted attention to her own family.

Weeks passed, and one day, while with her father, Clara slipped into the kitchen of the big house to ask about David and his family. The expressions of the women told her that the news was grim. The main cook hurriedly left the room, while a maid shook her head slowly and turned away. A young man who usually toiled in the fields stood by the door, staring down at the ground, unable to meet her gaze. Sensing the urgency of her need to know, Clara made the decision to go to the barn and search for David herself, despite the women's warnings against it.

Upon arriving at the barn, Clara discovered David's family huddled together, clinging to one another in desperation. David immediately asked her for food, and Clara, with an encouraging smile, retrieved some bread from her pocket and handed it to them. They devoured it with an eagerness that revealed how long it had been since they last ate. As she took in the scene, Clara's heart sank at the sight of David's father, tied up in a corner, a grim reminder of the realities they faced. Although it was a common occurrence for families to return home after capture, this situation felt vastly different. This moment marked Clara's first direct encounter with the stark tragedy of a slave being returned to their oppressor, shaping her perspective in ways that would resonate deeply within her.

Through it all, Clara's courage and determination shone brightly, fueling her belief that there was always a path forward and that hope could thrive even in the darkest of times.

Clara rushed back to the stable as her father and Master Smith returned. Ready to share important news, Master Smith alerted Paul about the escaped slave and his plan to make a strong point. Understanding the gravity of the situation, Clara's father hoped to leave quickly, wanting to shield them both from what was to come. However, Master Smith believed that witnessing the event would be an eye-opening experience for both father and daughter.

All the enslaved individuals were gathered nearby, forced to watch as the overseer restrained David's father to a tree. Though Clara had seen harsh moments before, nothing could prepare her for the chilling reality of that night. With her heart racing, she clung tightly to her father, closed her eyes, and listened, overwhelmed by the sounds that echoed the brutality of the situation. Despite the darkness, she held onto the hope that one day, things would change for the better. For a moment she thought it had begun raining, but when she opened her eyes realized that with every strike of the leather impacting his back, blood was being slung all over. There were two men beating him and with every occurrence he would let out a loud, strong yell, but as time went on the yells became weaker, by the end it sounded like a baby crying. Even when he stopped yelling, the beating continued.

Clara was filled with concern and curiosity about the family they once knew. The last time they visited the plantation, they'd mysteriously vanished, leaving Clara with unspoken questions. Though she longed to ask about them, she chose to hold on to the hope that they were safe. However, the haunting experience at the Smith Plantation weighed heavily on her spirit, making her increasingly anxious, quiet, and at times, unkind toward the younger girls around her.

After reliving this event, Clara rested her head on the table, tears streaming down her face. Isza approached her with compassion, gently placing a hand on the back of Clara's head. "I just can't stand the thought of one of my sisters being hurt," Clara lamented. Being on the run stirred up painful memories, and living in that cabin while contemplating her first love filled Clara with anxiety about what fate awaited them if they were caught.

With warmth and reassurance, Isza responded, "We're going to be alright, I promise. We truly will."

Isza recalled how Clara used to talk about a certain someone often, but that chatter had stopped abruptly. She found herself wondering what could have happened. Later, Clara confided that the family was no longer a topic of discussion, not even mentioned by their father. Isza tried to suppress Clara's fears, but found little comfort in her own attempts to reassure her.

"Isza, where are we? Who does this place belong to? What if someone comes through that door and questions us about what we're doing here? What should we do?" Clara implored; her eyes wide with concern. She yearned for a safer place, free from the vulnerability and fear that engulfed them. All Isza could do was offer her words of comfort, assuring Clara that everything would be alright.

"Trust me, this cabin is the safest sanctuary we could find. Have you noticed anyone suspicious since we arrived?" Isza asked gently. Clara considered this for a moment before shrugging her shoulders.

Eager to uplift their spirits, Isza gathered everyone around, ready to share a story.

"When I was still living on the plantation, I came across an old lady who didn't belong to our place. I'd see her sometimes by the barn or at the river. One day, she told me about a special cabin in the woods. She said that if I ever found it, my life would change in ways I couldn't yet imagine. At that time, I didn't completely understand what she meant, but the night we left, I felt like someone was guiding my way. I couldn't see who it was, but I felt an undeniable sense of safety in that moment."

Clara's eyes widened in disbelief as she absorbed Isza's words. During her own trip to fetch water, she had seen an old lady near the cabin, but assumed it was just a figment of her imagination. The lady had approached her and urged her to return immediately. When Clara turned to look at her, she heard dogs barking in the distance, but the woman had vanished. Confused and feeling disoriented, she hurried back home without mentioning it to anyone, worried they might think she was losing her grip on reality. Clara became curious about how Isza's old lady looked.

Isza explained, "The appearance of the woman can vary, but she's always an older figure who seems to just appear out of thin air. You might notice her coming towards you, but when you look away, she might be gone. When you're in her presence, it's a special feeling of peace that washes over you. So, if you do see her, pay attention to what you feel, heed her words, and act accordingly."

With each word, there was a sense of hope, reminding them that they were not alone, and perhaps there were forces watching over them after all.

After that morning, Clara felt a wave of relief wash over her; her fears melted away, and she joyfully returned to being her cheerful self. She was the sister full of laughter, ready to sprinkle joy and playfully tease everyone around her. A heartfelt conversation with her big sister had reignited her spirit, leaving her eager to jump into fun activities at a moment's notice. Occasionally, she would catch a glimpse of the mysterious old lady from a distance, imagining her as a watchful presence, perhaps even a guardian guiding her with love.

As time passed, Clara realized she hadn't seen the old lady in a while. This made her ponder, maybe the gentle figure was an angel who had completed her mission. One sunny morning, while she was joyfully picking berries, she suddenly heard the soft rustle of leaves nearby and instinctively called out, "Is anyone there?" When silence followed, a wave of uncertainty washed over her. A conversation with her sisters bubbled back to her mind; if you ever felt observed in the woods, you should get away from the cabin. With a rush of adrenaline, Clara decided to act on that advice. Though she longed to sprint away, a heavy instinct told her that someone might just be too close behind. She knew she needed to be cautious, so she pivoted quickly.

"Who's there? What do you want from me?" she called out, her voice mixed with curiosity and unease.

Clara held her breath, waiting for a response, but the forest remained quiet.

"Massa, I got lost. I was trying to find my way back..." she called, hoping that if someone was there, those words would encourage them to leave, thinking she belonged to another.

Not a soul appeared. Feeling the weight of her solitude, Clara settled under a comforting tree, acutely aware of a presence around her, the hair on the back of her neck stood up as if whispering that she wasn't alone. As she glanced around, her heart raced; everything looked foreign, unfamiliar to her.

Her eyelids began to flutter, and a soft breeze caressed her, gently lulling her into a serene slumber. When she opened her eyes again, she was startled to see a figure standing over her. The sun cast a warm glow, but its brilliance made it hard to discern the person's features. Suddenly, a voice broke through the brilliance.

"Clara, is that you?"

Her heart skipped a beat, and as she squinted to get a better look, confusion washed over her.
"Clara, it's me. Don't you remember?"

She hung on to every word, searching for familiarity. The voice felt close to her heart, yet she struggled to place it. If only she could see their face; everything would click into place. With determination, she attempted to focus, but the sun's rays made it a challenge.

"Sir, I'm so sorry, but I can't remember where I know you from. What's your name?"

Turning her gaze away from the blinding light, she strained to hear any name that might resonate with her. But once again, silence engulfed the moment, and when she looked back, the figure had vanished. Out of the corner of her eye, she caught sight of the old woman she had seen from time to time near their home. Feeling a quiet sense of bravery, Clara decided to follow her, hoping she might lead her back to familiarity and safety.

As they walked, Clara noticed the old lady occasionally glance back, ensuring Clara was still on her journey. Finally, they arrived back at the cabin, and just like that, the old woman disappeared. Clara returned, bubbling with excitement as she recounted the day's adventure to her sisters. Some were skeptical, suggesting it had been just a dream due to her napping under that tree. Clara smiled at them, feeling no need to convince them otherwise. After all, whether dream or reality, the experience was hers to cherish.

After sharing her heartfelt story, Clara stepped outside to find some solace in solitude. Just then, Isza appeared and took a seat beside her, offering her warmth and encouragement. "You're not alone in this," Isza assured her. "What you experienced was real, I promise. It's understandable that your sisters might find it hard to grasp since the old lady hasn't shown herself to them yet. Just remember, patience is important; she must have something meaningful to share with you, and in time, she will reveal herself." Isza went on to reminisce about her own conversations with the old lady, mentioning how they often wandered into the depths of the woods together, exploring and exchanging secrets.

One bright morning, as Clara was happily picking berries, she spotted the old lady in the distance. Excitement bubbled within her, but she focused on her task, keeping one eye on her berries and the other on that enigmatic figure. Over the next few days, the old lady would appear, yet each time Clara dared to approach, she seemed to vanish like smoke in the wind. This constant dance tested Clara's patience, compelling her to adopt a different approach. Instead of chasing after the mysterious figure, she resolved to sit still and wait for the moment the old lady might choose to reveal herself.

Then came a morning that sparked a flicker of hope; a voice called her name. Clara's pulse quickened as she scanned her surroundings, her heart racing with excitement and a touch of disbelief. For the first time, the old lady spoke, her voice echoing through the woods, urging Clara to follow her deeper into the forest. As they walked, the old lady introduced herself, saying, "My name is Florence, but my friends call me Flo. You can call me Mrs. Florence."

A smile spread across Clara's face at the warmth of the greeting. "Mrs. Florence, how do you know me? Have we met before?" she curiously asked. Although Mrs. Florence remained silent, she continued to lead Clara along the wooded path. Rounding a bend, Clara's eyes widened as she spotted a figure standing in the distance, her heart skipping a beat.

"Who's that?" she asked, her voice barely above a whisper. Still silent, Mrs. Florence merely nodded, and then the figure spoke, "Do you remember me?"

As they drew closer, recognition sparked within Clara. She rushed forward, placing a hand on the figure's chest in disbelief. "Is it really you, David?" she exclaimed, emotions swirling within her. There were no words from him; instead, he enveloped her in a warm embrace that reawakened the love she had always held for him.

"David, it's you," she murmured softly, letting the moment sink in. After what felt like an eternity of holding each other, he invited her to sit beside him, and in that moment, Clara felt an overwhelming sense of gratitude wash over her. She glanced at Mrs. Florence, realizing how deeply she understood Clara's heartfelt desires, the dreams she had whispered to the stars each night, yearning to be reunited with her first love.

As she rested her head in David's lap, he tenderly caressed her hair and began recounting his story; "After our last goodbye, my family was taken away to work on a plantation in Alabama. Life became a struggle. My father fought through physical pain, but it was the loss of spirit that truly haunted him. My mother remained a beacon of love, and through it all, she taught me the importance of never forgetting those we hold dear."

"David, we can be together now," Clara said earnestly. "I've never stopped loving you."

Her heart soared with hope as the bond they shared reignited, reminding her that love, no matter how tested, had the power to endure through even the darkest of times. This was just the beginning of their incredible journey together, a journey filled with love, resilience, and the rekindling of dreams that can't be extinguished.

He paused for a moment, gently stroking Clara's head with a comforting touch. Clara closed her eyes, and when she opened them again, she found herself lying beneath a sturdy tree, all alone in the soft afternoon light. A wave of uncertainty washed over her, and she decided to keep the experience to herself, unsure whether it had been real or just a vivid dream. One thing was clear, though; thoughts of him had been lingering in her mind. As she made her way home, the name Mrs. Florence popped into her thoughts, bringing an unexpected smile to her face.

"Mrs. Florence, that wonderful old lady's name, Mrs. Florence," she murmured, her spirit lifting at the fond memory.

One bright morning, Isza was busy picking fresh fruit when she heard a group approaching. Instinctively, she ducked behind a tree and observed them quietly as they ambled past her home, seemingly oblivious to her presence. Once the coast was clear, she hurried inside, her heart racing with worry that perhaps the girls had been taken. As soon as they saw her alarmed expression, the girls rushed over, curiosity lighting up their faces. Isza pressed her finger to her lips and gestured outside.

"I saw some people out there. I'm not sure it's safe to stay here anymore. I don't know where they came from or where they went, but I can't shake the feeling there might be more of them."

From then on, Isza took to sitting by the window at night, anxiously awaiting potential intruders. One evening, she must have drifted off to sleep, for when she finally opened her eyes, the kind old lady stood before her. In an instant, Isza sprang to her feet, startled.

"Sweetheart, there's no need to be afraid of me."

Relieved but still uncertain, Isza settled back into her chair.

"Darling, it's time for you to take the next step. Your sisters will be just fine without you."

She glanced at her sisters lounging around the room, worry flooding her thoughts.

"I can't just leave. Who will care for them?"

"Teach them to care for themselves, my dear."

With that gentle nudge, Isza knew she had to share her plans with the girls. It was time for her journey to New Orleans. She could see the fear in their eyes, but she felt a surge of confidence as she reassured them, "Everything will be okay as long as you stay close to the cabin and don't venture too far. I promise."

Over the next two weeks, Isza dedicated herself to preparing the girls for independence. She taught them essential survival skills, what foods were safe to eat, how to catch a meal, where to find fresh water, and the boundaries of the woods. It was crucial for them to be vigilant.

The girls listened with intent, promising Isza they would be okay. In turn, Isza promised them she wouldn't be gone too long, her heart warmed by their determination and bravery. Together, they built a sense of hope for the future.

Five

After Isza left, Hilda stepped up to take charge. Every morning, it was her mission to find food, and she tackled this responsibility with determination. One day, while she was on the lookout, she noticed footsteps approaching. Intrigued, she hid behind a tree and peeked out, only to be pleasantly surprised by a lively group of Negro individuals chatting and laughing together. Hilda felt a spark of excitement and a desire to introduce herself, but a voice of caution reminded her to be wary; it was widely known that some individuals might act as decoys to capture runaways. So, she decided to stay hidden for her safety. Later, when she returned to the cabin and shared her experience, everyone agreed it was best to avoid the woods alone.

As time passed, Hilda had not seen anyone walking through the woods and began to feel a bit more at ease about going out on her own, provided she stayed alert. One sunny morning, while the others were still asleep, Hilda took it upon herself to pick some delicious berries. She reminded herself to keep close to the cabin and remain aware of her surroundings. Upon discovering a patch of ripe strawberries, the sweet scent filled her with delight. In that moment, she couldn't help but wish her sisters were with her to enjoy the splendor of the vibrant red and green plants adorning the once-bare field. She envisioned the joy on their faces when she returned with a sack brimming with those luscious strawberries.

While Hilda was picking the fruit, she was startled by two women who approached her from behind and gently tapped her on the shoulder. Her instinct was to bolt, but she recalled Isza's advice that a free person had nothing to fear. Taking a deep breath, she composed herself and managed to smile, even if just a little.

"You must be the new girl," one of the women said warmly.

Hilda nodded, feeling a mix of apprehension and hope.

"Come on, that's enough strawberries for now," the other woman encouraged.

Curious, Hilda followed them deeper into the woods until they arrived at a sizable homestead. It was an unfamiliar sight to her; she saw both slaves and a number of free Negro people living there. Feeling a mix of emotions, Hilda found herself working diligently throughout the day, glancing out the window now and then, yearning to see the cabin. Unfortunately, all she could see were trees swaying gently in the breeze. As darkness started to descend, Hilda asked one of the women when she could head back, only to be surprised by the revelation that they only returned home on weekends. Conflicted, she pondered whether to sneak away at night or stay awhile longer to understand how everything functioned, hoping her sisters would be patient and wait for her.

Back at the cabin, the girls grew increasingly concerned when Hilda didn't return that morning as expected. Realizing something was amiss, they decided to search the woods, but it was as if she had vanished without a trace. In a state of concern, they gathered to discuss their options, finding it strange that they had never prepared for this scenario before. Banding together, they considered the idea of heading to New Orleans to seek out Isza and inform her that Hilda had been captured. However, it quickly became clear to them that this plan was unrealistic. How could five young Negro girls navigate the town without proper papers while searching for a sister who had escaped slavery and now lived disguised as a white woman?

After weighing their choices, they agreed to stay close to the cabin and monitor the situation from a distance, ready to react if anyone came looking for them. After hiding in the woods for a couple of days, they returned, resolving to take turns keeping watch. They each selected their own hiding spot where they would stay concealed until it was safe. They made a solemn vow that if one of them were apprehended, they would not reveal the others' whereabouts, regardless of the circumstances. Each girl also crafted her own story in anticipation of any unforeseen encounters. Together, they were determined to stay strong and find a way to support one another through this challenging time.

As the week drew to a close, Hilda found herself preparing for the journey back to the cabin, but not before receiving a generous sack filled with food for everyone. With a sense of excitement, she waited patiently for the workers to leave before setting off. As she approached the cabin, she could hear the rustling of leaves and the subtle sounds of movement in the bushes. Curiosity peaked, but when she stopped to listen, the noises faded away. Wondering if someone might be following her, Hilda chose to rest under a tree, hoping that someone would show themselves. When nothing happened, she decided it was best to hurry on. However, an unsettling fear gripped her at the thought of what might have happened to her sisters. Overwhelmed with worry, her feet instinctively started to run.

Upon reaching the cabin and finding it empty, Hilda dropped to her knees in despair, releasing a heart-wrenching scream. Her sisters, hearing her call, burst forth from their hiding spots, their faces lighting up with joy and relief. They rushed to her, yelling, cheering, and crying tears of happiness. The fear that a slave catcher had come to take her away had weighed heavily on their minds. Once the initial excitement settled, the sisters eagerly asked Hilda where she had been and why she left so suddenly.

Hilda reassured them, explaining that she hadn't really had a choice. Some women had approached her and beckoned her to join them, so she did. To her surprise, they explained that they only returned home on weekends. With a smile, Hilda placed the sack of goodies on their wooden table. Baby, her youngest sister, inquired about the contents of the sack, and Hilda happily explained that at the end of each week, everyone received a sack filled with delicious food and a special candy treat.

As she mentioned the candy, the sisters' eyes sparkled with delight; it had been so long since they last tasted any sweets. Hilda dove into the sack and pulled out a handful of licorice, placing it on a wooden box next to the table. They gathered around her as she began unpacking the bounty; eggs, potatoes, beans, cabbage, rice, and an assortment of meats. Among it all, at the very bottom of the sack, were sweet potatoes, something the girls had never tasted before. Hilda shared with them that these sweet potatoes were best when cooked at night over an open fire and enjoyed beneath the stars. That night, the girls drifted off to sleep content and full, their hearts warmed by the prospect of sharing delicious meals together.

The next morning welcomed them with the delightful aroma of a hot breakfast of eggs, biscuits, and pork. As they savored their meal, Hilda took the opportunity to share her story, weaving in every detail with enthusiasm.

"I was out picking strawberries when I felt a tap on my shoulder," she began, her eyes bright with the memory. "At first, I thought it was the old lady I often saw when I was alone, but when I turned and saw several women standing there, I realized it wasn't her. I briefly considered running, but then remembered I wasn't a slave. Instead, I acted as though I belonged there. They told me I had picked enough berries and that it was getting late, so I decided to follow them, not knowing what else to do. When we arrived at the house, I feared they would see through my pretense, but thankfully, no one said a word. To my relief, everyone treated me like I was one of them. I found out that they only went home on the weekends, and my role was to cook and keep an eye on little Susy May."

Hilda paused, a smile crossing her face. "Once the other ladies saw me in the kitchen, they quickly realized that I had much to learn about cooking. They started showing me how to prepare the food, and I was introduced to dishes I had never even heard of, gumbo, jambalaya, red beans and rice. The aromas wafting from the kitchen were so inviting that it felt like a warm embrace. Before long, I discovered that cooking was quite simple; the secret to any meal lies in the seasoning. Whether it's grits or gumbo, using the right amount of seasoning is crucial to achieving the perfect flavor. I admit, I was nervous preparing my first gumbo since it was such an important dish. Who knew that shrimp, crabs, onions, green onions, bell peppers, flour, and water could come together to create something so incredible?" Hilda chuckled, reflecting on the lessons learned during her time at the other house. "On this plantation, I've seen many slaves who are hesitant to leave, but I'm grateful for the experiences I'm gaining. With that thought, Hilda paused, gazing thoughtfully out the window.

Reflecting on those days of enslavement, if given the chance, we absolutely would have left in an instant. On the plantation, we rarely saw any free Negro individuals, but there, they are all over. It must be incredibly difficult for those who are enslaved. I wonder how often they think about escaping. They could walk away with the free Negro people.

But enough about my thoughts. I'd love to hear what you've been up to this week.

For half of the week, we lived with the fear that those who took you might come back for us. We rallied together and made a plan; if we heard anything alarming, we would hide in the woods, each choosing our own spot for safety. We took turns keeping watch at night while others rested, eagerly waiting for your or Isza's return.

I'm back now, but I'll have to return to the plantation.

Six

Isza's adventure to New Orleans was just beginning, and she was filled with excitement as she set her plan into motion. As she traveled along the railroad tracks, anticipation buzzed in the air. When the train arrived, she hopped on, her heart racing with the thrill of new possibilities. The other passengers were visibly surprised to see her seated at the back with the Negro passengers; their curiosity piqued. Among them was a woman who looked strangely familiar, sparking an instant connection. Their eyes locked, and the woman asked if Isza recognized her. Isza pondered the question, her mind racing with thoughts, perhaps she'd seen her at one of the plantations? This realization made her want to leap off the train, but she remembered her telling Clara how different appearances could indicate the presence of the familiar old woman. A comforting sensation of peace enveloped her, encouraging her to stay put.

As Isza gazed deeply into the woman's warm eyes, she noticed a gentle smile that radiated warmth and kindness. That moment brought her a wave of comfort, and she felt encouraged to share her story with the elderly lady. When the train rolled into the vibrant Tremé area of New Orleans, Isza was overwhelmed by a swirl of emotions. She couldn't help but notice the diverse tapestry of people around her, all interacting in a beautifully harmonious way. Negro individuals and Indigenous folks were laughing and chatting alongside white residents, displaying a sense of equality that warmed her heart. Children of every hue played freely, treating one another like family, and the joyful sounds of music filled the air, creating a joyful symphony of life. Later, she would learn about the Créole community, who proudly owned many of the city's beloved restaurants.

Upon her arrival, Isza didn't see plantations resembling those back in Mississippi; however, crossing the river opened her eyes to the reality of larger plantations and enslaved individuals nearby. She discovered that here, enslaved people had certain rights, many could earn a living working at various plantations or even venture out to visit family at other plantations in the area. It filled her with hope to think that New Orleans could be an ideal place for them. Her immediate goal was to find work, and thankfully, the wise old lady guided her across the river and introduced her to a family in need of someone to look after their child for a month while they traveled for business.

As their wagon rolled closer to the house, Isza caught sight of enslaved individuals toiling in the fields. A wave of panic washed over her, and her heart raced at the fear of being discovered as a runaway. Yet, as if sensing her anxiety, the old woman placed a reassuring hand on hers and whispered that everything would be alright. All Isza had to do was keep in mind her white identity and communicate accordingly. With a fond memory, she recalled her practice of speaking as the master's daughter during her time on the plantation.

After engaging with the couple and showcasing her knowledge, Isza was thrilled to secure the position. At first, it felt unusual to be in a different role compared to the enslaved individuals, but she soon realized that she had the opportunity to positively impact their lives. Keeping her true identity under wraps, she told them she was from the North, everyone knew that Northern whites were often perceived differently than their Southern counterparts, paving the way for any inconsistencies with her interactions with the slaves.

Isza's journey was just beginning, and she was ready to embrace the opportunities ahead with an open heart and a determined spirit.

Isza had a big heart and always made a point to ensure that the staff cooked extra food for them to take home to their families. And those special baked desserts? She made sure there was enough for everyone to enjoy. She even discovered a talented doll maker on the plantation and kindly asked her to create beautiful dolls for all the little girls. Isza fondly remembered how wonderful it felt to receive her very own doll from her father, and sharing that joy with the children was incredibly meaningful to her. The enslaved community sincerely appreciated her thoughtfulness, and as her time there drew to a close, they felt a deep sadness. Isza had brightened their days and made life just a bit easier for them.

Once her work was complete, Isza headed back to New Orleans, excited by the opportunities she heard awaited her in the French Quarter as an "everyday girl." While the pay wasn't overly high, it was a stepping stone that helped her gain recognition as a white woman in the vibrant city. People accepted her without question, especially when she mentioned her time working across the river, as it was known that few would leave their children under the care of a slave while gone.

After her experience as an everyday girl, Isza found a fabulous opportunity to work as an au pair for families visiting the city during its lively festivities. It was during this time that she discovered an even more rewarding job as a greeter, where she could earn twice as much as an au pair. With enthusiasm, she welcomed single men visiting New Orleans, showing them around and ensuring they had a fantastic time. Before long, Isza became the most sought-after and well-compensated greeter in the city, an accomplishment she was immensely proud of.

One of the most magical experiences for Isza were the weekends spent at Congo Square. The first time she heard the enchanting music coming from the Square, it took her by surprise. At first, she didn't understand the beautiful yet complex message behind the beats and rhythms. Music was a lifeline for the enslaved people, serving as a medium to convey important information about their lives; for instance, if they sang "Down by the River," it was a signal that someone was planning to escape, inviting others to join them at the river.

When she heard the lively drums and cheers from the Square, her initial thought was that something terrible was happening. However, as she approached, she was filled with relief when she saw people dancing joyfully. The atmosphere transformed as someone began to sing and the crowd joined in with "Hey Pocky A-Way."

The joyous scene was a true melting pot of community, free Negro individuals, enslaved persons, whites, Indigenous folks, Créole's, and Frenchmen all came together to celebrate life. This incredible gathering provided enslaved individuals with a rare glimpse of freedom, connecting everyone through music, dance, laughter, and delightful refreshments. Isza was mesmerized by the distinct and uplifting tunes played at Congo Square. The music wasn't just sound, it was a culture, a bond reflecting the joy of being alive.

Yet, Isza was often left astonished by the stark contrast of life in New Orleans. Just a day after reveling at Congo Square, she could witness the brutal reality of an enslaved person being beaten in the streets. It was a heartbreaking paradox that left her both puzzled and reflective about the complexities of society.

After nearly a year of building her life in New Orleans, Isza realized her dream by purchasing a small piece of land with a charming house right off the river. Living in an area where people of various backgrounds coexisted in harmony was beyond anything she'd imagined. It was a beautiful surprise to witness free Negro individuals living alongside whites, and Negro and white families sharing homes together. She also had her first encounter with a Negro Indian and learned that these individuals were free, which meant that their children would also share that freedom, an inspiring realization that highlighted the beautiful tapestry of community life in her new home.

Her neighbor down the road was in a loving relationship with a wonderful Negro woman. However, Isza later learned that they weren't actually married; he was simply providing for her. This sort of situation wasn't uncommon. Many white men had Negro families that they supported but didn't honor the commitment of marriage.

Isza spent a lot of time thoughtfully crafting a relationship dynamic that blended a sense of authority with the care of a family bond. She wanted to ensure that no one would question her when she began bringing her sisters in as part of that new arrangement. Although people were aware that such dynamics existed, she believed that with careful planning, she could create a safe haven for them.

The moment had finally arrived for her to fetch her beloved sisters from the cabin. However, upon her arrival, her heart sank as she found the place empty, with no sign of anyone. A wave of sadness washed over her, and she felt lost in that moment. The worry that their old master might somehow find them and force them back to the plantation, or worse, harm them, gripped her heart. There was no evidence of any struggle, yet she couldn't shake the feeling that if they had returned to the plantation, they might have managed to come back, whether alive or otherwise. It had been over a year since she had seen her sisters, and uncertainty clouded her thoughts. In her despair, she sat for days contemplating her next steps. Though returning to the plantation felt like an option, there was no assurance that her sisters were there. She even toyed with the idea of searching the grounds, wondering if any unfortunate incidents had befallen them. Surely, if there were graves, they would have marked them, knowing she would eventually return. But what about the last survivor? Surely something should have been visible.

After two long days of searching without a trace, Isza resolved to set out and find them. If that meant retracing her steps back to where everything began, then so be it.

Early the next morning, a delightful sound of rustling leaves stirred her from sleep. She hurried to the window, and to her absolute joy, she spotted all six of her sisters, Hilda, Clara, Teacee, Viola, Picola, and Baby, laughing and enjoying each other's company. Isza couldn't contain her excitement and dashed to the door, joyfully announcing her return. The six girls ran over, surrounding her in an explosive outburst of happiness. Each sister took a moment to share her joy with Isza, showering her with hugs and kisses. When the initial excitement settled, Isza bravely opened up about her fears that they might have been taken back to Mississippi, expressing how unbearable it was to think of them back on the plantation, and she was prepared to risk everything to find them.

After savoring a moment of closeness outside, they headed back into the cabin. Eager to catch up, Isza wanted to know everything that had happened since she last saw them. They explained that they had been living and working on a plantation, but they would regularly return to the cabin to check if she had come back. Hilda shared how she initially found work, but as time passed, it became increasingly challenging to leave. One day, while out, Hilda heard a woman crying. Curiosity led her closer, where the distressed woman urged Hilda to leave immediately and never look back. Unsure but compelled, Hilda turned and walked away. Suddenly, she heard shouting and then a gunshot, which propelled her to move faster. The following week, when she went to meet the ladies, she often walked with, no one appeared. Whatever danger had loomed over the plantation, she felt she had narrowly escaped.

Isza shared with them the troubling rumors she had heard about free women being shipped from New Orleans to South Carolina and sold back into slavery. It was heartbreaking to think of families waiting for their loved ones to return, only to be met with silence.

After that experience, the sisters vowed not to leave the cabin, until eventually, a kind elderly woman visited and shared valuable insights about finding legitimate work. Encouraged, Hilda took the first step, followed weeks later by Teacee, and soon enough, everyone had secured jobs. Thankfully, no one questioned their freedom; they realized Isza was right; if you carried yourself differently, people would treat you accordingly.

Isza excitedly recounted her own escapades, sharing tales of her first job on a plantation as a white woman, her adventures at Congo Square, and the fascinating people she had encountered. To top it off, she revealed that she had purchased a lovely piece of land, complete with a charming Creole cottage where they could all live together harmoniously.

Much to her surprise, her sisters expressed a heartfelt desire to stay where they were, happy with their newfound lives. Teacee chimed in, sharing her plans to jump the broom in just two weeks with a wonderful man named Joseph. Isza felt a mix of emotions; her original vision was for them all to be united and free. After contemplating for a bit, she decided to stay a while longer, regardless of whether her sisters ultimately chose to join her in New Orleans. The essence of family, love, and freedom would guide her decisions moving forward.

Joseph's journey began on a plantation where he was born to a remarkable Indian mother and a loving Negro father. Thanks to his mother's heritage, he was born free, which opened up a world of possibilities. As a young boy, his adventures took him to New Orleans with his mother, where they danced joyfully in Congo Square. Joseph was captivated by the vibrancy of the city and dreamed of one day calling it home. With his heart set on this dream, he planned to move there after marrying his beloved Teacee.

On a touching day during the broom-jumping ceremony, Isza found herself overwhelmed with emotion, thinking about her parents and how proud they would have been to see her standing there. In the past, many individuals had little control over their partnerships, but Isza's parents, Viola and Paul found true love after Viola was finally free from her previous obligations.

Joseph and Teacee decided to remain on the plantation with Joseph's wise and loving grandmother, Mrs. Carrie, until they could earn enough money for their family to move to New Orleans. Mrs. Carrie was a treasure trove of enchanting stories, and when she spoke of water, it felt as if you could hear the gentle drip or the wild splashing against rocks. She painted vibrant pictures with her words, describing the trees swaying as water embraced their trunks, and the playful creatures that shared their world. By the end of her tales, you could almost taste the water she described, so rich were her vivid details.

For Baby, Mrs. Carrie was more than just a grandmother; she was a lifeline. Baby had come into this world as a little one, unable to remember her parents who were sold away, and Isza filled the maternal role with affection. Mrs. Carrie became Baby's steadfast grandmother, showering her with the love that every child needs. Now, with a few years of freedom behind her, Baby had little memory of the harsh life on the plantation, which, in many ways, was a blessing. Enslaved parents often hoped their children wouldn't carry the burdens of those memories, aspiring for a brighter future. But she was learning in a world that still posed challenges; meaning she needed to navigate her interactions carefully. Remarkably, Baby played carefree with the white children, who eagerly taught her to read and write, allowing her a taste of freedom.

Isza was filled with pride the first time she heard Baby read aloud. While other children gathered in a cozy corner, engrossed in their books, Isza noticed Baby's voice break through the soft chatter. She glanced apprehensively toward the father sitting at the desk. The urge to whisk Baby away quickly rose within her, but then she realized that everyone else continued as normal. It was a stark reminder of the times. That evening, Isza gently advised Baby to be cautious about where she read, recognizing that even New Orleans had its silent rules regarding education and race. Baby's bright spirit shone as she shared that Grandma Carrie and her playmates were her teachers.

Mrs. Carrie was born in the early 1800s, and Isza could hardly believe that someone of her age had learned to read. With a twinkle in her eye, Mrs. Carrie explained how her love for storytelling had made reading a natural extension for her. She had learned words through the tales she spun and simply needed to discover what they looked like on the page.

Reflecting on her childhood, Mrs. Carrie fondly remembered her anticipation as a little girl waiting for her turn to pick cotton, eagerly looking forward to joining her siblings in the fields. She vividly recalled her first day; her mother gently woke her, saying it was time for work. Little Carrie jumped out of bed with pure joy, as though it were a holiday celebration. Her older sister watched, bemused, wondering how this innocent child would fare in the long day ahead. What would become of her bright smile after the hard labor? But that spirit of joy and eagerness for life was something truly special and to be cherished, an emblem of hope that even in challenging circumstances, dreams and warmth could thrive.

As Carrie made her way to the fields, her heart swelled with excitement at the thought of working alongside the grown-ups. It was a chance to be part of something bigger. However, by the end of the day, she found herself struggling to see the bright side. Her fingers and knuckles were sore and covered in grime, and she felt a bit overwhelmed. She confided in her mother that cotton picking was tougher than she had anticipated. But her mother, always the voice of wisdom, reassured her that in time, her hands would adapt, and she would master the art of cotton picking.

Carrie listened intently; she appreciated her mother's encouragement. Yet, she couldn't ignore the realities around her. She had seen those who hadn't learned the technique, some facing unfortunate injuries, and even one woman who had lost an arm to an infection. This only fueled her determination. Carrie resolved that if cotton picking was in her future, she would become the best there ever was. With persistence and practice, she surpassed her own expectations, often helping fill her mother's bags with cotton.

One of Carrie's favorite tales was about her family's journey to New Orleans. When they lived on a plantation in Arkansas, they developed a close bond with a nearby Indian family. Even though that family wasn't enslaved, they faced their own struggles without rights. On chilly nights, the children would sometimes be invited over to share warmth in their cozy shack. One day, the father of that family visited to express his gratitude for the friendship they shared. He shared the exciting news that they would be moving to a reservation, a place where they could live freely and thrive.

Imagine the joy and hope that filled the air when he returned just two months later to invite them to join him on the reservation alongside other free Negro people. Carrie's family took a leap of faith, leaving the past behind, and embraced their new life on the reservation for a couple of years. When the tribe eventually split, they joined the group traveling towards New Orleans, ready for new adventures.

While working on the plantation didn't require papers, the bustling streets of New Orleans called for a different kind of vigilance. Freedom papers were essential, and the anxiety of showing them weighed heavy on Carrie's heart. She had seen how quickly papers could be torn apart before a crowd, leading to heart-wrenching consequences for those deemed runaways. Even with papers, the path to equality felt steep, and people were often judged not by their freedoms, but by societal expectations.

But as Carrie continued to navigate the complexities of her world, she held onto her dreams and determination, ready to carve out a brighter future for herself and her family. With resilience in her heart and hope in her spirit, each day became a new opportunity to learn, grow, and make her story one of inspiration and courage.

Weeks later, Isza successfully persuaded Picola and Hilda to accompany her on the journey. Though initially hesitant, they embraced the spirit of their original plan. They practiced their travel demeanor, preparing for anything that might come their way. Isza took charge, assuring them that as long as she was there to speak for them, everything would be alright. She taught them to keep their gazes focused on the ground if approached by a white person and to await her guidance in any conversations.

On their journey to vibrant New Orleans, Isza and the girls spotted two scraggly-looking white men approaching on horseback. Isza sensed they could be trouble and kindly whispered to the girls to keep their heads down and stay calm. As the men drew nearer, Isza felt a flash of apprehension, but she quickly realized that running might only escalate the situation.

As the men passed, Isza mustered her courage and cheerfully greeted them, saying, "Good morning." To her relief, the men tipped their hats and continued on their way. The girls glanced up at Isza with smiles, and she gently reminded them to keep their eyes lowered, just in case the men were still watching. Just as she finished speaking, she heard horses approaching from behind.

Determined to stay composed, Isza picked up her pace without seeming frantic, but soon enough, the men caught up to them and ordered them off the carriage. One of the men roughly grabbed Picola, lifting her onto the back of his horse, insisting they leave. Isza, filled with fierce determination, firmly asserted that he had no right to take her. She explained that the sheriff of New Orleans was expecting them that very morning and that she would report this incident.

As she turned, hope surged within her that they would let Picola go. Suddenly, she heard footsteps behind her and then the sound of horses riding away. To her relief, Picola stood there, tears glistening on her face but strong nonetheless. Isza longed to embrace her sister, but knowing they might still be watched, Picola climbed back onto the carriage, and with renewed hope, they continued their journey together.

Seven

During their exciting journey, Isza shared some important insights with the girls. At first, it might feel like they were simply working for her, but soon enough, they would have the chance to achieve their own freedom. Isza encouraged them to be cautious in certain parts of the city, especially when it came to crossing the river. For a Negro person, the waters could be perilous, papers or not. With a twinkle in her eye, she assured them that she would be there to guide them if they were curious about exploring that side of New Orleans. However, she also advised them to steer clear of an area known for its outlaws, safety first. As Isza spoke, she couldn't help but notice the girls' expressions, which seemed to convey a vibrant curiosity mixed with a hint of confusion, as if they were wondering, "What's New Orleans really like?" Recognizing that she was throwing a lot of information their way, Isza felt a sense of hope about the new chapter in their lives. She painted a vivid picture of the freedom-filled city, describing the lively French Quarter, bustling French Market, and the heart-pounding atmosphere of Congo Square, where the music danced through the air.

Upon their arrival in New Orleans, Isza, Picola, and Hilda wore the marks of exhaustion. The journey had been long, and the mental fatigue from being questioned and fearing discovery as runaways weighed heavily on their hearts. There were moments when they longed to retreat back to the comforting embrace of the woods, where safety seemed guaranteed. However, they reminded themselves that their adventure was part of a carefully crafted plan leading them to a future filled with freedom to explore the country without fear.

The first trip on the ferry was a bit of a rollercoaster for Picola, who unfortunately felt unwell. Isza, with her nurturing spirit, encouraged her to focus on the swirling water around the ferry. "Look closely, Picola," she said. "Let the rhythm of the water match your own." This thoughtful advice helped Picola regain her balance, though she realized that ferry rides might not be her favorite pastime just yet.

Next up on Isza's itinerary was the enchanting Congo Square. As soon as they arrived, the vibrant atmosphere swept them off their feet. The music was absolutely mesmerizing, and the beat of the drums seemed to awaken something deep within them, making their bodies sway in beautiful, soft movements. Some moments were so moving that tears of joy and nostalgia flowed freely. Every note wove a tale, evoking memories of their past, celebrating a jumping-the-broom ceremony, rejoicing in the birth of a child, or mourning the loss of a home or loved one. They began to understand how laughter and music were intertwined, both having the special ability to touch the heart and soul.

It was as if the rhythm of the drums called out to Picola. While she sat on the grass, her feet tapped in eager response to the beat, as though her body couldn't contain its rhythm. The drummer, sensing her engagement, picked up the tempo, and Picola felt the beat pulse through her chest with exhilarating energy. Before she knew it, she leaped to her feet, dancing around joyfully, her arms high above her head, twirling in circles with pure exhilaration.

Meanwhile, Hilda was captivated by a talented trumpet player. The moment he began to play, the music enveloped her, creating a beautiful symphony that brought a sense of calm to her mind. She swayed gently, allowing the uplifting notes to wash over her while tears brimmed in her eyes from the sheer beauty of it all. As her gaze lingered on the trumpet player, with sun-kissed skin and striking steel-gray eyes, she felt a mix of vulnerability and newfound maturity. Isza gently tapped her shoulder to bring her back to reality, but for a moment, Hilda was lost in the enchanting melody. She was so enchanted that when Isza suggested they explore the park, Hilda asked them to go on ahead, eager to stay close to the source of such wonderful music. Isza and Picola exchanged a smile before continuing their adventure, leaving Hilda happily swaying next to the band, completely absorbed in the moment.

As they strolled through the park, Picola was astounded by the dazzling array of music that surrounded them. One moment, a brass band would fill the air, and just a few steps away, a group of talented violinists brought a different flavor; further down, guitar players strummed cheerfully, while drummers and even bagpipe players contributed to the celebration, along with creative individuals tapping on tin buckets. If something could create music, it was alive and thriving on the weekends at Congo Square. It was an incredible experience.

Just as Isza and Picola were returning, the lively brass band was taking a well-deserved break. The trumpet player sauntered over to Hilda with a friendly smile.

"Hey there. I don't think I've seen you around here before. Where do you come from?"

Hilda felt a wave of shyness wash over her. She found herself looking down at the ground, shuffling her feet nervously. The urge to blend into the crowd was strong, yet her curiosity about this charming musician tugged at her. Just as she was gathering her thoughts to introduce herself, Isza emerged from the bustling crowd.

"She's with me. What's your name young man?" she asserted with harshness.

Surprised, the trumpet player stepped back, his gaze darting briefly between the two women before understanding dawned. He had encountered people like them before, those who had to adopt a different pretext for their families' freedom. He tipped his hat gracefully and replied, "Good evening to you, ma'am. I'm William, William Armstrong."

With a smile, he returned to his band, seamlessly picking up where he left off while keeping a watchful eye on Hilda, who was particularly taken by his talent. Though William was not free himself, the music brought him some privileges, and over time, he and Hilda formed a bond. He would pop by to visit, and occasionally, he would invite her to see him perform. She adored his shows, especially when he played for Negros, it felt like home. Just as their friendship blossomed, William's departure loomed as travel season approached. He shared his dreams with Hilda, saying that upon his return, he hoped to purchase his freedom and would ask her to marry him. Her heart soared at the thought; she cared deeply for him and felt that life had taken such a beautiful turn. Not long ago, she had been enduring life on a plantation, devoid of any hope of finding true love.

Things seemed to be falling into place for the sisters until an unexpected twist darkened their days. Isza began to feel unwell at work, her head spinning. She tried to find a seat but collapsed, hitting her head on the edge of a table. When she was rushed to the hospital, it was several days before Hilda and Picola learned of the incident. Sadly, when they attempted to visit, they were denied entry. The hospital was strictly reserved for whites.

Isza had enjoyed some success, but her accomplishments stirred envy in others. They seized the chance to remind her of her "place," insisting that women like her ought to marry and serve men, not be independent property owners. While Isza was hospitalized, her inability to manage her financial obligations sparked the city to start selling off her properties, and this was a disaster for the sisters. In the rush, Isza hadn't finalized the paperwork for their freedom. When word spread that the sheriff would be auctioning off Isza's belongings, panic set in. They contemplated fleeing back to the woods but knew it would put them in grave danger since others would be searching for them. Tragically, they were sold to the highest bidder without any chance for resistance.

Isza felt a crushing weight in her heart as she learned that her beloved Hilda and Picola had been sold so swiftly. She was devastated, feeling as though she had betrayed them after being the one to plan for their freedom. She had no idea where they could be or who had bought them; it felt as though the friends she thought she had disappeared when she needed them most. Due to her illness, her search was painfully narrow. Isza was tormented by the conversation she would need to have with her sisters when she finally found them.

Caught in the grips of despair, Isza found herself back in the hospital, feeling as if she were waiting for an end. The thought of her sisters suffering as they once had was unbearable. The hospital staff struggled to encourage her to eat, to move, or even to step outside and bask in the warmth of the sun. It was evident that she was battling a significant hospital blues.

One night, as the darkness fell, Isza was jolted awake by a loud noise. Sitting up straight in her bed, she strained her eyes to determine where the sound had come from. As she scanned the room, she noticed a shadow in the doorway.

"Isza?"

She blinked, trying to sharpen her focus in the dim light. The voice called out again.

"Isza, daughter of Paul and Viola?"

With those words echoing in her mind, Isza felt a surge of panic. She attempted to leap up, but her weakened state restrained her. The voice continued, reassuring yet poignant.

"Are you the daughter who vowed to watch over Paul and Viola's daughters?"

Isza felt a mix of confusion and concern as she lay in the hospital bed surrounded by the bright white walls of the room. She sensed that if this mysterious person truly knew her parents, things could get complicated. She took a deep breath and gently reclined as thoughts of her mother and father consumed her. She hoped the figure would move closer to reveal their identity. As she waited, sleep overtook her, and when she opened her eyes, morning light filled the room. She wondered, was it all a dream? Thoughts of their harrowing escape and the sacrifices they made along the way enveloped her. May left them, understanding that some sacrifices were necessary for all of their freedom. But this time, the stakes were different. Now, two more family members were lost. The weight of the news about Picola and Hilda being sold back into slavery filled her with dread. The thought of sharing this tragedy with other girls. She feared they would feel disheartened and might struggle to be around her. Just picturing that outcome was exhausting.

Once again, she was gently roused from her thoughts.

"Isza, daughter of Paul and Viola?"

With a deliberate openness, Isza blinked awake from her thoughts to find an older woman standing by her bedside. "Are you Isza, the daughter of Paul and Viola?"

This time, there was no fear in her heart. She understood now that her dreams offered her comfort instead of fear. Sitting up eagerly, she replied with pride, "Yes, I'm the oldest daughter of Paul and Viola."

Yet, as she glanced around, the darkness encroached again, signaling that this too was a dream. Memories of her family's resilience flooded her mind; they had instilled in her the strength to protect her sisters and the conviction to survive. Tears streamed down her cheeks as a powerful realization struck her; she had to endure and thrive. In her dreams, the old lady continued to visit, imparting strength and encouragement. Isza gradually began to nurture herself, eating, standing tall, and eventually stepping outside to welcome the warmth of the sun.

One joyful morning, while savoring breakfast, a familiar voice broke through her reverie.

"Isza, the doctor said you will be checking out today. You've made incredible progress; I'm so proud of you."

Isza felt a flutter of apprehension at the sound of the voice, was this truly the old lady? If it wasn't a dream, she had shared everything about herself. Mustering her courage, she turned to find a young white woman before her. Isza paused, momentarily speechless.

"Isza, are you alright?" the nurse inquired with genuine concern.

Isza closed her eyes, convinced she was still dreaming. However, as the nurse spoke soothingly, a part of her felt a deep warmth and familiarity. Opening her eyes again, she focused on the young woman, who then reached out and placed a gentle hand on Isza's forehead. Stepping back, the doctor winked, filling Isza's heart with comfort. The connection reassured her, and she smiled brightly, sharing her excitement about going home.

Even though she didn't have a traditional home anymore, having lost all her belongings, she welcomed the prospect of leaving the hospital with hope in her heart. Starting over felt daunting, yet she believed she had the strength to face whatever came next. Moving back to the French Quarter, Isza dedicated herself to building a new life and earning money.

One bustling day at the French Market, she caught sight of someone who looked strikingly like Picola. It was hard to be certain through the layers of dirt on the woman's face. The figure struggled under the weight of a large sack of grain, and when she stumbled and fell, a nearby young white man rushed over, urging her to get back on her feet. Isza felt a wave of emotion wash over her as she locked eyes with Picola; a single tear slid down her cheek. It was indeed Picola, but she appeared worn and beaten by life's harsh challenges.

Isza hurried towards her, a sense of determination igniting within her. As she reached where Picola lay, she dropped her purse beside her, and when she bent to help, their eyes met. There was a flicker of life in Picola's gaze, and Isza felt a surge of urgency. Standing tall, she called out with strength, "What did you say to me? Who does this slave belong to?"

The man stepped from behind a wagon and said it belong to me. Isza asked him if he had never taught her any manners, and now he was insisting that she stand up. As she rose, Isza stepped closer, curiosity in her gaze.

"Do I know you?"

Silence hung in the air as she only focused on Isza.

"My name is Miss. Isza."

"Oh, Miss Isza. I remember you well. My name is Picola. I used to belong to you."

"Picola. It's wonderful to see you again. I've missed you so much, and little Suzy has been asking about you too."

Isza could see that the young man was intrigued by her words.

"If you can give me a hundred dollars, I'll let you have her back."

"My husband is currently out of town, so I'll need to speak with him and get back to you about that. She doesn't seem well, and I'm not sure he'll agree to that price. What plantation do you live on? We can come in a couple of days."

Though it pained her to think of letting Picola go, she realized that making the deal in that moment could draw unnecessary attention. Isza felt a rush of determination to ensure Picola was safe because the young man now believed that someone would be willing to pay for her. This meant he saw value in her well-being, even if he had little use for her otherwise. Upon returning to the plantation, Picola felt a newfound sense of freedom. They treated her well, and for the very first time since her arrival there, she slept indoors, feeling a hint of comfort.

It took Isza two weeks to make the trip to the plantation. When she caught her first glimpse of Picola, surprise illuminated her face. But when the owner quoted them a price of one hundred fifty dollars, they turned away, determined not to be exploited.

"You told my wife one hundred dollars. "

They kept walking, signaling that they wouldn't be manipulated. The young man called out after them.

"That was two weeks ago. Look at her; she's worth a hundred fifty dollars now. Your wife told me your daughter really adores her. It's one hundred fifty dollars, or nothing".

Sticking to their plan, Isza clutched her companion's hand and earnestly urged him to purchase Picola. He met her gaze with kindness and, after a moment of reflection, smiled.

"Alright, one hundred fifty dollars. I'll do this for my wife."

With that, Picola was gently placed in the back of the wagon, and they started their journey home. Isza longed to talk with Picola about Hilda and whether she knew where their sister was, but when she turned around, she noticed that Picola was fast asleep. It seemed as if she hadn't had a moment's rest since the day she had been sold.

Weeks passed before Isza and Picola had the chance to discuss her experiences. One morning during breakfast, Picola's voice broke the silence. "Hilda's dead."

Isza's heart sank, and tears welled in her eyes. "When did she pass away?"

"A while ago."

Unable to contain her sorrow, Isza stood up from the table and stepped outside. She lifted her face to the sky and cried out, "I'm so sorry, Hilda. "

Kneeling on the ground, she covered her face with her hands, allowing the grief to wash over her. Picola wanted to comfort her but chose to give Isza the space she needed to mourn.

Isza spent the day outside, lost in thought about how different choices might have changed their fates. She recalled the excitement of their escape plan from the plantation, the bittersweet realization of having to sacrifice May for their freedom, and the joy that had filled their hearts when they finally grasped that they were free. As Picola and Hilda decided to venture to New Orleans, Isza found happiness in knowing it was a step towards a brighter future. She remained hopeful for what was to come, ignited by the memories of their shared resilience.

After a couple of weeks, Isza felt it was time to uncover what had transpired with her sisters during her hospital stay. She settled into the cozy rocker while Picola gazed thoughtfully at the river from the porch, clearly searching for the right words. Isza wanted to be patient, but the suspense was palpable, swirling around her thoughts like a whirlwind. Suddenly, fueled by a surge of urgency, she sprang to her feet.

"Picola, please share with me, what happened while I was away? How did Hilda die?"

Picola turned to her, her eyes glistening with emotion, ready to share the truth.

The day you entered the hospital we felt a wave of concern wash over us. A thoughtful colleague from your workplace visited us, sharing the news and offering support. His daily updates brought us comfort and confidence in your recovery. As the days went on, he kindly began to take us to his home to work together, making sure we stayed connected and focused. His generosity and friendship truly brightened our challenging situation.

One day while we were over there, he grabbed me and began pulling me into his room. I started screaming, and Hilda came running. She told him to let go of me because we didn't belong to him. He walked over and back handed her across her face. Her head snapped to one side than slowly turned toward him. Her eyes looked as if they were sitting on the outside of the sockets. As he stared at her, I could see and feel the fear entering his body. The hand that had a grip on me was becoming warm and clammy. I felt the grip gradually loosening around my arm. He told the overseer to teach her a lesson and said we now belonged to him.

Unusual events began to unfold for him, sparking a whirlwind of disbelief. He stumbled down the steps, which led to a sprained ankle, and had an unexpected fall from his horse that resulted in a cut on his head. To add to his misfortune, a mule kicked him in the back. As if that wasn't enough, when his wife fell ill, a lingering suspicion crept into his mind that Hilda might be involved in some kind of voodoo. He'd catch her smiling at him, and a flicker of fear would flash across his face, prompting him to quickly turn away, often stumbling in his haste.

Then, one morning, a group of men barged in where we were resting and declared us their property. One of the men seized Hilda, dismissing her with a wave as he scoffed at the idea of voodoo. In response to his aggression, Hilda maintained her graceful smile, even when he forcefully threw her across the barn. On our journey to the plantation, a tree branch knocked him off his horse, and once more, he found Hilda smiling at him. Overcome with anger, he struck her, causing her to lose a tooth, yet her unwavering smile remained, a testament to her resilience.

He backed away from her, but it was clear that it wasn't over. He was determined to show her who was in control. When we arrived at our destination, he tied her to a tree for weeks. She told me that she was okay and that she was doing this for my sake. One morning, when I woke up, she was gone. I thought they had killed her, but later I found out she had run away. She didn't get far, but she felt she had to try. They beat her mercilessly; some of the other slaves said they had never seen anyone beaten like that, especially not a woman. Her back looked like someone had attacked it with a machete.

Difficult times began to envelop the plantation, and a sense of trepidation towards her grew among the people. It almost felt like she reveled in their fear. One day, she opened up about her desire to escape, fully aware of the risks involved. While I wished for her to stay, I recognized her need to forge her own path. She bravely pursued her freedom, but tragically lost her life. In the end, I was sold, but her spirit and courage inspire me every day.

Picola fell silent, her gaze fixed on the flowing river, lost in thought. Isza watched her, feeling a deep sense of compassion. She moved closer and wrapped her arms around Picola, offering reassurance that everything would turn out fine and that the shadows of the past would not darken their future. As she held her, Isza felt the subtle, poignant reminders of Picola's past struggles in the bones of her shoulder, a testament to resilience and healing. She was eager to delve deeper into the story of Hilda, but was mindful that Picola had already shared so much.

As the days passed, Isza became increasingly aware of Picola's progress. The limp that had once defined her movements was fading, a clear sign of healing from the hardships she had endured. Picola eventually shared the details of her recent accident, a fall from the back of a wagon that led to her being run over by a horse. Fearing for his own safety, her master had sold her to work on a nearby plantation, where she had spent only a few short days before their fateful meeting at the market. Isza felt a rush of empathy and stood up to envelop Picola in a warm hug. Picola shared how the legacy of Hilda's courage kept her safe; the whispers of what they believed Hilda could do, even from beyond, ensured no one laid a hand on her.

"Hilda's sacrifice was a testament to her love for me," Picola reflected. "She knew she couldn't survive as a slave, haunted by the memories of fear and helplessness. She would see young girls taken away, their cries echoing in her ears, she couldn't bear to witness that again." Both of them felt tears welling, a mix of grief and profound connection pouring forth.

"I wish I could have done more to protect you and Hilda. I truly regret that," Isza said earnestly.

"Hilda always believed you would come for me. She had a way of knowing," Picola replied, a hint of hope in her voice.

Tears of joy mingled with sorrow in Isza's eyes for both Picola's newfound freedom and Hilda's sacrifice. With a newfound sense of purpose, Isza suggested they pay a visit to their sisters. Together, they would share the story of Hilda, celebrating her spirit and ensuring that the legacy of love and protection would continue to thrive among them.

Eight

Isza hadn't visited the cabin for several years, and she found herself hoping that her sisters were still keeping an eye out for her return. One beautiful Sunday morning, she felt an undeniable pull to make the trip. Over the years, whispers about the brewing conflict between the South and North had echoed through the plantations, but nothing ever came to fruition. This time, however, the unease among the plantation owners was palpable. If war did erupt, Isza dreaded the thought of not knowing when she could make that cherished journey again.

With optimism and determination, she and Picola set off, packing only the essentials. As they journeyed, Picola's memories began to bloom. She recalled the last time she ventured through those woods, a time filled with fear that men might take her away, never to see her family again. When she had been taken from the wagon, it had felt as though Isza was letting her go, but the warmth in Isza's gaze provided Picola with a reassuring sense of peace. Deep down, Picola understood that whatever Isza needed to do was for the greater good of their family. When Isza turned and walked away, Picola had feared that her freedom had slipped away forever. Yet, Isza was fueled by a fierce resolve; they would either find their way to freedom together, or they would face whatever came their way side by side.

As Isza began reminiscing about their parents, she realized that Picola had only a few scattered memories of them. With a heartfelt sincerity, she started sharing all the beautiful stories of their life on the plantation, the tale of how their parents had met, the immense love they held for their children, and their steadfast belief that one day they would all be free. Viola and Paul had instilled in them a powerful belief that slavery did not define their identity, but was merely a situation they had been thrust into. Their parents constantly emphasized the importance of family bonds, something that Isza cherished deeply.

On the plantation, every action, every song and dance, revolved around the common goal of attaining freedom. Joyful dances filled the evenings, songs carried messages of hope, and the children's games were joyful expressions of their spirits. Each note sung and each dish prepared served a greater purpose. If the air was filled with the aroma of a particular meal, it was a signal that something significant was about to unfold, whether it was someone planning to escape or offering food to a traveler on the run.

A laugh escaped Picola as she recalled the games they played. Although the specifics were hazy, the joy of those moments lingered. She remembered being encouraged to play even when fatigue weighed her down, and now she understood the importance behind those moments.

Amidst the laughter and stories, Picola suddenly asked, "Was our mother's name May?" The question struck Isza, who realized that Picola had a faint memory connected to that name. Picola remembered a moment from the past involving Hilda and a reassurance from May that everything would be alright, a comforting presence that had seemed maternal to her.

"No, May is our sister, not our mother," Isza gently clarified. "Viola is our mother."

The air shifted as Isza fell quiet for a moment, taken aback. It had been a long time since she had thought of May. May had sacrificed everything for her siblings, giving them the hope of freedom. Isza vividly recalled May's words before their parting, that she would find her way to the first Free State. A flicker of hope sparked within Isza; perhaps, with her lighter skin, she could search for May and bring her back to join them. This thought brought a fleeting smile to her face until the haunting dream of May's tragic end in the swamps clouded her mind. Yet even then, Isza felt an unwavering sense of purpose; the possibility of reuniting with May was too precious to ignore. There was still hope to cling to, and that made the journey meaningful.

They arrived at the cabin nestled in the woods, the special place where they always found solace. When Picola caught sight of the familiar structure, tears of joy and nostalgia flowed freely down her cheeks.

"I remember this place," she began, her voice trembling with emotion. "I remember the first time we arrived here. I felt so cold and weary. I remember my sisters, and I remember my mother. Back then, so many memories were lost to me; I couldn't even recall how I ended up on that plantation. But now, it's all coming back. I remember it all."

With warmth and care, Isza wrapped her arms around Picola, gently rocking her back and forth. She whispered softly into her ear, assuring her that their sisters would be arriving soon to join them.

They spent two weeks in the cabin, sharing stories about their pasts and joyfully exploring the surrounding area, though they stayed relatively close. Inspired by her neighbor's craftsmanship, Isza suggested they try their hand at making a table and some chairs for their gathering spot. They set out to collect cypress logs that lay on the forest floor, carefully choosing the perfect pieces of wood to transform.

As days went by without any sign of her sisters, they decided to allow themselves just one more week to wait before embarking on a search. In the meantime, they threw themselves into building the chairs, using vines found around the cabin and at the base of nearby trees. When they completed the two chairs, they couldn't help but feel a sense of pride in their handiwork, even though they were slightly rickety when sat upon.

One bright morning, while resting on the floor in a cozy corner beneath the window, Isza suddenly heard a soft rustling outside. She jumped up, filled with both excitement and trepidation, unsure whether it was her sisters or perhaps the owners. She wished to keep her presence a secret just a little longer.

Peering through the window, Isza spotted a figure running toward the cabin. Clothed in a flowing, sheer white dress that danced in the breeze, the woman looked ethereal as though the very wind was urging her onward. Through the mist, Isza struggled to identify her, and though the figure was moving swiftly, it seemed almost as if time were stretching, keeping her just out of reach.

As she scanned the room, Isza realized Picola was nowhere to be found. Panic rose within her, and she instinctively lowered herself, hoping that the mysterious visitor would drift past without entering. Sitting there, arms wrapped tightly around her knees, Isza focused on the door, her heart racing. A wave of unease washed over her, as if something ominous lurked nearby. She thought of Picola and vowed that if anyone dared to take her sister, she would shout out that they were family and would return for her.

In that moment, Isza fought to keep her body steady, battling the urge to flee like a leaf caught in a storm. She reminded herself that caution was her ally in this uncertain moment, and so she waited, full of hope and anticipation for what was to come.

For the first time in what felt like ages, Isza found herself grappling with a sense of fear, acutely aware of her identity and the precariousness of her freedom. Sitting there, she caught herself anxiously staring at the door, her heart racing at every creak as she listened to the approaching footsteps.

In that tense moment, she reminded herself that in order to truly embrace her freedom, she needed to rise above fear, so she took a deep breath, stood tall, and lifted her chin high.

The doorknob slowly turned, and it felt as though time stopped, every moment stretched as she watched. When the door finally began to open, her voice broke through the quiet, "Who's there?" She held her breath, anticipation coursing through her veins. As the door swung open fully, she couldn't believe her eyes; standing there was May. Joy surged through her as she rushed forward and wrapped her sister in a heartfelt embrace, overwhelmed by the happiness of their reunion.

With excitement bubbling over, Isza quickly recounted the incredible journey they had shared, how they had escaped and were living their lives as free individuals, even as she felt the weight of sorrow linger in the memory of Hilda, who had tragically lost her life while still in bondage. Looking deeply into May's eyes, Isza sensed that May understood the gravity of their situation, recognizing the sadness reflected there. Isza felt a shift in the air, this moment was different.

As she glanced around the cabin, it appeared unchanged since that fateful night when she and her sisters first arrived. Turning back to May, Isza saw a bittersweet smile cross her sister's face as May shared her own harrowing tale of escape.

"I finally found a way to freedom only to be captured and sent back," May said, her voice steady yet heavy with emotion. "They tried everything to make me reveal your whereabouts, but I refused to betray you, no matter the cost. One day, they talked about letting me go, thinking I would lead them to you. That was when I knew I had to make a run for it. I remember the night vividly; I could hear them close behind me. I crept along the banks, seeking refuge where the land was higher, desperately trying to find a safe place to rest. I stood at the top, arms outstretched, and I heard a voice say, 'Come home.' When I hit the water, it felt like pure peace, a glimpse of what freedom truly felt like."

Isza listened with rapt attention as they both heard a rustle outside. Her heart leaped, and she called out, "Picola, is that you?"

As the door creaked open once more, she felt a wave of courage wash over her. And then, to her astonishment, there was Hilda standing there. Overwhelmed, Isza fell to her knees, her heart full, pleading for forgiveness. "Hilda, I'm so sorry for going to New Orleans. If I would have known the pain it would cause, I would have stayed behind."

With a gentle smile, Hilda spoke, "Isza, none of this was your fault. Because of you, I tasted freedom and experienced love, something I wouldn't have known otherwise. Thank you for that."

As Hilda's form began to fade, Isza cried out, "Hilda, please come back. I love you."

Turning to see how May was doing, Isza noticed her sister also beginning to disappear. They shared a profound moment, their voices intertwining as they said, "We love you."

Fueled by a surge of emotion, Isza sprang to her feet, shouting, "Come back. Please, don't leave. I love you both."

In that moment, amidst the swirling feelings of love, loss, and the unbreakable bond of sisterhood, Isza understood the power of hope and the strength that love gives, even in the darkest of times. Her heart brimmed with optimism for the future, knowing that their spirits would always be intertwined.

As Isza took another look around, she noticed Picola standing in front of her, tears glistening in her eyes. With genuine concern, Picola asked whether she was alright. and who she was hoping would return.

Sitting down with Picola, Isza decided to share the dream that had been weighing on her heart. She explained that they'd stay a few more days together to see what might unfold. However, when no one showed up, they came to the mutual decision to head back to New Orleans. It would be seven long years before Isza returned to the cabin again.

The long-anticipated war among the enslaved people finally arrived, bringing about a monumental change; the end of slavery. One of the remarkable aspects of this war was the significant part that enslaved individuals in the South played in their own liberation, a fact that often goes unnoticed. Contrary to popular belief that they idly waited for the North to rescue them, enslaved men and women actively fought for their freedom.

It was a transformative era for Negro's who suddenly found themselves free to craft their own futures. In the years following the war, many embarked on journeys, some traveling west, others heading north, while some who had originally come from the North returned South in search of long-lost family.

Unfortunately, the excitement of newfound freedom was soon tempered by the harsh reality that came with it. The South was none too pleased with the outcome of the war, and racial violence surged. Many Negro people found themselves targeted during the night, facing horrors such as lynching, arson, and other brutal acts. For those who hadn't yet left the South, the path to safety became increasingly treacherous. Life felt crueler than it had during slavery, as individuals who were newly freed lacked legal protections, now, no one felt accountable for their lives.

In light of this danger, Isza took it upon herself to help escort people from the perilous South to the safer North. She used the simple strategy of claiming that those traveling with her were her workers. It was an uncertain time, where the threat of recognition loomed large. Each time someone directed a light on her face, the chilling fear of being spotted lingered.

One evening, while traveling with a group of Negros from Mississippi, that fear materialized. As they made their way through Tennessee, a commanding voice cut through the night saying, "Stop the wagon."

Isza's instinct was to keep going, though she knew it was futile. The man's question rang in her ears, "Who do you have with you?"

In that moment, she focused on maintaining her composure and replied quickly, explaining that she was heading to her mother's house to deliver some hands for her farm. "My father passed away, and my mother could use the help. After the war, she lost all her enslaved people. These have been working with me since they were born; they love me."

As the man shone the light into her face, he inquired about her name. With a steady voice, she answered, "Suzy Jackson from DeSoto, Mississippi." He scrutinized her for what felt like an eternity before finally allowing them to continue. Isza felt an overwhelming wave of gratitude that he hadn't recognized her as his own granddaughter. The night was dark, but she knew that if he sensed her presence, her distinct scent or the vibration of her voice, or even the movements of her horses, he might have picked up on her deception.

Once they were safely away from danger, Isza rode into the night, a heavy realization settling in; this could very well be her last journey. Though they had achieved freedom, the lingering issue of runaway slaves made the stakes incredibly high, and she fully understood the dire consequences that loomed should she be caught.

With a newfound perspective, Isza recognized it was time to invest in her own life and ambitions. The dynamics had shifted; she no longer bore the burden of her sisters' safety, despite not having seen them for years. They often crossed her mind, and she remained watchful for any signs of them. Whenever she had vivid dreams about one of her sisters, it felt real, as though they had truly spent time together. Isza held on to the belief that they knew where to find her, and perhaps one day they would seek her out in New Orleans. With hope in her heart, she was ready to chase after her own dreams.

Nine

Meanwhile back at the plantation near the cabin, Baby lived, with Teacee and Joseph, she had the opportunity to meet Cooper, a charming young man visiting from New York for the summer. Cooper was there to spend time with his grandmother, affectionately known to everyone as Nanny. Teacee was the first to notice the spark between Baby and Cooper; she felt an undeniable chemistry between them that seemed to grow stronger each day, even as they tried to brush it aside. It wasn't long before Cooper, too, became aware of Baby, yet she seemed to look right past him, completely oblivious to his attempts to catch her gaze.

One bright Saturday morning, as Baby and Teacee embarked on their morning walk, everything changed. Baby finally locked eyes with Cooper, and in that instant, she felt a thrilling connection. It was clear he felt it as well; the way he looked back at her suggested a mutual spark that was hard to ignore. Teacee couldn't help but chuckle quietly at the moment, sensing the electricity in the air and the tension between the two that was simply too palpable to miss.

Feeling that their silent game of pretense was growing a little tiresome, Teacee decided it was time to help them break through the barrier. She cleverly sent Baby to Nanny's house to retrieve a sack of potatoes. Baby's heart raced with excitement at the thought of finally having a chance to speak to Cooper, hoping that once they were in a more familiar setting, he might feel at ease. Although she didn't quite understand why he made her feel a blend of excitement and nerves, she was determined to unravel the mystery. As she approached Nanny's house, she felt butterflies in her stomach and her palms grew clammy. It was as if her heart was creating its own rhythm, leading her like a drumbeat towards something wonderful. By the time she reached the house, she hesitated, leaning against a nearby tree to gather her thoughts. She took several deep breaths to steady herself. Spotting someone on the porch made her realize just how much this moment meant to her.

Just then, someone called out to Cooper, asking him to bring the sack of potatoes to the front door. The moment Baby arrived at the house, there he was, tall and lean, casually carrying the sack of potatoes over his shoulder. Baby stepped further into the yard, heart fluttering, and he nodded in her direction. Inside, she thought, Oh no, not just a nod.

Looking deep into his eyes, Baby managed to say, "Good evening." For a few seconds, he stood there, wide-eyed and momentarily speechless. As she waited with bated breath, she noticed his lips begin to move. Time seemed to slow as a sound escaped him, she didn't catch every word, but it didn't matter. She took a seat on the porch, Baby chatted with Nanny while Cooper set the sack of potatoes down before turning to head back into the house. Though she felt a pang of disappointment, wishing he would sit down and join them, she relished the moment.

As it came time for Baby to leave, she picked up the sack of potatoes, swinging it over her shoulder. In an attempt to appear nonchalant, she stumbled slightly under its weight. Suddenly, the screen door burst open, and Cooper dashed out, exclaiming, let me carry those potatoes for you.

Baby felt a warm blush creep onto her cheeks as she lowered her eyes. With a shy smile, she handed him the sack, only to watch him lift it effortlessly, as if it weighed nothing at all. He could see that she was enchanted. Baby stood there, utterly captivated by the handsome young man in front of her, trying her best not to smile too widely, though her heart betrayed her with excitement when he smiled back. The moment was sweetened further, as Nanny chimed in with a playful tone, "Are you two going to take those potatoes, or are you planning to bake them right here in the sun?"

With a bright smile directed at his grandmother, Cooper replied, "Yes, ma'am, we're on our way."

In that magical moment, the energy between them felt like just the beginning of a beautiful adventure.

As they meandered down the dusty road, Cooper warmly shared stories about his family with Baby, painting a picture of resilience and history. He spoke of Nanny, whose early life was marked by hardship; when she was just a baby, the Master made the decision to sell her mother, Mary, separating them forever. Raised by her grandparents, Nanny grew up surrounded by tales of her mother, who had shown incredible courage and determination in her struggle for freedom. Despite everyone urging her to stay, Mary was resolute, expressing her fierce desire to escape the bonds of slavery, unwilling to endure such a life for herself or allow her precious baby girl to suffer the same fate. Tragically, during her attempt to flee, she was captured, vanishing from their lives forever.

Although Nanny's grandparents eventually bought their freedom, they chose to remain on the plantation, clinging to the hope that one day, Mary would return. Sadly, that hope was never fulfilled. After the passing of her grandparents, Nanny found herself still at the plantation, holding onto dreams of reunion. However, when Cooper's grumpa suggested they move to New York, she made the difficult decision to let go of that dream. In her new journey, she discovered her talent as a seamstress, having learned from her grumpa, who was a tailor. They began by repairing clothes, and before long, their skills attracted attention, leading to requests for custom pieces. This blossomed into a thriving shop on Broadway, one of Brooklyn's busiest streets, where Cooper was born and raised, contributing to the vibrant fabric of their community.

Nanny recounted the incredible moment of reuniting with her mother on a frigid winter night, its coldness more biting than anything she had ever experienced. It was one of the reasons Nanny fled New York; she simply could not bear the chill. That evening remained etched in her memory, the fire crackling and a large pot of water steaming on the stove, yet she still could feel the icy grasp of the night.

As she passed by a window, something outside caught her eye, prompting her to pause and focus. Perhaps it was her neighbor, who lived just across the way with her twelve children, coming to seek warmth from a too-cold home. Standing there, she watched intently before eventually stepping away from the window to warm herself in front of the fireplace. Suddenly, a knock echoed through the house, igniting her excitement as she raced to the door, anticipating her neighbor's arrival. But when she swung the door open, it revealed an elderly woman enshrouded in snow, her features almost unrecognizable. Without hesitation, Nanny wrapped her warm blanket around the stranger, feeling an inexplicable familiarity with her.

After the old woman had warmed up and found her breath, they started to share stories, leading Nanny to the astonishing realization that this woman was her mother, Mary. Through a journey filled with heartache and longing, they had finally found each other again, and Mary was resolute in her commitment to never let her daughter go again.

As Cooper finished sharing this heartfelt tale, they discovered they had arrived at Baby's home. Teacee was on the porch, beaming down at them, and Baby felt a pang of anxiety, hoping she wouldn't embarrass her in front of Cooper.

"Hi, Cooper. How are you doing today?" Teacee called out cheerfully.

At the sound of his name, Cooper paused mid-story, acknowledging her.
"Ma'am, I'm doing well. My grandma asked me to bring you these potatoes. Where would you like me to put them?" he responded politely.

"Could you place them on the back porch?" Teacee suggested with a friendly smile.

As Cooper headed to the back, Teacee followed closely behind him. Baby, feeling a stir of unease, wished she could intervene, fearing Teacee's playful teasing might make Cooper hesitant to visit again. They spent some time outside, and Baby found herself anxiously waiting on the porch, wishing she had joined them but too late to change her course now. When the sound of their voices drew nearer, she scrambled to mask her anticipation, pretending to have forgotten Cooper was even there.

"I'll see you at five o'clock sharp. Thanks again." Cooper called out as he prepared to leave.

Baby watched him walk down the road until he vanished from view. Once he was out of sight, she quickly turned to Teacee with curiosity, eager to know the meaning behind Cooper's promise to return at five, anticipating what might unfold. Teacee simply chuckled and replied, "That's just dinner time, as it always is at five."

In that moment, Baby felt a sense of excitement brew within her as the day unfolded with promise.

Baby stood there, gazing at Teacee, her mind a whirlwind of thoughts about whether inviting him over was the right decision. Teacee believed that this could bring Baby great joy, but a flicker of guilt lingered in her heart at the thought of being mistaken. Observing their interactions, it became clear that someone needed to encourage a connection.

Suddenly, Baby turned and took a few steps back, but just as Teacee began to feel uncertain about how to respond, Baby sprinted toward her, arms flailing with sheer excitement. At first, Teacee was taken aback, but then she caught sight of Baby's radiant smile.

"Thank you, thank you. You've made me the happiest girl in the world. Thank you, I love you. Baby exclaimed; her joy infectious.

With that, she dashed into the house, and Teacee quickly followed, eager to share in the moment.

"What are you up to?" Teacee asked with a curious smile.

"I need to find the perfect outfit for tonight." Baby replied, her eyes sparkling with anticipation.

"It's still noon; you have plenty of time," Teacee reassured her.

"But I want to look my absolute best." Baby insisted, her enthusiasm unwavering.

"Absolutely. You have all the time in the world, and I'd love to help you find the ideal look," Teacee said, feeling a rush of excitement for what the evening held.

As the delicious aroma of dinner wafted through the air, Baby's nerves about her outfit heightened. Eventually, she emerged proudly clad in her Sunday best, beautiful though Teacee thought it might be a tad formal for the occasion. Despite this, Baby was resolute in her decision, and Teacee respected her choice. Once Baby set her mind to something, there was no swaying her.

Around four-thirty, a cheerful knock echoed from the door. When Teacee opened it, she was greeted by Cooper, dapperly dressed in his Sunday suit.

"Good evening, ma'am. I'm here for supper," he said with a warm smile.

"Come on in. We've been eagerly awaiting your arrival," Teacee welcomed him in.

As he walked past her, Teacee felt a joyful realization wash over her; Baby's outfit was just right; they were both perfectly in sync with the spirit of the evening.

As dinner unfolded, Cooper was lively and engaging, showering Baby with compliments about her beauty and raving about the delightful smothered potatoes. He expressed gratitude for the invitation and entertained them with vibrant tales of New York, where he worked alongside his father. He shared that his mother was a talented seamstress while his father was known for making and repairing shoes, renowned by many who traveled far and wide for his craftsmanship.

"I made these shoes myself," he proudly said, extending one foot to showcase his handiwork beneath the table.

Both women couldn't help but smile at the evident pride he took in his work. After dinner, Baby and Cooper settled on the porch, engrossed in each other's company. He painted a vivid picture of New York, the bustling streets filled with people and towering buildings that seemed to scrape the sky. He even shared a thrilling encounter with the President of the United States, and Baby listened in wide-eyed amazement, a smile blossoming on Cooper's face as he spoke.

As the evening progressed, Baby yearned to hear more about his family's stories, but she sensed that time was fleeting; soon Teacee would come out to nudge him away. They sat, spellbound under the stars, exchanging glances filled with unspoken words. Just as the warmth of the moment lingered, Teacee stepped onto the porch, gently reminding them that it was time for Cooper to head home. Baby shot her a hopeful glance, silently requesting a reprieve, but Teacee merely took a seat beside her. Acknowledging it was time to leave, Cooper stood, offered a warm "goodnight," and headed home, leaving echoes of laughter and joy in the air.

Baby and Teacee were enjoying a quiet evening on the porch when Baby decided to share her thoughts about Cooper. With a curious expression, she asked Teacee what she thought of him. Teacee, always genuine, replied that Cooper was a wonderful boy, but she gently reminded Baby that he was just visiting Atlanta and would soon be headed back to New York. That realization struck Baby anew; she had forgotten he lived so far away and would be leaving at the end of summer. As mid-July approached, a wave of sadness washed over her as she imagined the day he would depart.

After bidding Teacee goodnight, Baby climbed into bed, but sleep eluded her. Guilt tugged at her for not having spoken to Cooper earlier, and frustration bubbled inside. When she finally drifted off, her dreams alternated between the joy of being with him in New York and unsettling nightmares about not seeing him again. She was eager for morning, hoping the night's turmoil would finally subside.

In one vivid dream, Baby found herself in a quaint house nestled in the woods, a feeling of loneliness enveloping her without any clear reason. Just as she began to ponder her surroundings, a knock at the door broke the silence. To her surprise, Cooper stood there, looking as if he had just run a marathon, sweat glistening on his brow. Even after all this time apart, she felt an unexplainable connection to him. "The dogs are on my scent," he exclaimed, urgency in his tone. "We need to leave together to avoid capture." His words puzzled her, as the house seemed familiar; it was a place from her childhood, long ago.

Just as she began to ask what was happening, loud gunshots echoed outside, accompanied by the frantic barking of dogs. In a surge of instinct, Cooper grabbed her hand, leading them both to dash outside. As the sounds of pursuit grew nearer, he urged her to run in the opposite direction as a diversion, but in her heart, she felt the desperate need for him to stay by her side.

Startled awake, Baby gasped, her heart racing. Teacee, alert to her distress, rushed into the room, concern etched on her face. Baby told her she had a bad dream. Teacee thoughtfully suggested that perhaps it reflected her anxieties about Cooper's upcoming departure.

The next morning, Teacee awoke to find Baby sitting quietly in the kitchen, her expression hinting at a difficult night. Baby opened up about her restless sleep and the emotions swirling inside her. Teacee wanted to delve deeper into Baby's feelings, but she wisely decided to wait for Baby to express herself when the time was right.

Later that day, Cooper stopped by for a visit. Baby was attempting to rest in her room when Teacee entered, beaming as she informed her that Cooper was waiting on the porch. Suddenly invigorated, Baby leaped to her feet, eager to see him. She paused at the door, taking a moment to catch her breath before stepping outside to find Cooper grinning broadly. His smile instantly brightened her mood.

"I've been worried, this is my second time checking in on you today" he shared, his eyes sparkling with concern. "I thought maybe you didn't want to see me, or worse, that I had upset you somehow."

Baby felt a surge of gratitude for his dedication. She explained that she had struggled to sleep, restless and anxious, and that she might be coming down with a cold. His persistent kindness truly meant the world to her, and she couldn't help but smile back.

In that moment, surrounded by good company and heartwarming friendship, Baby felt a sense of hope. Whatever the future held, she knew they cherished this time together, and that made all the difference.

One sunny afternoon, they made their way downtown in search of a delicious root beer float, and the timing couldn't have been better. Hand in hand, they strolled down the road, enjoying the warmth of the day. Suddenly, Baby caught some unsettling noises coming from the nearby woods. Cooper, with his New York background, felt a natural curiosity to investigate, but Baby's instincts told her a different story. She was all too aware of the harsh realities that could unfold in those woods, instances where innocent lives were tragically altered due to the color of their skin.

With concern etched on his face, Cooper suggested seeking help in town, but Baby felt a strong urge to return home, sensing that discretion was the better part of valor in that moment.

Back at home, Baby shared with Teacee what they had witnessed, her heart heavy as she revealed that the boy being attacked was none other than the Butler's oldest son. It wasn't long before word spread, and the Butlers began their frantic search for him. The first place they rushed to was the very woods where Baby and Cooper had seen the horrifying scene unfold. Together, Baby and Cooper led them there, their hearts pounding in unison with every step. Thankfully, they found no horrifying evidence of the boy's fate hanging from a tree, an image that had haunted their minds.

Their next stop was the hospital, but when they inquired, they found he wasn't there. They then turned towards the jailhouse and discovered the shocking news that he had been arrested for being drunk in public. Everyone in their community knew that this was an outright lie; he was a devoted young man who didn't drink and was even on the path to becoming the pastor of their church.

As they spoke with the sheriff, three men entered the room, their laughter echoing off the walls as they jostled each other. Cooper's heart sank as he recognized them; he couldn't contain himself as he pointed and shouted, "That's them. They were there."

Baby instinctively tightened her grip on his arm, her voice low and urgent. "No, what are you talking about? You must be confused. Come on, let's go home." She led him towards the door, but as soon as they stepped outside, Cooper pulled away, frustration coursing through him.

"Why did you say that? You saw them." he insisted.

"Of course, I saw them," she replied, her voice steady but anxious. "But did you notice that they were wearing uniforms?"

Silence hung between them as he grasped her hand tightly, and they began their walk home. Later, while reflecting on their experience, Cooper expressed his disbelief at witnessing the law, those meant to protect, turning against the very people they were supposed to safeguard. Having grown up in New York, he had heard stories from many who had fled the South in fear of the law, yet it never truly registered until now. He couldn't fathom how Negro families chose to endure such conditions while living in the South.

In the days that followed, they cherished every moment they could share together. However, the atmosphere grew tense, and with increased police presence in their community, Baby wisely advised Cooper to remain cautious with his words; a silent agreement that they would navigate this with care. With more people staying indoors unless absolutely necessary, Baby grew anxious when Cooper stopped visiting. Fear crept in; she wondered if something had happened to him or if he had been taken away during the night. Teacee did her best to comfort her, assuring Baby that he was likely alright, yet Baby couldn't shake her worries. She needed to see him for herself.

Seeing her distress, Teacee joined her, and together they knelt in prayer. "Our Father, who art in heaven..."

A few days later, the community was rocked again when the Butler's son was found hanging in the woods, a chilling confirmation of Baby's worst fears, making it all the more dangerous to step outside. The atmosphere shifted; people returned to their daily routines as if nothing had transpired. The Butlers held a quiet service for their son, but the weight of what had happened loomed over everyone.

Cooper found it impossible to forget the grave reality of a young life lost at the hands of those who were supposed to protect him. He longed for Baby to come to New York, but they both recognized the limits of their youth. She wanted him to stay close to his grandmother, yet this was a decision neither could truly make alone. Ultimately, they decided to stay connected through letters, eagerly awaiting the next summer when they could reunite. Together, they held onto hope, cherishing the love and understanding they had found in each other.

Ten

After Cooper's return to New York, Baby underwent a remarkable transformation; she was blossoming into a young woman before Teacee's eyes. It was a new chapter, and with each passing day, Baby eagerly awaited any word from Cooper. The highlight of her day was seeing the mail carrier approach their home. But when no letter arrived, her spirit would dim, leaving her feeling heartbroken and puzzled. The silence bred her worries, leading her to imagine troubling scenarios about Cooper's fate. One recurring nightmare haunted her, a fear that he had been taken from the train by law enforcement and taken deep into the woods, left in dire straits. Baby confided in Teacee about her fears and dreams, and though Teacee tried to reassure her, reminding her that Nanny would surely have communicated any bad news, it did little to ease Baby's longing or questions about why she hadn't heard from him.

Feeling the weight of the situation, Teacee decided to take action. She approached Nanny, hopeful that there might be some news about Cooper's well-being. Teacee expressed her concern, explaining how deeply Baby felt connected to him and how distressed she was about the lack of communication. If only Cooper could send a simple letter confirming his safe arrival, it would do wonders for Baby's heart. Teacee kindly asked Nanny to keep their conversation private, fearing that Baby's emotional state might worsen. However, as the days turned into weeks, it became painfully clear to Teacee that Cooper might not feel the same way about Baby. His silence spoke volumes, indicating that perhaps he wasn't inclined to reach out, not even to reassure Baby of his safety.

Determined to lift Baby's spirits, Teacee suggested outings to the market and times to spend with friends, hoping to distract her from thoughts of Cooper. Despite her good intentions, Teacee couldn't shake the guilt of having introduced them. She wondered if her involvement had led Baby into a whirlwind of emotions that now overwhelms her. Teacee understood all too well the intensity of first love and how challenging it could be to navigate those feelings. Memories of her own first love surfaced, the joy and turmoil wrapped in those early experiences. She reminisced about Wes Brady, a spirited young man who had also worked at the plantation as a free man. Their conversations had been filled with hope and dreams of a better future, especially his desire to venture beyond the plantation.

Wes had shared his aspirations of leaving for New Orleans, a place where the stories of freedom and opportunity were tantalizing. He painted a vivid picture of life in the city, where many freed slaves thrived and built their own lives. Since he had his papers, he could carve out a space for himself and pursue his passion for cooking, a talent he had honed from a young age. The way his face lit up at the prospect brought Teacee so much joy; she felt deeply that he was destined for great things. They spent weeks immersed in discussions about his future, and the spark of excitement in him was contagious. Each time Wes showed her his documents of freedom, the reality of his situation became clearer, it was only a matter of him making the pivotal choice to embark on the journey.

Yet, the reality of leaving weighed heavily on him, particularly as the weekends approached. Each Friday, when many would set out toward newfound possibilities, he would shy away, avoiding her company. The first time they planned to meet at a certain time, he didn't show up, sparking Teacee's hope that perhaps he had taken the leap to New Orleans. As she walked home, her mind swirled with the hopeful vision of their future together, she envisioned him returning to sweep her away to adventure and new beginnings. However, when she shared her excitement with her companions, their laughter rang hollow. They dismissed her hopes, insisting that Wes would never leave the plantation. But Teacee held firm to her faith in his dreams. She recognized the fire in his heart and believed that, since he had shared his aspirations with her, there was every reason to trust his sincerity.

Teacee took a while to understand that Wes Brady had no intention of leaving the plantation. Intrigued and concerned, she felt a strong desire to discuss with him his reasons for wanting to stay in a place where both he and his mother had suffered so deeply. It was hard for her to grasp that a man who held freedom papers would choose to remain in such bondage. Wes hadn't realized that his freedom came at a heartbreaking cost, his mother's life. As she drew her last breath, she must have thought he would be safe, having sacrificed everything so he could be free. Teacee recognized that she needed to get to the bottom of this situation and decided that Friday would be the best time to talk with him, even though she knew it might be challenging, as he often kept his distance on that day.

Determined, she approached him early and asked if they could chat. They found a comfortable spot under a large shade tree, where they could speak freely.

"Wes, why do you want to stay here? You could go to New Orleans and be free, or head north for that same freedom. Why choose to remain?"

He gazed ahead; a deep weight of shame evident as he struggled to meet her eyes.

"I can't leave. Only part of me is free," he replied, his words hanging in the air with an unsettling gravity.

Teacee felt a flicker of confusion. "What do you mean, part of you is free? You have your papers; you're a free man."

He stood up abruptly, motioning for her to follow him. "Let me show you something," he said, guiding her to his cabin at the far edge of the plantation. Teacee's heart sank when they arrived and she saw a young girl and two small boys sitting together.

"This is why I can't leave," he explained, his voice heavy with emotion. "She is mine, but those boys aren't. If I leave, I can't take them with me."

This revelation struck Teacee like a thunderbolt. "What do you mean, she belongs to you?" she asked, trying to process the implications.

Lowering his gaze to the ground, he shared, "The Master gave her to me when I turned thirteen. She was my 'gift.'"

Teacee took a step back, grappling with the reality of his words. She had envisioned leaving the plantation together, starting a new life in New Orleans, but that dream now felt utterly out of reach. The pain within her was multifaceted, was it the fact that Wes had another woman in his life, or the fact that she was enslaved? Observing his sorrow, she realized he saw the look of disappointment on her face. Wes wanted to clarify that their lives often required sacrifices to protect those they loved, so he pleaded with her to hear his story, and she nodded in agreement.

"My momma told me that when I turned thirteen, I would receive a gift from the Master. It was a part of his tradition; she had been the Master's gift. When I received her, my momma expected me to treat her the way I would want someone to treat my own mother. She always reminded me that having ownership of someone doesn't give you the right to treat them poorly. When she came to me, she was sixteen and had been through a lot already. Sometimes just her shadow would frighten her. I followed my momma's advice; I treated her well. I fell in love with her, and though we didn't have a formal marriage, I consider her my wife. Those boys are my heart, yet they belong to the Master."

As Wes spoke, Teacee couldn't help but notice the pride that illuminated the young girl's face as she heard him profess his love. It became clear to Teacee that they were the anchor holding Wes to the plantation. Though he yearned for freedom, the thought of leaving them behind was unbearable. He shared his fears, that if he left, they might be sold off. The very notion was terrifying to him. He had to maintain the illusion that his true love was merely a gift, forcing himself at times to pretend interest in someone else. Teacee felt a mixture of joy and sorrow; joy for witnessing such a profound love, and sadness for realizing that she couldn't be a part of his life.

Years had passed since Teacee lost her first love, yet she frequently thought of him, often wondering how his journey unfolded. Wes Brady remained on the plantation long after her own work there concluded. After the war led to the end of slavery, he was sometimes spotted working in restaurants around Atlanta. Tragically, Wes and his family left the vibrant city after enduring the loss of their only daughter, who had been born free. Teacee later learned that this wasn't a mere separation, his daughter had become a victim of the heartless tradition. Wes had been warned that if he sought her out, there would be dire consequences. Faced with the possibility of losing everything he loved; Wes couldn't stay in Atlanta either. With heavy hearts, he and his sons departed, and that was the last time Teacee would lay eyes on him.

In reflecting on Wes's journey, she felt a deep appreciation for the complexities of love, sacrifice, and the many forms freedom can take. Even amidst their struggles, what shone brightly was the undeniable strength of connection, and Teacee knew that their stories, while intertwined with hardship, were also filled with immense love.

Teacee came to a heartfelt realization; the most powerful way to support Baby was to surround her with love and connection. Inspired by this insight, Teacee committed to spending more quality time with Baby. They strolled along the winding red clay road, where the remnants of the slave quarters stood silently, echoing stories of the past. The sight of those humble structures served as a poignant reminder, offering a deeper perspective on life's challenges. As night fell, some claimed that walking past the shacks meant hearing the whispers of those who endured slavery. It was as if the very ground held their sorrows, and by the end of their walks, both sisters often found relief from their own burdens, feeling uplifted and renewed.

During their walks, Teacee observed something that caught her off guard; Baby couldn't recall much about their parents. Eager to fill that gap, Teacee began to share her cherished memories of their mother and father. Despite the heavy shadows of slavery around them, their parents had instilled in them a profound sense of freedom, encouraging them to think for themselves and recognize that happiness is truly a choice, one that was eternally available to them.

In the softest tone she could muster, Teacee turned to Baby and said, "I know you love him."

Baby's response was immediate, filled with passion, "Yes. Why hasn't he written to me yet? I thought he loved me too. He said he loved me, and I believed him. Why hasn't he written?"

Teacee knew the importance of choosing her words carefully in this tender moment. "I truly don't know. But it's important for you to move beyond this. You deserve to live fully and not be weighed down by sadness."

Baby appeared taken aback by her sister's honesty. "Why do you say that? I do love him, but I don't want to die."

With sincerity, Teacee replied, "You may love him, but it seems like you've forgotten to embrace life. Many have sacrificed greatly so you could have this opportunity. You are here, and your life is precious."

Baby absorbed Teacee's comforting words, feeling a glimmer of understanding bloom inside her. "I do love him, and I hoped he'd reach out, but I'm okay. Just talking to you lifts my spirits. Thank you; I love you too."

Standing before the last shack, Baby felt an incredible lightness as if her troubles were being shed. As they continued their daily strolls, Baby blossomed with each step they took together. Her smiles returned, and she began reconnecting with old friends. She also cherished her visits to Nanny, where she assisted with reading letters from family members, which brightened her days.

One day, upon arriving at Nanny's house, Baby found her standing at the doorway, a letter in her hand. Nanny hesitated, unsure about Baby's feelings towards the letter from her grandson, fearing it might bring more heartache. Yet, as Baby looked into Nanny's eyes, she sensed an unspoken change. She glanced at the letter, its importance palpable, and then back at Nanny's hopeful expression.

When Nanny extended the letter toward her, Baby hesitated as she recognized the sender's name. For a fleeting moment, she considered tearing it up in frustration, but then realized it wasn't directed to her; it was for Nanny. Nanny gently acknowledged Baby's emotions, expressing understanding if she chose not to read it. However, since it was the first letter from him, she valued Baby's insight and hoped she might give it a chance. After reflecting, Baby made a conscious choice to set aside her hurt; it was clear he had different feelings, and while she couldn't change that, she could still support Nanny.

"Dear Nanny,

I hope this letter finds you in great health, and I hope Baby is reading this to you."

As she read on, a mix of emotions filled Baby's heart, a reminder that life has its ups and downs, but love and hope can guide us through.

When Baby said those words, it felt as though the world around her paused. She dropped the letter, glancing around with a mix of confusion and curiosity, as if someone else had spoken the sweet affirmation. The letter lay at her feet, and she found herself standing there, momentarily lost in the significance of what she had just read. After taking a deep breath, she gently picked it up, feeling a rush of emotions, and began reading it again.

"I hope this letter finds you in great spirits, and I truly hope Baby is reading this to you. Upon my return to New York, I excitedly shared with my parents that I had found the woman I wish to marry."

Once again, Baby dropped the letter, and as she reread those heartfelt words, she heard Nanny's playful voice.

"There must be butter spread all over that paper because you can't seem to hold on to it. "

She chuckled, a blush warming her cheeks, then refocused on the letter, reading on with eager anticipation.

"Baby, I love you so deeply, and Nanny, if she isn't reading this, please let her know how much she means to me. I will be with her as soon as I can. The reason I'm writing to you instead of Baby is that my parents have forbidden me to reach out directly. They've gone through my letters, and now they believe it's not advisable for me to visit. After sharing my concerns regarding that boy in the woods incident, my parents told me that you would be visiting New York next summer. Nanny, I can't wait to see you soon, and Baby, I love you."

Overwhelmed by the revelation, Baby could hardly contain her excitement. "Nanny, can I keep this letter?" she asked, a hopeful plea lingering in her voice. Nanny's eyes twinkled with understanding, and she agreed, knowing it was rightfully Baby's. Cooper had found a way to express his deep feelings for her; despite the hurdles he was facing from family.

When Baby returned home, she was practically breathless, her heart racing with exhilaration. Teacee, concerned, thought someone might be after her and quickly retrieved a gun. Upon seeing the weapon, Baby instinctively dropped to the ground, shielding her head as thoughts swirled in confusion.

"What's happening? Is someone after you?" Teacee shouted, eyeing her with concern.

Baby struggled to find her voice, finally managing to say, "No, no one is chasing me. "

Teacee lowered the gun, her brow furrowing in disbelief. "Have you lost your mind? What was all that commotion?"

With gleaming eyes, Baby could hardly contain her joy. "Look at this letter. " She exclaimed, her voice bubbling with excitement. "He loves me. Cooper loves me. "

"Who loves you?" Teacee replied, puzzled but intrigued.

"Cooper, Cooper loves me. " Baby declared, handing the letter over, only to snatch it back before Teacee could read it. All day long, Teacee couldn't help but notice Baby sitting on her bed, completely absorbed in the beautiful words, a soft smile gracing her lips.

Fast forward to the next summer, Cooper came to visit Nanny, and the visit turned into something grander, he moved in with her. Baby and Cooper began dating, nurturing their love over the next couple of years, leading to a joyful marriage. They settled in New York, where Cooper worked alongside his father as a shoemaker. Over time, his parents grew to cherish Baby, especially after she blessed them with their first grandchild, which brought immeasurable joy.

However, when Baby moved to New York, Teacee and Joseph found themselves grappling with an unexpected void. Though Baby was Teacee's sister, she had always felt like a daughter, and their bond filled a space in their hearts that had long been cherished. Now, with Baby's absence, Teacee felt a profound sense of loneliness, a reminder of how much love and warmth Baby had brought into their lives.

Eleven

O n a warm summer night, Isza found herself tossing and turning in bed, enveloped by a profound sadness that weighed heavily on her heart. The source of her distress eluded her, heightening her sense of confusion and concern. With a history of depression, Isza was apprehensive; she recalled her doctor's warning that a return to that dark place could lead her back to the hospital. As she wrestled with her feelings, it felt as if her entire being was enveloped in grief, leaving her overwhelmed and vulnerable. By morning, the heaviness in her heart had only intensified, and anxiety seeped into her thoughts, leaving her disheartened and restless.

In her isolation, Isza contemplated reaching out to someone who might understand. Picola had married Samuel Sr. and now lived across the river, raising their two boys Samuel Jr. and Lester. They were in route to visit their grandmother in Baton Rouge.

Over the next few days, Isza's feelings deepened, taking over her thoughts and overshadowing her daily life. She was acutely aware of the seriousness of depression and the dire consequences it could bring if left unaddressed. It was clear to her that action was needed, yet she felt lost in a fog of despair. Eventually, overwhelmed by her emotions, Isza stopped going to work and began barricading her windows with wooden planks. Her worried friends and neighbors tried to reach out, but she told them grotesque tales of soldiers coming for her, convinced that they thought she was helping enslaved individuals escape. The fear of being captured loomed over her, and she imagined herself facing the worst fate possible.

During the late eighteenth century, anxiety and depression were prevalent in the Southern states, especially among former slaves living under the shadow of constant fear. The concept of freedom was often an illusion, weighed down by the harsh realities that many faced. Some individuals, driven by despair, isolated themselves, becoming fearful of any human contact, while others exhibited violent behavior out of fear of losing what little they had. The atmosphere of dread was pervasive, creating a landscape rife with psychological turmoil.

Upon returning to New Orleans, Picola quickly learned about Isza's difficulties and felt a compelling need to check on her sister. When she arrived at Isza's home, her heart sank at the sight. The once vibrant and welcoming exterior now lay in disarray, with litter scattered about and the once-beautiful garden in shambles, as if someone had tried to destroy it. Picola knocked on the door, the anxiety of what she might find rising within her.

"Isza, it's me, Picola. Are you alright?" she called out, hopeful she would respond.

"Isza, please open the door. It's me, Picola," she urged, listening intently for a reaction.

"Picola, is that you?" came Isza's faint voice from within.

"Yes, it's me. Please, open the door," Picola pressed.

When Isza finally opened the door, she rushed into Picola's arms, and warmth enveloped them both. "You are safe now; I was so worried about you." Picola said, concern etched across her face.

Looking deeply into Isza's eyes, Picola recognized the urgency for help. Without hesitation, she took Isza to the hospital, where she stayed for several weeks, receiving the care and attention she needed. Upon her release, Isza started to feel a renewed sense of self and purpose.

One quiet evening, she woke suddenly with a start, calling out for her sister, Viola. She sat up, her heart racing and tears streaming down her cheeks. The weight of longing for her sister struck her profoundly, and she realized how many years had passed since they last saw each other. Thoughts of Viola consumed her, intertwining with her concern for her sister's safety and well-being.

As a little girl, Viola had a beautiful voice and a passion for singing. Their mother had warned her to keep her talent hidden, fearing that if the Master discovered it, he might sell her. This reality shaped their lives, as a talented Negro was seen as a prized curiosity, often showcased in demeaning circus acts to entertain white audiences, where her voice would be compared to that of white singers in an unjust way.

These dangerous comparisons could lead to chaotic scenes where audience members shouted cruel remarks, dismissing the authenticity of her talent. Such disrespectful displays served only to highlight the precariousness of their lives. Whenever a circus passed through, the haunting strains of singing could sometimes be heard coming from the tents, but the joy of those moments quickly turned to turmoil when the public responded harshly. By morning, the chaos often left their memories behind as if the circus had vanished without a trace.

In moments like this, Isza knew she had to find Viola. The bond of sisterhood and the struggles they faced resonated deeply, igniting a spark of hope within her, a reminder that connection and love could help uplift even the heaviest of hearts. With determination blooming in her spirit, Isza began to embrace the possibility of reunification and healing, promising herself that she would find her sister and reignite the joys of their shared past.

Isza fondly remembered a special circus that marked a historic moment, the first time Negro people were welcomed to attend. She and Viola buzzed with excitement as they anticipated seeing an elephant for the very first time. The Master's daughter eagerly shared fascinating tales about these majestic creatures, the largest animals in the jungle, hailing from Africa, the homeland of Negro people. While she spoke about the past and offered her perspective on history, Isza and Viola exchanged knowing glances, aware that the true feelings of gratitude within their community were quite different. They understood the importance of embracing their heritage and celebrating their own narrative, filled with resilience and hope for the future. This experience only deepened their pride and curiosity about their roots.

The day the children on the plantation learned they would get to attend the circus was filled with pure joy, reminiscent of the delight they felt receiving treats like rock candy or fruitcake at Christmas. Some had heard amazing stories about the circus, even if they didn't fully grasp what it was all about. Viola was bursting with excitement, especially knowing she would finally see an elephant.

On the morning of the big day, they set off to the river to collect some water, their laughter echoing in the air. As they splashed playfully, a beautiful melody floated toward them from the water. As they got closer, they discovered it was the enchanting sound of someone singing, adding to their day of anticipation and wonder. What a magical experience it was turning out to be. They settled down comfortably by a tree, eagerly listening, knowing how important it is to approach others with care and kindness. They wanted to make sure their presence was felt gently, so they chose to wait for the perfect moment. When the beautiful singing paused, they made a little noise to let anyone nearby know they were coming. As they reached the top of the riverbank, they exchanged astonished glances, taking in the scene before them. There, standing confidently, was a completely free-spirited Negro woman, radiating natural beauty. They were captivated, and though Viola felt a bit tongue-tied in that enchanting moment, her heart was full of curiosity and wonder. The woman looked at them and said, wow, have you never experienced the joy of a talented Negro woman singing? Then she smiled at them and asked, if they were coming tonight? They both nodded enthusiastically. As they walked away, she yelled, don't forget to grab your water, wouldn't want you to get in trouble if you return without it.

As they strolled away, a cheerful voice called out, promising to see them at the circus that night. Bursting with excitement, the two of them started racing and laughing. Just then, Isza noticed her Master approaching, curiosity etched on his face as he asked what was so amusing. Viola, unable to contain her joy, exclaimed that they were heading to the circus to see a talented Negro woman perform in a way that was reminiscent of a white woman's style. Isza instantly sensed the tension in the air; her heart raced as she stepped in front of Viola, concerned about what might follow.

To her astonishment, her Master burst into laughter, responding, "A Negro person who sounds like a white woman, that's quite a concept." He rode off, still chuckling and nearly losing his balance.

Isza looked at Viola in disbelief, questioning her reckless choice of words. "What were you thinking?" she asked, genuinely worried for her sister's safety. Viola admitted that her exuberance had simply taken over, and the words slipped out before she could catch them. Isza gently reminded her of the need for self-control, emphasizing that as a Negro girl, she had to be mindful of her words. She nodded earnestly, understanding the importance of their conversation and feeling grateful for her sister's guidance.

As Viola arrived at the event, she nestled close to her mother, holding her hand with warmth. Excitement filled the air when the Ringmaster stepped into the spotlight, followed by a majestic elephant carrying a beautifully dressed performer. Little people in colorful outfits darted joyfully around them, igniting the crowd's energy. Everyone erupted into applause, with some startled attendees rushing outside, but not Viola. She recognized that the elephant was from her homeland, and rather than fear, a sense of peace washed over her. When the man invited anyone to come meet the elephant, Viola eagerly attempted to rise, but her mother's firm grip reminded her to stay in her seat. This protective gesture was familiar; it often shielded her from circumstances that could harm her. Nevertheless, Viola felt a spark of hope and wonder as she soaked in the enchanting event around her, cherishing the moment.

Later on, their mother shared a powerful lesson that resonated deeply; society often dictated that Negro people should not be brave. She explained that if Viola had taken that courageous step forward and the white children had hesitated to follow, significant trouble would have arisen. At the very least, she would have faced harsh consequences for publicly embarrassing them.

After the incredible performance of the elephant, the clowns, and the jugglers, anticipation grew as it was time for the Negro woman's song. As they brought her onto the stage in a cage, her worn and tattered clothing and the dirt smudged across her body told a story of endurance. When their eyes met, the woman's gaze was filled with a melancholy that felt almost like an apology to them. Yet, as she began to sing, something transformative happened, all the Negro's saw her for who she truly was. The crowd fell silent, completely enveloped by the beauty of her voice. When the final note lingered in the air, it marked the end of the circus, and a sense of longing filled Viola heart. The next day, driven by her desire to connect with the singer, Viola returned only to find the cage, her spirit had disappeared along with the performance.

A few years later, fate intertwined their paths again. However, when Viola approached the woman, eager to rekindle their connection, the singer hesitated and claimed they had never met. Over time, she opened up, revealing that she had closed herself off from those memories, stating that her time at the circus was behind her. She reflected on that night with both sorrow and relief, acknowledging that she felt lucky to have survived. The ringmaster had been angered by the beauty of her voice, and she had paid the price. A man had intervened, offering to buy her freedom, which ultimately spared her life. It was a bittersweet acknowledgment that, while it was a momentous occasion for the Negro audience to hear her sing, it came at a great personal cost. She said, "Negro people have died for far less than my song." Normally, she would restrain herself, as the crowd often held the expectation of her failure, viewing her talent as an affront to their assumptions. Reflecting on her harrowing experience, she found solace in being sold and mentioned a previous singer whose fate had ended tragically, a stark reminder of the risks involved. Viola's heart swelled with gratitude for witnessing that unforgettable performance.

Inspired, Viola began experimenting with her voice more often at home, discovering the profound beauty and tranquility that singing could bring. One afternoon, while harmonizing in the barn, an overseer walked in, curious about the enchanting sound. Upon discovering Viola was the source, he exclaimed that she should be a star at the circus. Yet, the memory of the caged singer held her back; the desire to perform was overshadowed by the realization that such a life was not one she wanted for herself.

Isza's thoughts were consumed with her sister Viola, as if an invisible thread connected them. She felt an overwhelming urge to find her. After days of contemplation, Isza decided to take action, she would return to the last place she remembered seeing her sister; the cabin in the woods. This place held a special significance, feeling like a haven where they could discover who they truly were, even if they hadn't grown up there. It signified hope and a new beginning.

As she approached the cabin, an unfamiliar feeling washed over her. Was it possible that someone else now claimed this space? Isza lingered outside, waiting for a sign, and when no one came, her curiosity nudged her inside. As she opened the door, a rush of memories enveloped her, greeted by the fragrant scent that brought tears to her eyes, its subtle sweetness was reminiscent of the magnolia blossoms on that first magical evening they had spent there. The way the trees stood and the wind carried that scent to the room felt like a beautiful embrace of nostalgia.

That night, Isza settled by the window, her gaze wandering into the enveloping darkness of the woods. She found comfort in the tranquility, interrupted only by the sounds of nature, a gentle rustling of leaves, the whispers of night-time creatures. The peace was a stark contrast to the fears of her past; the acoustic backdrop felt like a soothing lullaby. After all, the noises she'd faced on the plantation were far more intimidating. Now, in this serene moment, the night felt welcoming, a reminder that safety and hope could still exist.

One day as Isza sat by the window, she heard footsteps drawing closer. For a brief moment, her instinct was to slip away. However, she quickly dismissed that thought, eager to see who was approaching. If it turned out to be the owner, she planned to explain that she had paused for a moment to rest on her journey to her mother's home. It felt like an eternity as she waited, but eventually, Viola stepped out of the shadows. Isza could hardly believe her eyes; it was Viola, the very person she had been dreaming of, the one she longed to hold in her arms. They stood together in the dim light, a mix of gratitude and joy washing over them as they embraced. Slowly, they made their way inside, and Isza felt a delightful anticipation fill the air, leaving her momentarily speechless. She let Viola take the lead in their conversation.

Viola shared with Isza that this place had never left her thoughts. She had been reflecting on the family for quite some time but was unsure of everyone's whereabouts. Her return was driven by love and hope; she recognized how significant it was to the family and wished for any sign that could lead her to them. Lately, she had felt a persistent energy, almost a spirit guiding her to make this trip one more time.

Viola recounted how things had deteriorated since their last gathering due to the war. At first, life had seemed relatively unchanged, but as whispers about the end of slavery spread, tensions escalated. With the war nearing its conclusion and freedom within reach, many former masters and overseers had gone off to fight, thrusting their families into the care of those they had historically treated like animals. In a powerful turn of events, those who had endured brutality were rising up, fighting back against their oppressors burning their homes to the ground, and some kill their tormentors. Some white families even sought refuge in the very quarters that had once served as a prison for the enslaved.

As Isza shared her own experiences, she painted a picture of the long walks she took through the woods to visit the house, miles of solitude with no other dwellings in sight. Reflecting on Teacee's broom jumping ceremony, she admitted that she hadn't ventured through the trees much and recalled little about the distance. Viola reassured her that the old plantation where they once worked still stood strong, promising to show it to her before they left.

Isza went on to talk about May and Hilda, mentioning that Picola was thriving and had married and they have two boys. However, her heart felt heavy as she expressed uncertainty about Teacee and Baby's current situation, recalling their last visit when they were contemplating a move back to New Orleans or a nearby place.

With tears glistening in her eyes, Viola cried for her sisters. She explained that following the end of slavery, she returned to the old plantation in search of family. She discovered one elderly cousin, Henry, who, although he didn't remember them, held onto the echoes of their family's history. Henry had endured a lot of brutality during slavery, and even after gaining his freedom, the thought of facing the world alone felt overwhelmingly daunting to him. It was a reality that Viola had noticed everywhere; people trapped by the chains of their past.

Henry shared tales of the sisters who had escaped without a trace, tales that had become part of their family's legacy. Their master had attempted to convince everyone that they were dead, but the community knew the truth. If they had truly perished, their bodies would have been displayed to serve as a warning. Cousin Henry celebrated our bravery, but advised me to leave the area, after all, the master could never forgive us for escaping. He had been mocked for allowing eight spirited girls to vanish from his plantation. We became legends in our own right, known for our audacity, as if we had taken flight like birds at dawn. Some claimed we had disappeared right before his eyes, while others believed our parents had come to take us away.

A few years post-emancipation, Viola found herself as the only sister still living on the plantation near the cabin. She had chosen to stay because of a man she believed could be her partner for life. However, he remained bound to the plantation due to debts, unsure of when or if he would ever be free. Their love blossomed in secrecy, understanding the dangers that came with their situation. They both felt the weight of his status, knowing that if their relationship became known, she could be viewed as part of his property, responsibly entangled in his debts. Yet, the deep connection between them was undeniable, drawing them closer together despite the uncertainty of their circumstances.

In this moment, amidst whispers of their shared past, there was a beautiful knowledge that, no matter the challenges ahead, they would face them together with hope and resilience.

When Viola found out she was pregnant, she realized that staying in her current situation was no longer an option for her. She made the courageous decision to leave and sought shelter at a small house nearby, but soon found that it was too late to travel. With her delivery date fast approaching, she had to confront the reality of her situation, alone, scared, and with no one to turn to. With determination, she gathered grass to create a makeshift corner for herself and covered it with a piece of rag.

She was reminded of a time spent working in the fields with her mother, when a fellow slave had suddenly called out for help. A group of women rushed to assist, and amidst the chaos, a baby fell into her mother's arms. That memory gave her hope, and she set up a small area by the window, praying for the wellbeing of both herself and her baby.

As time passed, waves of anxiety washed over her as she would leap up to grasp the window sill, convinced it was time for her baby to arrive, only to realize it was merely the baby shifting inside her. Then one night, a wave of pain surged through her, a pain she had never felt before, and instinct told her that the moment had come. With each contraction, she gripped the sill, the intensity overwhelming her. Just as fear threatened to take hold, a gentle voice echoed in her mind, urging her to remain calm and trust that everything would be alright. That comforting presence helped her find her strength, and soon after, she heard the sweetest sound; her baby's cry. She gazed down at the most beautiful child she had ever seen, naming her Angel, a tribute to the force that had guided her through the ordeal.

Viola eventually found herself on a plantation in Virginia, striving to escape the South. Fortunately, she had no trouble finding work; the plantation owner had recently given birth and needed help feeding her child. Viola had an abundance of milk, which she happily shared with their baby alongside her own. As Angel grew to be three years old, she was moved into the house, joining their daughter. At first, she felt a twinge of skepticism since the situation reminded her of her past, but she reassured herself that as long as she could keep a watchful eye on her child, things would be alright. And though her new living arrangement involved sleeping on the floor, it was a significant improvement from where they had been.

However, a sense of unease began to creep in when she overheard white people commenting on how beautiful Angel was, and suggesting that she would make the perfect gift. She was stunned, realizing they were discussing her child as if she were an object. When someone mentioned that James would be turning thirteen soon and speculated about Angel as a possible present, she knew they had to act swiftly. She had seen what could happen to young girls who were treated as gifts, and she was resolute in ensuring that her daughter would never face such a fate.

Determined to protect her daughter, she felt a nagging sense that they were being watched, as if there was a plan occurring to take Angel from her. Refusing to let that thought manifest any further, she made a plan to leave. In the dark of night, she gathered her baby and made her break for freedom. Even though she and her child were free, it didn't matter to them. As they escaped, the distant sounds of barking dogs and footsteps began to echo behind them, a stark reminder of her family's own desperate journey to freedom. Grasping that this was their only chance, she ran as fast as she could.

During her flight, Viola found refuge in the homes of other Negro families. It dawned on her that she wasn't alone; many others were bravely seeking liberation from the oppressive grip of slavery. After living years on plantations, Viola had forgotten what true freedom felt like. But as she interacted with those who had broken away from bondage and carved out their own lives, she began to see that there was a different, hopeful path ahead. Although she initially thought staying on the plantation to earn a living was their only option, being surrounded by those who successfully escaped filled her with inspiration and renewed belief.

For nearly a year, Viola and Angel stayed with supportive families, drawing strength from their shared journeys. After this time, they returned briefly to the cabin before setting off in search of her family, with newfound hope in their hearts and freedom on the horizon.

During her stay at the cabin with her child, extraordinary events began to unfold. Viola found herself immersed in vivid dreams about her sister, Isza, from the moment they first arrived. In those dreams, Isza expressed a profound wish that their escape had been the right choice. Viola could sense the overwhelming fear Isza felt about the uncertain future that loomed before them.

After a couple of weeks at the cabin, Viola felt a growing determination to find them. Conversations with people from the nearby plantation revealed that they had moved away years ago, though they mentioned that Isza sometimes returned to check on anyone searching for her. Encouraged, Viola asked them to convey her message, that she was looking for her and would be at the cabin from time to time.

They lingered a bit longer, but Viola soon decided to visit the plantation where Angel's father was living and working. Yearning for stability, she envisioned a life where they could be a family. However, her heart sank when she discovered he had already built one. He urged her to leave quickly, revealing that his entire family was entrapped in a harsh cycle of labor for mere food and shelter. If they became aware that Angel was his daughter, the same fate might befall her. He implored her to escape as far and fast as she could.

Then, without warning, Angel vanished the following morning. No one could grasp what had happened to her, but mere days later, Angel's father and his family walked away from the plantation as free individuals. It turned out he had settled his debts by using Angel as payment, leaving Viola at a loss. After fleeing from the North to save her daughter, she now faced losing her to a man she once believed would protect them. Initially overwhelmed by grief, she faced a tumultuous storm of emotions, contemplating revenge but ultimately recognizing that vengeance wouldn't heal her heartbreak. Deep down, she understood he likely had no real choice in this cruel situation.

Viola ventured North, where she met her husband, Jim. Jim had been free since running away with his brother when their owner sold their parents. When the war erupted, he fought alongside soldiers of all backgrounds, celebrating newfound freedoms when peace returned. Viola enjoyed a fulfilling life with Jim, yet memories of Angel never left her. Jim believed that if they had a child, Viola could find peace. They tried, but to no avail. After several years, Viola felt an undeniable urge to see, hold, and breathe in the essence of her baby. She needed to discover where her child was.

Determined, Viola embarked on a journey from state to state in search of her daughter, unable to find rest until her baby was back in her arms. Viola recounted her relentless search for Angel after leaving Jim, sharing disheartening reports of people who claimed to have seen her child traveling with a family of white individuals. The mere thought of her daughter being trapped in bondage plagued Viola's mind, stealing her peace and leaving her fatigued.

As Isza listened intently to Viola's heartfelt story, an instinct prompted her to pause, by a sound outside that caught her attention. She turned to Isza, wondering if her sister heard it too. Without hesitation, Isza stepped closer, wrapped her arms around Viola, and reassured her that everything would be alright. Yet, deep down, she recognized that what Viola truly sought was the certainty that her baby was safe.

Suddenly, Viola's attention snapped back to Isza, eyes wide with anticipation. "Did you hear that?" she whispered. With a knowing silence, Isza eyes darted outside toward an image moving toward them. She could feel the tension building between them. The sounds grew closer, and as a shadowy figure emerged, Viola gasped, "It's Angel; it's her. I knew she would find her way back." Without a moment's hesitation, Viola burst forth from the cabin, eager to reunite.

Isza felt a mix of emotions as she watched Viola run toward the sound. Her feet felt anchored to the ground, unable to follow. She observed the joyous reunion unfold as they embraced, moving back into the fog. While Isza felt a twinge of sadness at seeing her sister depart, a wave of happiness washed over her for Viola's long-awaited reunion. She lingered for a couple of days, hoping to see them return. When they didn't, she resolved to head back to her home in New Orleans, her heart filled with curiosity and hope.

Upon her return, she pondered the mystery of that day. Did she truly witness her sister's reunion? Were Viola and Angel finally together forever? Those questions lingered, but one thing was certain, love and hope were powerful forces that could reunite families in ways nothing else could.

Twelve

The sisters had originally planned that if Isza ever stopped visiting, they should continue with their lives and not dwell on her absence. Clara had developed a strong connection with one of the enslaved boys, Jake, and though this relationship could jeopardize her own freedom, something about him truly captivated her. Jake shared an inspiring vision; if they escaped together, they could achieve their freedom. The thought of being with him excited Clara, but she found herself questioning why he would want to risk becoming a fugitive when they were already close on the plantation. Jake opened up, sharing a somber truth; while Clara enjoyed her freedom, his fate was uncertain, and if his master decided to sell him, he would be taken away without a chance for a farewell.

Jake recounted the heart-wrenching day he lost his parents. He vividly remembered his father being taken first, carted away without a moment to say goodbye. When his mother was put up for sale, he instinctively shouted out a bid of two hundred, not fully grasping his actions. The crowd found it amusing, but their laughter didn't stop her from being sold. Clara realized that if they wished to remain together, Jake had to be free. He expressed his deep feelings for her and insisted that if she truly loved him, she should join him in his plan to escape, as he was resolute about leaving.

Clara understood the stakes; being caught would mean severe consequences. The night before their intended departure, she found herself outside, staring up at the stars and pondering what their future might hold. In that moment of contemplation, a soft voice resonated, "Clara, there is no reason to fear. Sometimes, your destiny leads you to unexpected places. If you love him, embrace that love and go with him."

That was the encouragement she had been waiting for, and she couldn't wait to share the good news with Jake. However, when she returned to their meeting spot, her heart sank, he had already left. Clara felt a wave of uncertainty wash over her. The voice had urged her to take a leap of faith, but now that Jake was gone, she stood at a crossroads, unsure of her next steps. Still, deep down, she felt a flicker of hope, knowing that true love often comes with its own guiding light.

Clara spent the next week contemplating what to do. One night, she heard the dogs barking furiously and rushed to the door, just in time to see Jake being dragged by his heels. He was kicking and screaming in pain as he was pulled over the rocky ground. A trail of blood followed him as they continued their journey to the barn. He yelled out, "I AM A MAN." Clara felt his pain; tears began to overflow from her eyes, and she realized it was her turn to donate her tears to the well of her ancestors.

She wanted to run to his side to comfort him, to tell him how proud she was. The master understood that the other slaves viewed runaways as heroes, so even making eye contact could be dangerous for anyone involved. As Jake passed by, their eyes locked. Clara could see the fear in his face; he knew what he had tried to avoid was about to happen. He would either be sold or beaten to death. Either way, she would be forced to witness his departure, whether through sale or death.

Clara couldn't believe he was back and remembered the voice that had told her to leave with him. She had to act quickly. Of all the sisters, Clara was the one who was most afraid of everything, but she knew something had to be done if Jake was going to have a chance to live. She slipped into the barn to tell him that they had to leave together; otherwise, he would surely die, and she would probably face the same fate soon after.

He shared with her that once the dogs had discovered him, it would be a breeze for them to pick up his scent again. With earnestness, he pleaded for her to set him free, emphasizing that he had made a choice rooted in his faith. She grasped the rope that held him to the rafters and confidently led him out of the barn. Off in the distance, she spotted Mrs. Florence, a glimmer of hope sparking within her, at that moment, she felt certain everything would be alright.

After wandering for a while, she suggested it was safe to take a break. They nestled down in a delightful strawberry patch, enveloped by the sweet aroma of ripe fruit, and sensed it would now be impossible for the dogs to track their scent. With Mrs. Florence guiding the way, they ventured north. Jake, unaware of the guiding spirit, occasionally turned to Clara, asking if she was confident in their direction. She wished she could tell him who was leading them, but knew he might not fully grasp the extraordinary situation.

As their journey neared its end, Jake emerged as a free man. He landed a job cleaning a saloon, and before long, Clara and Jake found a cozy place of their own, living together as husband and wife. Jake cherished his newfound freedom; he understood that danger could surface at any moment, someone with a gun demanding his return. He often expressed to Clara that now that he was free, he would choose to live and die on his own terms.

However, one day, Clara's heart sank when she spotted a bounty hunter speaking with him. Her mind raced with concern. Usually, they would interrogate him and eventually let him go, but this time felt different, he had been recognized.

When asked his name, Jake instantly understood the impending threat, having witnessed it countless times before. Recognizing the bounty hunter from another plantation, Jake dreaded that this might be his final moment of liberty. He and Clara had a plan in place; a discreet signal for her to escape if he sensed danger approaching. When their eyes met, he signaled to her, and without hesitation, she packed her belongings and left.

Clara was filled with uncertainty; returning to the plantation didn't feel like an option. Even if they didn't suspect her of aiding Jake, it would seem suspicious for her to be around when he was caught. Tragically, she later discovered that he had been killed, his body returned to the plantation as a sobering reminder of the harsh realities faced by runaway slaves.

In a twist of fate, Clara soon realized she was pregnant, and she decided to use this unexpected news to her advantage. First, she visited the cabin, taking a moment to gather her thoughts on what to share with everyone. As she sat there, memories washed over her; the loss of her parents, the harrowing escape from slavery, and the pain of love and loss, leading her to this exciting new chapter of motherhood.

With her resolve firm, she headed to the plantation to see her sisters who were working there as free negros and joyfully announced that they were going to become aunts. This clever plan shielded her, as no one connected her to Jake. Clara shared that she was visiting from New Orleans, where her husband was a free man toiling on a farm. Given that many of the women there had husbands working in New Orleans as well, her story flowed seamlessly, and it felt reassuring to connect with her community in this time of uncertainty.

When Clara finally shared her true story with her sisters, their surprise was palpable. They had been in the dark about her ordeal while numerous rumors swirled around their community. Some speculated that whoever had taken the runaway must have taken Clara as well. Others theorized that perhaps the runaway had teamed up with a group, who then returned to rescue him from captivity. Although Clara's sisters searched high and low for her, they felt trapped by fear and couldn't ask anyone for help, worried that inquiries might mistakenly suggest that Clara had run off, drawing unwanted attention to themselves. Deep down, Clara understood she wouldn't remain undetected forever. When the baby came, it would be hard to hide the fact that Jake was the father, making it property of the master. She reassured her sisters that she was safe and headed north to seek a better life.

Her journey brought her to Warren, Ohio, where she knew she'd be away from slave states. To her excitement, her arrival coincided with the exhilarating stagecoach races in downtown Warren. Clara was captivated by the sight of Negro and White spectators' side by side, cheering for the riders. At that moment, Clara felt a spark of hope, maybe Warren was the fresh start she had been looking for. When one of the riders caught her eye, all she could think was how she had to explore the possibility of calling this vibrant place her new home. The man who had captured her attention was Poindexter Anderson Jr., a proud, confident resident of Ohio. Their brief encounter felt serendipitous; Clara had a strong feeling it was fate that allowed them to meet just days before he was set to move to Boston.

Clara felt a positive connection with Poindexter, and the thought of following him to Boston was tempting. However, she faced a roadblock, she was pregnant, and the uncertainty of his reaction gave her pause. To avoid falling deeply for him, Clara chose to keep her distance, believing that less time together would mean fewer feelings to navigate. Yet, Poindexter was persistent in getting her attention, even extending his stay in town by a month just to be close to her. Once he finally departed, Clara realized she might have underestimated their connection and regretted not embracing it sooner. Fate had other plans, as Poindexter soon returned to find her, only to discover that Clara was visibly expecting. They made a heartfelt decision to marry and together made their way to Boston.

On December 17, Clara welcomed a beautiful daughter into the world, naming her Willa Mae in honor of her mother-in-law. This little girl quickly became a daddy's girl, often found spending time with her father fishing at the pond or helping him in the barn to tend to the horses. Of all the horses, Clara's favorite was Molly, a sweet and gentle two-year-old filly.

Clara's family grew with the arrival of her second daughter, Edith, in Boston. But life took a heartbreaking turn when she lost her husband in a hunting accident. Despite the grief, Clara knew she had to be brave and embarked on a journey south, driven by the hope of reuniting with her sisters. Poindexter, being born free, may never have completely understood why Clara or any Negro individual would choose to return to the South.

Sharing stories of her past with her daughters was essential to Clara, giving Willa Mae and Edith a snapshot of their family and their little house filled with memories. It was time for them to return to the New Orleans area and hopefully reconnect with family.

The reunion with Picola was heartfelt and warm. Clara and Picola reminisced about their shared past, while Willa Mae listened in awe, captivated by the tales of yesteryear. She would often close her eyes as she imagined herself in the stories, as if she could see the cotton fields, the cabin through the trees, breathe in the scent of magnolias, and feel the gentle breeze as it brushed against her skin. In one instance, while Picola vividly described a downpour, Willa Mae was momentarily confused, thinking she was magically experiencing the rain, only to realize that it was indeed falling outside. She couldn't help but laugh at the whimsical mix-up.

When Picola wasn't around, Willa Mae eagerly turned to her mother for stories. She often imagined how her mother and aunts must have silently guarded their family secrets from prying eyes. Day after day, they hoped that their true identities would remain undiscovered. As time passed, however, Willa Mae noticed the weight of sadness that sometimes cloaked her mother while sharing their stories. Among all the tales Clara told, none struck Willa Mae with more anxiety than the one about the troubling practice of "the gift," where little girls would occasionally go missing, even in the post-slavery era. Though they weren't common occurrences, each mention sent a shiver down her spine and an unwavering resolve to protect her family.

Through it all, Clara and her daughters remained resilient, filled with hope for brighter days ahead as they navigated their shared journey with love and determination.

Thirteen

The cabin nestled in the woods had become a sanctuary for Isza. Whenever the chaos of city life became overwhelming, she sought refuge there to clear her mind and find peace. Losing contact with her sisters had left her feeling particularly isolated, as they had always been her anchor, helping her navigate a world filled with lies and deceit. What troubled Isza the most was the persistent question of why the charade continued long after slavery had ended. Despite being free, she was still living as a white woman, and this façade was slowly corroding her spirit. There were moments when she yearned to burst into the streets and declare her true identity to everyone, shedding the heavy burden of pretense. The serenity of the cabin gave her the space to reflect on her journey and to seek answers to her haunting questions.

Isza observed the stark realities of racial inequality all around her; the color line was unmistakable, and she often found herself pondering why anyone would choose to perpetuate such deep injustices among themselves.

Just when she thought happiness might never return to her life, fate intervened when Mathew walked into the place where she worked. The moment her eyes met his, she felt an overwhelming urge to leap into his arms, but a glance at his expression reminded her to maintain some distance. Mathew took a seat with a group of Negro men waiting for work. As a wagon approached, the men surged forward, eager to be chosen. However, Mathew's attention remained fixed on the door where Isza was. A voice called from the wagon, urging him to come over, but Mathew, lost in thought, didn't register that he was being addressed.

"Boy, I'm talking to you," the man shouted, jolting Mathew back to reality.

Hearing that word shook him; it reminded him of the past he had left behind. Although he hadn't lived in the South since emancipation and had settled in Canada, he had returned to the States with a singular purpose; to find his family. Suddenly aware of his surroundings, he sprang up and hurried to the wagon, stumbling slightly in his haste. Mathew understood all too well that nobody wanted to hire a Negro man who couldn't stand tall and confident. Dusting himself off, he looked up at the man in the wagon and said, "Yes, boss, I want some work."

The man gazed down at him in distaste and barked, "Boy, what you good for?"

With a dusty face but a fierce spirit, Mathew replied, "My daddy says I ain't good for nothin', but I could work hard for you, sir."

The man shrugged and signaled to a couple of others to get on the wagon. As it rolled away, Mathew returned to the shade of a nearby tree with his fellow workers, laughter bubbling among them as they settled down.

"Man, you sure didn't seem eager to go with him. Your daddy said you were good for nothin" I've never heard that one before.

Laughter erupted again, and Mathew joined in, his spirits lifted.

"Honestly, I'm not working for anyone unless it feels right. The last time I took a job like that; I ended up stuck on a plantation for six months. I had to flee without the pay they promised me. During my time there, I met a young man who struggled under the owner's scorn. The plantation owner taunted him, calling him good for nothing, and those words haunted me; what kind of father would say that about his child?

Eventually, the owner paid him what he was owed and cast him off. As he walked away, he stumbled, glanced up at me with a wink, then picked himself up and continued on. I think about him often; he showed me the way out if I ever found myself trapped in that situation.

When I finally tried to claim my pay, they told me I owed them money. So, I bided my time until the moment was right and made my escape. Since then, when someone offers me a job that doesn't sit well with me, I pull out that "good for nothing" tripping story as my excuse. I'm here in this city for a purpose; I'm waiting for Miss Isza. I used to work for her; she knows who my mother is, and I'm determined to find her."

Each word Mathew spoke was infused with hope and resilience. His story inspired those around him, reflecting the strength found in struggles shared. It was a reminder that even in the face of adversity, the bonds of family and friendship could light the way through the darkest times.

As Mathew engaged in conversation, Isza stepped outside and surveyed her surroundings, her eyes lighting up as she spotted him. Excitement bubbled within her as she began her walk home, and Mathew couldn't help but admire the graceful way she moved down the street. Once she had reached a safe distance, he decided to follow her, wanting to keep their connection under wraps, hiding that they both were slaves on a plantation in Mississippi.

Arriving home, Isza waited with a fluttering heart for the familiar sound of a knock. When Mathew finally stepped through the door, she couldn't contain herself any longer. In a burst of emotion, she jumped into his arms, feeling an overwhelming need to connect with him. Wrapping his arms around her, Mathew held her close, offering the comfort she desperately sought as she let her emotions flow.

As Isza's tears subsided, she took a deep breath and whispered, "I love you." The sentiment surprised her, but it was a truth she could no longer keep inside. She had thought her chance to see him again was lost forever, yet here they were. She wished she could pull those words back, fearing they were too bold, but deep down, she knew they needed to be said. Eagerly, she looked into his eyes and asked him how he felt about her, because she wanted the truth right then.

Mathew gazed at her, his eyes shimmering with emotion as a few tears escaped. Before he could collect himself, Isza watched as the tears rolled down his cheeks.

"I love you, Isza, and I always have. This journey has taken me to places I never expected. I set out to find my family, and I think I've found her right here with you."

Joy surged through Isza as she leaped back into his embrace, feeling like the luckiest person alive.

"How long do you plan to stay?" she asked, her heart full of hope.

Mathew gently kissed her forehead and replied, "Forever, if that's what you want."

Although Mathew had reservations about living in the South, the thought of losing Isza again filled him with determination. However, the reality of their situation loomed large; Isza was living as a white woman, which made their love forbidden and their relationship a secret. Initially, he thought he could manage the secrecy, but the sight of other men interacting with her became a heavy burden. Anger simmered within him, and he knew he had to act before he did something reckless.

He told Isza he needed to leave, expressing his love for her and inviting her to come with him. But Isza felt tied to her roots; this place was where her family would come looking for her. Mathew gave her space to ponder their choices, but he made it clear that he would eventually have to leave, whether she chose to join him or stay behind. Isza found herself torn. How could she possibly leave a place that had liberated her spirit? Yet, she realized this same place had also confined her to a role that wasn't her true self.

In search of clarity, she decided to revisit the cabin. She told Mathew she would be away for a couple of days and asked him to wait for her. This time would be crucial for her decision; to stay or embark on a new life with him. Upon her arrival at the cabin, everything felt different. The sun struggled to break through the dense trees, casting an unexpected chill over the place, which seemed so dreary for a summer day.

As Isza stepped inside, an intense wave of fear washed over her. She felt a strange sense of displacement, as if the cabin itself was gently urging her to move forward. Sitting in the corner under the window, a spot that had once brought her comfort, she took a moment to reflect. Memories, vivid and warm, began to resurface, each one a reminder of the joy the cabin had nurtured in her sisters. She remembered laughter ringing through the wooden walls and long walks in the woods with the kind old lady who had shared her wisdom.

As she prepared to leave for New Orleans, excitement mixed with trepidation surged inside her. This visit had been essential; it reinforced the love and memories she cherished. The entire night was a tapestry of dreams, each one like a page from her family history, she saw herself as a carefree girl playing with friends, she remembered broom-jumping ceremonies with her mother and Paul, and the sweetness of her first taste of warm bread.

She reflected on the joy of welcoming her sisters into the world, May, Hilda, Teacee, Viola, Picola, Clara, and the youngest, Baby. The warmth of their playful moments filled her heart as she thought about how their parents had prepared them for the future. Then came memories of the escape, the fear that had gripped them, and the myriad people she had encountered along her journey. Each recollection was a thread in the fabric of her life, teaching her about love, resilience, and hope.

As the sun rose, casting a warm glow over the house, Isza was enveloped in the comforting embrace of cherished memories. It reminded her of the love and protection that filled the space. Her thoughts naturally drifted to the remarkable women who had come before her; May, who gave everything for her family's freedom; Hilda, whose selflessness saved her sister; and Viola, who had finally reunited with a daughter she had tirelessly searched for. While her other sisters had stepped forward to build new lives, Isza felt deeply rooted, knowing that her time would soon come. She had achieved so much, and she could sense her parents' pride in her accomplishments.

Even with clarity about what lay ahead, the idea of not being able to return to this area whenever she wished to feel close to her family was heart-wrenching. She often found herself sitting in the cabin, feelings of nostalgia washing over her as relatives arrived, sometimes right as she had been thinking of them. They would share laughter, reminisce about joyful days gone by. Leaving behind this sacred place was a profound challenge.

As Isza made her way home, she heard footsteps behind her, and upon turning, was elated to see an old friend, the wise woman who had guided her to that little cabin on that wonderful yet daunting night. It was that woman who had helped her navigate uncertainty and doubts in the past. Isza eagerly inquired about her sisters, and the old woman smiled, reassuring her that one day they would all return to the cabin together.

Walking through the woods, Isza felt herself shedding layers of her past with every step she took. "I am not a slave," she declared with conviction. With each stride, she reaffirmed who she was; "I'm not a runaway slave." As she said it again, "I'm not white", an incredible realization washed over her, and she dropped to her knees, gazing upward.

"I'm colored, daughter of Paul and Viola."

In that moment, Isza understood that living as a white woman had kept her from fully embracing her true identity and her family's legacy. She recognized that this chapter of her life was coming to a close and that she would soon embark on a journey with Mathew to fully embrace her identity as a proud colored woman.

Upon returning home, Isza found Mathew was not there. Panic set in initially, as she assumed he must have stepped out temporarily. As night descended, worry took hold, was he safe? Had he left her? With a heavy heart, she sat by the window, longing for news. The next morning brought an explosion of joy when she opened her eyes to find him standing before her. She rushed into his embrace, relief flooding her.

"I thought I had lost you again. I'm ready; let's leave right now."

"I'm so sorry for not being here. People were looking for you, and when I didn't have answers, they became suspicious. I had to make myself scarce."

"I want us to go together, right now."

"If we leave immediately, they'll think I've done something to you, and they will come looking. You need to tell them you're going to stay with a sister or a friend. In a few days, I'll follow. It's necessary for your safety."

He provided her with an address, assuring her that he would be there soon. For the next couple of weeks, Mathew remained in New Orleans to ensure their story held up. After reuniting, they set off for Canada, where Isza got a job at the same hotel as Mathew. Six months later, they joyfully tied the knot, and for the first time in her life, Isza felt a genuine sense of liberation.

Two years into their marriage, Isza discovered that she was pregnant, and joy bubbled within her. She hoped for a son, inspired by her life spent among daughters, eager to raise a boy. Mathew, however, cared less about the gender and simply wished for a healthy, free child. Though slavery had officially ended, the shadow of fear lingered, reminding them that some still worried it could return, even in the safety of Canada.

With love and optimism, Isza and Mathew stepped into their vibrant future, ready to embrace all that lay ahead.

The day her daughter was born, Isza felt a mix of emotions, but deep down, she knew her love for her would be boundless, just as it would be for any child. She often found herself affectionately calling her "Baby," even though she officially named her after her beloved sister, May.

Mae blossomed into a joyful little girl, thriving in the care of two devoted parents who cherished her and were determined to nurture her happiness. Inspired by her love for Mae, Isza made the heartfelt choice to stop working and dedicate her time to being present with her child. She immersed herself in books of all kinds, enthusiastically teaching her numbers, the alphabet, and even how to spell and write her own name. As onlookers marveled at Mae's brilliance, they began to approach Isza, eager for her to share her teaching talents with their children. This newfound passion led her to embrace the role of a teacher.

One day while out in town, Isza had an unsettling encounter. A man approached her from behind, tapping her on the shoulder and asking if he knew her. In that instant, Isza's heart raced, gripped by a wave of fear. She had long feared being recognized and dragged back to New Orleans, her identity as a Negro woman revealed while she lived her life as a white woman. In the South, such a breach of social norms was perilous. She had heard horror stories of women who had suffered grave consequences for such deceptions.

So, when she felt that tap and heard his question, an overwhelming terror enveloped her, and she struggled to find her words.

However, when Mae sweetly called her "Momma," the man's expression shifted as he glanced from Mae to Isza and muttered that he must have made a mistake, he hadn't realized she was Negro. Seizing the moment, Isza quickly scooped up Mae and hastily walked away, aware of the man's gaze following them. It wasn't long before he recognized her, and Isza knew that danger was once again lurking close by. Once home, she shared the incident with Mathew, articulating her fears that someone might snatch their precious child, viewing her as some sort of 'gift.' Mathew looked puzzled, not quite grasping the depth of her concern. Isza painstakingly explained how it had happened to her mother, sister, and her sister's daughter, who had been taken away, each child a "gift" for little white boys.

That encounter profoundly changed Isza. She felt as though eyes were always watching her, and an unshakeable belief that they were not safe, settled over her. Despite reassurances from others, the weight of her fears only grew. One day in town, she spotted the man again, this time fixated on Mae. Acting on instinct, she quickly whisked Mae away and returned home, urgently insisting to Mathew that they needed to leave for their safety. Although Mathew had planned a birthday celebration for Mae, who was turning four in just two days, Isza felt they couldn't afford to wait.

On Mae's birthday morning, Isza entered her daughter's room, only to find it empty. At first, she thought Mathew was playfully illustrating the absurdity of her worries, so she patiently awaited his return with Mae. Hours passed, and anxiety turned from a whisper to a shout in her mind. Concerned, she made her way to Mathew's workplace. The moment he saw her without Mae, his expression shifted to one of immediate alarm. Isza fell to her knees, pleading for news about their daughter. The look on Mathew's face told her everything; he had no idea. In a surge of panic, she bolted from him, and he instinctively chased after her. As he caught up, the reality of her warnings sunk in, but she brushed him off, heading home, packing a few belongings, and leaving without another word. With a heavy heart, she embarked on a lifelong quest to find her stolen child.

Decades passed in her quest, but eventually, Isza felt it was time to return home. While she thought "home" meant Canada, she found herself walking down a familiar dirt road, surrounded by memories of lessons learned, love shared, and heartaches endured since her last visit. The chill of her previous journey came rushing back. Suddenly, she paused, looking up through the trees as the sun broke through, warming her face just as it had long ago. Right then, she knew it was the perfect moment to come home.

Strolling through the woods, everything looked just as it had the first night she laid her eyes upon it. She settled beneath a tree, feeling a mix of apprehension and anticipation about what awaited her in the cabin. Just then, she sensed someone approaching from behind; she didn't need to turn around to know who it was. It was the familiar presence that always welcomed her on her visits. The old woman informed Isza that they were waiting for her. Filled with curiosity, she wanted to ask who they were, but when she turned around, no one was there. With a heart full of determination, Isza opened the door and stepped into the house, ready to embrace whatever lay ahead.

TheirStory

Fourteen

Edith was one of the first generation to be born legally free. Her journey began on a picturesque plantation along the shores of Lake Charles, where she met Larry, a man who would soon become her husband. At twenty-five, he was captivated by her spirit, and at just twenty-three, Edith felt the thrill of a blossoming romance. Their courtship lasted a little over a year, filled with laughter and connection, until Larry found the courage to talk about the next step, marriage.

It wasn't Edith's vibrant personality that made him uncertain; rather, it was Willa Mae, her sister, who had a strong presence that left most people intimidated. Many speculated that Willa Mae's fierce demeanor was the reason Edith remained unmarried for so long. Larry, in particular, tried every possible approach to win Willa Mae's approval, as he knew that her blessing was essential before he could even dream of asking Edith's mother. Willa Mae carried with her a weight of fear and protectiveness that stemmed from childhood memories. Even though they had always been free, their mother Clara had instilled in them a deep-rooted apprehension.

Clara, who had once faced the harsh realities of being a runaway, often urged her daughters to prepare for the unthinkable. She would tell them that if she disappeared, they should gather their important papers, pack a few clothes, and wait in the woods. If she didn't return, they were to make their way to New Orleans and find Isza, who would help them. Clara always reminded them how much she loved them, making her children's hearts swell with a mix of anxiety and devotion. For Willa Mae, this fear was a constant shadow, echoing the terrible knowledge that at any moment, she could lose everything.

Even in communities far from plantations, children played carefully orchestrated games that echoed the constraints of their past. If there were bounty hunters nearby, the kids played hide and seek; if someone needed protection, they joined hands in a circle and played ring around the roses. For Willa Mae, these innocent games were reminders of danger, signaling to her that their mother could be at risk.

Despite the end of slavery, inklings of fear continued to linger. Would the promise of freedom really hold? The tumultuous after-effects of war made trust a heavy burden to carry. Willa Mae struggled with the notion of safety in a world that had historically turned a blind eye to injustice. The reality of random violence against Negro people persisted, and she found herself clinging tightly to the lessons she had learned long ago; to be wary and to stay guarded.

Larry's family shared a similar history; they had experienced life on an Alabama plantation until freedom was secured. With a hopeful heart, they initially believed they could work freely for pay. However, that optimism soon faded, leading them to relocate to Louisiana in pursuit of genuine freedom and opportunity.

When Larry announced to Edith his desire to marry her, excitement bubbled within her, though a sense of trepidation about informing her mother clouded her joy. The mere thought of approaching her mother sent chills down his spine, as he wondered what kind of resilience he would need to muster. When he sought advice from his own father, he was reassured that Clara was kind-hearted. Yet, when Larry met Clara's penetrating gaze, he sensed a complexity that made him unsure.

After six challenging months of contemplation, Larry finally worked up the courage to approach Willa Mae. To his surprise, he encountered a soft-spoken, gentle person who was far more approachable than he had imagined. With Willa Mae's blessing in hand, it was time to face the ultimate test, speaking with Clara. This would be their first real conversation, and Larry's heart raced as he broached the subject of marrying Edith. Clara's stoic expression hardened, and he could feel a wave of panic threaten to overtake him. He thought about bolting from the room, but love anchored him in place.

Just as he felt the weight of his worry blossom, he heard an unexpected giggle. Turning around to find its source, he saw no one behind him. When he looked back at Clara, he was stunned to see a smile flicker across her face. The sound of

Clara's laughter felt like warmth in the room, lifting Larry's spirits.

With newfound courage, he asked Clara if that joyful moment signified her blessing for him to marry Edith. Clara's laughter grew, and she nodded in agreement. In that instant, Larry felt a sense of triumph, she had said yes. He embraced her with gratitude, filled with excitement as he raced to find Edith, eager to share the incredible news. As he made his way home, he couldn't help but announce to everyone that he and Edith were getting married, joyfully proclaiming that both Willa Mae and Clara could smile, after all, he had witnessed it with his own eyes.

After getting married, they moved in with Clara and Willa Mae, who generously insisted they stay there until they could afford to buy their own home. Homeownership meant everything to them; it signified stability and the freedom that came with it. In a world where exploitation was a constant threat, particularly from White landlords who imposed unaffordable rents and left them drowning in debts for basic necessities, owning a house felt like a beacon of hope and security. Slowly but surely, Negro families began to purchase properties in parts of the city that others overlooked, carving out their own spaces and making their mark.

Their time with Clara lasted for two years, filled with laughter and support. Finally, they were able to buy a charming one-room house on Esplanade Avenue in New Orleans. With Larry's knack for building and a vision for growth, he planned to expand the house as their family blossomed. He worked as a doorman at the renowned Place

D'Armes Hotel, where he often returned home bubbling with fascinating tales of the paranormal. Rumor had it that the hotel stood atop the remnants of a schoolhouse engulfed in fire long ago, claiming the lives of many teachers and children. Guests claimed to hear the soft whispers of their spirits and the distant booms of cannonballs echoing from the War of 1812.

Although Larry relished his job and the opportunities it provided, his spooky stories made Edith hesitant to visit the hotel. Larry, however, loved every moment, his warm smile was his biggest asset. He believed that a Negro man confidently showcasing his smile brought an undeniable charm, that nostalgia of the "good old days" resonating with guests. His cheerful attitude often meant that his tips were sometimes even more lucrative than his regular earnings, turning his work into a delightful experience.

There was one bustling day during Mardi Gras, the highlight of his work year. The city was alive with excitement, and Larry was receiving generous tips from joyful visitors pouring in from all corners of the nation. It was one of those happy times when everyone simply wanted to celebrate, share, and shower kindness.

As he stood proud on the banquette, he spotted a carriage approaching in the distance that stirred something deep within him. As it drew closer, an unsettling mix of emotions washed over him, overwhelming his senses.

When the carriage finally reached him, recognition jolted through him like a thunderclap, it was the plantation owner who had once enslaved his family, the man his father had always talked about. He told Larry that this man was the worst slave owner in town. His father told him, that even after arriving in the vibrant city of New Orleans, the specter of being found and returned to Alabama haunted his thoughts. This encounter would be a turning point, as it marked the first time, he would meet the man who once held authority over his family.

Larry stood tall, prepared to confront the past. Although he enjoyed his newfound freedom, he couldn't shake the feeling of vulnerability that lingered around him. In a world where racial tensions prevailed, he knew that any misstep, a sideways glance, not stepping aside quick enough, or even declining a petty request, could lead to serious trouble. He had to walk a careful line. When he spotted the buggy and recognized the passenger, he forced a smile, trying to engage the guest courteously. The man didn't even acknowledge him, yet he left a generous tip behind. It was startling to realize how one could share space with another human being and remain utterly oblivious to their existence. Deep down, he understood that to some, slaves were reduced to mere objects, not individuals with thoughts or feelings.

Three years had passed since they achieved self-sufficiency, but then Willa Mae fell ill, prompting Larry and Edith to invite her into their home. This was the only way for Edith to care for her beloved sister, especially after their mother had decided to move north. Willa Mae chose to stay behind, feeling a deep connection to New Orleans, she believed it was her true home. Meanwhile, Larry and Edith had faced challenges in their journey to parenthood, taking several years to conceive. Throughout that period, Willa Mae remained unwell, but the news of the baby sparked a fire in her spirit. She had always longed to become an aunt, and this joyful disclosure seemed to breathe fresh life into her.

One day, Larry joyfully burst into the house to tell Edith that Willa Mae was in the backyard, energetically pretending to jump rope without a rope. At first, Edith didn't believe it until she stepped outside and saw her sister, full of determination, practicing her moves. Willa Mae was gathering strength to help with the baby, proudly claiming that a child needed a strong NanNan.

Edith cherished memories of her aunties and the joyful moments spent together during their visits. She held dear the tales they spun, immersing herself in their narratives. Yet, there were times when Willa Mae would leave the room when the stories began; they echoed memories of a troubling past that weighed her down. Meanwhile, Edith hungered for every detail of her relatives' lives, despite knowing that some tales were likely embellished. In her mind, the stories came alive, where she imagined herself in harrowing situations on a plantation, escaping from fierce hounds or tied to a tree, stories that, while chilling, captivated her imagination.

On the morning of July 20, 1900, at 7;00 AM, Edith joyously welcomed her baby girl into the world, naming her Magnolia after Larry's mother. This little girl represented a new generation, she was the first child born to parents who carried no memories of the shackles of slavery.

Willa Mae was absolutely enchanted with her niece. All the bitterness that once occupied her heart faded away, revealing a tenderness that radiated from within. Edith felt immense gratitude knowing that Willa Mae was there to nurture little Magnolia. She took charge of feeding her, ensuring her cleanliness, and attending doctor visits, always ready and present. Whenever Edith glanced out the window, she was met with the beautiful sight of Willa Mae and Magnolia beneath the large magnolia tree. She watched as her sister pointed out the colorful flowers dotting the garden, with the baby gazing about, as if fully engaged in the conversation. Edith reveled in witnessing the blossoming bond between her sister and her daughter, and it filled her heart with a profound sense of joy and optimism for the future.

Fifteen

Willa Mae was filled with delight as she watched her niece Magnolia dash around, absorbed in play, radiating the carefree spirit of childhood. It reminded her of a story their mother had once shared about the games they used to play. Willa Mae recalled her mother telling her about one day on the plantation her and her sisters were lost in the joy of a lively game of tic tag with other children. How it all began was a mystery to her, but the laughter and excitement were unforgettable. However, in the midst of their merriment, a sudden chaos erupted as the adults began to run frantically. Confused, the children thought the grown-ups were joining in the fun. As the dust settled, their parents called them in and expressed their concern for playing without permission. It was only later that the girls learned the harsh truth behind that day; their innocent game had coincided with a serious reality. The sound of tic tag had echoed across the plantation at a time when people were seeking refuge and freedom, a reminder that not all games were devoid of deeper meanings.

Another one game they played was "a tisket, a tasket.", this game always filled her with excitement because it often meant that a family with children would come to visit and stay for a couple of days. There were moments filled with laughter, but one particular day took a darker turn. As they waited in eager anticipation for their guests, an eruption of terrifying screams pierced the air, accompanied by the growls of dogs. The chilling noise shook her to the core. Later, she learned that the screams belonged to those who had been desperately searching for freedom but had been captured by the dogs. It was devastating to realize that even the youngest among them had not been spared. The shadows of that story loomed over them, and whenever they saw children playing that game. It served as a solemn reminder of a painful past.

For a time, they feared that these games would fade away entirely, and indeed, there was a long period when they seemed to disappear. Yet, she now noticed a beautiful revival. Watching Magnolia play tic tag with only joy in her heart began to heal the wounds of the past, filling Willa Mae with warmth.

There was a sense of hope brewing for Colored people across the South. No longer were they resigning themselves to the injustices that had plagued their community; they were rising with courage and determination. Conversations bubbled with passion at barbershops, hair salons, churches, schools, and even at the shoe-shine stands. People were gathering, united in their desire to advocate against the injustices that remained. It was a brave and perilous time; Colored people still faced the threat of violence simply for asserting their dignity, be it through a glance or refusing to step aside on the sidewalk. Their belief was that the Jim Crow Law would bring about a safer environment, but the reality was far more complex.

In the 1890s, a pivotal moment emerged in Louisiana when Colored citizens boldly argued that their state was violating both the Thirteenth Amendment, which abolished slavery, and the Fourteenth Amendment, which promised equal rights to all U.S. citizens. This pressing matter culminated on June 7, 1892, when a determined man named Plessy purchased a first-class ticket at the Tremé Press Street Depot and bravely boarded a Whites-only car of the East Louisiana Railroad in New Orleans. His courageous act led to a landmark case that would reach the Supreme Court, setting the stage for the introduction of Jim Crow laws and cementing the notion of "separate but equal." State enforcement of this idea brought forward a new chapter, and Colored people recognized that their struggles were deeply rooted in the challenges posed by state governing.

Amidst the trials, there was undeniable strength in their spirit, and Willa Mae looked toward the future with cautious optimism, holding on to the belief that brighter days were ahead.

Jim Crow laws forced the Negro community to seek solace and togetherness among themselves. It was during this critical period that Josephine, affectionately known as Aunt Josie, returned to her roots. Willa Mae often reminisced about the moment Aunt Josie shared her remarkable life story for the first time.

She recalled, her first day of freedom, a day that came about because the Misses had chosen to free her in her will. It was a bittersweet moment; the family that had enslaved her urged her to remain with them, gently pleading with her to accept the role of what they called a 'house nigger.' she stood there, her feet firmly planted, feeling a strange hesitation wash over her. After waiting her entire life for this moment, she found it hard to take that first step. she could hear voices from the plantation, people cautioning her with thoughts of danger, saying things like, 'If you leave, the night riders could find you,' or 'You won't find a home; no other plantation will accept you.' Then she heard the Master's voice, a man who was an authority figure for so many of them, stating, 'No one will treat you better than he does.' His words somehow ignited her resolve, giving her the strength to move forward."

Despite having lived that life for so long, she was resolutely determined to carve out her own path. The end of slavery signified a new era where she would be respected as an individual, able to work and earn fair wages for her efforts. That day felt like a rebirth. She could almost feel the remnants of slavery evaporating from her very being, as if the chains that had bound her were finally falling away. She understood that the only way to truly escape that past was to step away and never look back. With each step, her pace quickened, and her confidence soared. Suddenly, she found herself moving so quickly that she nearly stumbled. As she ran, sweat streaked down her face, and an instinctive drive propelled her forward. It was as if her feet knew that stopping would mean returning to the plantation.

Though the air was thick and heavy, it parted as she dashed through it. Her hair flew wildly in the wind, and she remember glancing down at her dress, seeing her body outlined against the fabric, and for just a moment, the pounding of her feet felt like she was soaring. As she fled, a whirlwind of emotions flooded over her; the pulse of fear, the exhilaration of newfound freedom, and a growing pride in her bravery to leave it all behind.

The dream that all slaves had yearned for had come true for her. She held the papers that declared her freedom high above her head, shouting her triumph to the heavens. In that moment, she felt the weight of her ancestors surrounding her, sharing in the joy of what it meant to be free.

Willa Mae cherished every opportunity to take Magnolia, to visit Aunt Josie. They would sit and listen intently to her captivating stories and enjoy the company of their cousins. Aunt Josie had a warm way of welcoming them, bringing out a large pitcher of lemonade and a special treat to share. The excitement always bubbled up when Aunt Josie had a lengthy tale to tell because it meant they could stay longer. On this beautiful day, an unmistakable sense of joy filled the air as Aunt Josie prepared to share a story that would surely captivate everyone present. It was as if her excitement radiated from within, and the children, recognizing the significance of the moment, sat in rapt attention, eager for the adventure that awaited. With a thoughtful gaze cast across the river, Aunt Josie seemed to be connecting with something beyond the waters, a spark of inspiration ready to flow into her words. The atmosphere was electric, and everyone could feel it. They patiently waited for her to select someone to fetch the jars, a clear sign that the storytelling was about to commence.

With a twinkle in her eye, Aunt Josie scanned the circle of children, her gaze sparkling as it met each hopeful face. She was searching for just the right person to embark on the quest. The anticipation was almost palpable, and just when Magnolia thought her heart might burst from excitement, Aunt Josie declared, "Magnolia, I think it's your turn to get the jars. "

Pure elation surged within Magnolia as she sprang to her feet, her eagerness leading her to dash towards the house. In her excitement, she forgot about the old screen door, and with a gentle thud, she collided with it. Laughter erupted around her, and though she felt a bit shamefaced, she couldn't help but giggle at the moment as she backed up, opened the door, and quickly grabbed the jars inside. As she emerged, balancing them carefully in her arms, everyone was pleasantly surprised by her success in choosing the right container.

Once Aunt Josie poured refreshing lemonade into each jar, they all took a sip and set the jars beside them, eyes gleaming with anticipation. Aunt Josie encouraged them to listen closely, foretelling an important story that promised to unfold. This was a lively tradition; every story began with such enthusiasm, but today she seemed particularly charged, hinting that this could be her greatest tale yet.

As Aunt Josie began to weave her narrative, the moment she spoke the name Isza, the children quickly realized they were about to hear a precious part of their family history,

HerStory. Magnolia's heart raced with recognition; Isza was her aunt, the eldest sister of their grandmother. Curiosity bubbled within her, urging her to ask questions, but she knew better than to interrupt Aunt Josie mid-story. Years of experience told her it was wiser to listen intently, and it was this very beauty of Aunt Josie's storytelling that always seemed to answer unsaid inquiries. By the time the tale concluded, all thoughts of her questions had dissipated into the magic of the story.

One particularly riveting story Aunt Josie told was about a runaway slave, racing along the riverbank, the splashing of his feet mingling with the distant barking of dogs in a frantic chase. Each child gathered closer together, feeling as if they were witnessing the scene unfold in real time. The thrill was contagious, and for a moment, they all shared a sense of suspense, imagining someone bursting through the trees in search of refuge. Aunt Josie emphasized how storytelling had been a cherished family tradition, a gift that resonated through generations, bringing them all together.

Magnolia cherished the memory of Aunt Josie's last story before she passed, a day that felt distinctly different. On that day, Aunt Josie's vitality shone through as she appeared eager, as if planning a joyful outing to her favorite shops downtown. When Magnolia approached the house, Aunt Josie was already stepping off the porch, heading towards her beloved magnolia tree, its broad leaves inviting her beneath their shade. In her youth, Aunt Josie often spun tales beneath that very tree.

On this meaningful occasion, she gathered her listeners, her tone shifting to one of gravity. "This is a family story I want you to remember," she said, a sparkle in her eye. "You must share it with your children one day. When I talk about an ancestor, it's as if they are present with us. Pay attention, and you may feel their spirit."

Aunt Josie began, "My daughter Rose was born free. We lived in a world where there was a semblance of freedom. It was complex, though in some areas, slavery seemed a given, others like us had learned what it meant to live unshackled. Even if one possesses papers, asserting their freedom, I witnessed so many lose their papers, and they would inevitably lose themselves, forgetting their worth. Even freedmen from the North understood the importance of navigating the South with dignity."

With heartfelt emotion, she elaborated, "Rose was my firstborn. At that moment, I experienced true dignity myself. It was then that I understood the unseen chains that slavery had placed on so many Negros lives."

Her heartfelt account captured everyone's attention, as she spoke with such sincerity that it felt like she was drawing each of us into her memories. Her eyes, glistening with tears, conveyed the depth of her emotions as she paused and shook her head gently, as if grappling with the weight of her reflections. Then she shared;

"From the moment Rose began to understand who she was, I took her on inspiring trips to New Orleans. I had a dream for her, one where she could become part of a vibrant community of free Negro people, a community that had never tasted the bitterness of enslavement. I wanted Rose to embrace the beauty of that life. Although some in the community were hesitant about welcoming newcomers, I believed in Rose's spirit and knew she would shine brightly, drawing others to her. I dedicated myself to making this dream a reality.

As Aunt Josie spoke, tears flowed openly down her cheeks, creating a poignant silence around us so profound that you could almost hear the soft rustle of a lizard in the nearby leaves.

One of the most important truths I needed Rose to understand was that she was born free. However, everything changed when she reached the age of ten. We learned a devastating truth; because her father had been born into slavery, the law deemed Rose a slave as well. It was heart-wrenching to realize how the times we lived in allowed the law to twist and turn, leaving us feeling powerless against such deep injustices.

In my desperate attempt to shield her from harm, I tried to take her away, but forces beyond my control wrestled her from my arms. They promised that she would lead a happy life as a companion to someone's niece. It was heartbreaking to see families torn apart this way; too many parents would never see their children again. Yet, I counted myself fortunate that, one day, while sitting on that porch, I saw her walking back up the road.

As she neared, she lifted her arm, and all the children turned in unison to follow her gaze.

Without a single word spoken, I instinctively knew it was Rose. My heart swelled with joy at our reunion, and in that moment, we began to weave our lives together once more, her with her mother and me with my daughter. It was during this time that she started to share her incredible journey with me.

Aunt Josie engaged the children, recalling how she once sat in their position, intently listening to her daughter's experiences.

She recounted how, after settling into her new surroundings, she came to understand that this was her new reality, and she was filled with eagerness to absorb everything she could. The white children became her unexpected teachers, involving her in their lessons. Over time, she learned to read, count, and write. One day, the youngest girl, Susan, curiously asked her if she was a slave. This question caught Rose by surprise since slavery had officially ended by then. Remembering my insistence that she was born free, she knew in her heart she was not a slave, but cleverly chose to keep that thought to herself, aware that openly declaring her independence could attract unwanted attention.

When Susan posed her question, Rose replied that she worked for her family, but she was not a slave. Curiously, she then asked Susan why she wanted to know. Susan simply shook her head and walked away, as if to say that if she wanted to believe that, there was little more to discuss, after all, the reality of Rose's life still bore the marks of servitude.

Day after day, Susan would ask about Rose's status, and each time, Rose's answer remained the same, until one day when Susan surprised her with a book written by an ex-slave and began to read it aloud. The timeless story of the Underground Railroad left a lasting impression on Rose, filled with themes of resilience and hope in the face of adversity. Susan became a true friend, helping Rose realize that what was happening wasn't legal and that she had the right to leave. What Susan didn't grasp was that Rose belonged to her brother.

In sharing these stories, Aunt Josie drew us all in, igniting a spark of understanding and reflection within each of us. It reminded us that even amid challenges, hope and resilience can pave the way for brighter futures.

One day, Rose had a powerful realization inspired by Susan and decided to leave that challenging situation behind her for good. However, this choice led to an unexpected and tough moment. As she began to gather her things in her room, Johnny, Susan's brother, burst in. Overwhelmed by his emotions, Johnny became aggressive, and Rose couldn't believe what was happening.

In her moment of need, she called out for help, and thankfully, Susan rushed in. Together, they stood strong against Johnny's outburst until their father, Mr. Toby, arrived and helped to separate them. Johnny voiced his frustrations, claiming Rose couldn't leave because she belonged to him.

In that intense moment, Rose felt a wave of clarity. She recognized that her options were limited, and that realization was both frightening and liberating. Before she knew it, she found herself in a dark, suffocating room, but deep down, this experience sparked a seed of determination in her heart, planting the idea that brighter days were ahead. Rose had been in the room for quite a while, lost in her thoughts about her life and how she ended up in that moment. It was a time of reflection, a time to grasp how much everything had shifted.

The turning point came with the tragic death of a young Negro girl, slightly older than Rose, who lived on the plantation. Whispers emerged suggesting that Johnny was somehow involved, but few took those rumors to heart. Strangely, after that incident, Johnny began to regard Rose in a new light. To her delight, she received an unexpected invitation to his birthday party, which felt like a chance for reconciliation after the earlier tensions between her and Susan and Johnny. Clad in a lovely white dress, Rose felt a wave of joy wash over her, believing that their misunderstandings were finally behind them.

As she stepped into the party, she was greeted by a lively gathering of workers and family. She noticed the workers' eyes darting away, their discomfort palpable as it dawned on her that they were aware of tensions that she had yet to grasp. She wanted to reach out, to comfort them, and express that everything would be alright, that the earlier consequences were not so dire. Just then, she spotted Johnny near his father, beaming with a joyful smile. His happiness lifted her spirits; perhaps he truly had let go of past grievances. Yet, as she glanced at Susan, she noticed the same shade of worry mirrored in the eyes of the workers. When Susan waved goodbye, a sense of unease began to settle in Rose's heart.

Eager to mingle, Rose attempted to join the workers, but they gently guided her back to the center of the room. This behavior puzzled her. She tried moving to another group, only to face the same barrier. Unsettled, she remained at the heart of the gathering, searching for Susan, but she was nowhere in sight. Later, it became clear why, Susan had been sent away to school, the result of disagreements with her father regarding the troubling behavior of the men in their family. Despite the uncertainties, Rose held onto the hope that understanding and change could come in time.

Rose stood in the center of the room, filled with anticipation as she waited to see what would unfold. Mr. Toby and Johnny approached her, and she noticed Johnny was full of life, his laughter echoing in the air. It was a side of him she had never witnessed before. When they reached her, Mr. Toby gently placed his hand on her shoulder and said warmly, "As I promised, son, happy birthday."

In that moment, Rose felt a mix of disbelief and a flicker of hope. She had heard daunting tales about a time long gone, stories tied to a painful past, but never thought they would manifest her own life. The words that lingered in her mind, spoken by Susan, reminded her of the struggles ahead. Part of her wanted to retreat into hiding, yet she knew deep down that she had a path to follow, and she was now bound to serve, enduring each day with resilience in a foreign land. When her entire family made the move to Arkansas, she realized how far away her dream of being reunited with her mother had become.

Once in Arkansas, thoughts of escape began to seed in her mind. Rose envisioned running away someday, seeking her family and freedom. She diligently performed her tasks, all the while recalling stories about how slaves had to act to stay safe, shaping herself into the ideal obedient servant. When Johnny decided to share her company with friends, she complied without complaint. One day, he sent her down the road to help with preparations for his aunt's birthday celebration. In a stroke of luck, she managed to convince one of the workers to let her stay with him for a couple of days before she was taken to the train station. There, she stepped onto a train, filled with hope and determination, ready to forge a new beginning.

Her journey led her to Chicago, where she found love in Samuel Taylor. He was a wonderful partner, and though they never had children, their bond brought them joy and strength. After his passing, Rose chose to remain in Chicago, carrying the wish to reunite with her mother close to her heart, and now she was in my company again.

The last time I saw Rose; I reminded her to always remember that she was born free. In that moment, I felt an optimistic certainty that we would reunite, unaware that our time together was drawing to a close. If only I had known, I would have spoken more words of love, whispered how truly special she was, and held her a little longer.

Aunt Josie shared that when Rose finished recounting her story, a profound sense of closure enveloped her. That evening, they sat together on the porch, cherishing their time and each other's presence. The next morning, Rose walked back the way she had come, and while she didn't ask when she would return, deep down, she knew that their paths would cross again.

Sixteen

After Aunt Josie's passing, Edith observed something remarkable about Magnolia; she seemed to have picked up some of Aunt Josie's charming traits, even mimicking a slight limp on her right side. Initially, this development startled Magnolia, but a soft voice in her heart comforted her, assuring her that everything would be alright. For days, Magnolia would sit on the porch, gazing dreamily into the distance and softly muttering to herself. Edith noticed this change and wanted to reach out, but she also understood Magnolia's need to process her emotions in her own time. One thing was certain; Magnolia preferred to navigate her feelings before confiding in anyone else.

As the weeks passed, a touching moment arrived one night when Edith awakened to find Magnolia standing beside her, beaming through tears. With a heartwarming smile, Magnolia reassured her mother that all was well and that Aunt Josie had peacefully found her resting place.

Magnolia excitedly shared that Aunt Josie had imparted a beautiful message to her; just because she was gone didn't mean they couldn't still see their cousins. Magnolia had felt a sadness creeping in, believing that Aunt Josie's departure signified losing those cherished family gatherings, where stories and laughter flowed freely.

Edith took a moment to reflect on Magnolia's words. It dawned on her that indeed, they hadn't gathered as a family since Aunt Josie's death. While she recognized the grieving process was essential for everyone, she felt a spark of inspiration, it was time to embrace a sense of normalcy, just as Aunt Josie would have wanted. With that in mind, Edith reached out to family members to brainstorm ways to revive their beloved Sunday gatherings. They all agreed to rotate locations each week, and so it began, starting with an invitation to host at her home. Edith kept the plans a delightful secret from Magnolia, aiming for a wonderful surprise.

On that beautiful Sunday morning, Magnolia awoke to the sweet scent of her mother's cooking, reminiscent of the festive atmosphere during Christmas. She rushed to the kitchen, where her mother was whipping up a meal while singing joyful church songs. Thrilled, Magnolia exclaimed, "Momma, Momma, what's happening today?"

Edith's face lit up with a radiant smile. "Sweetheart, it's just Sunday, that's all."

However, the joy in Magnolia's expression faded as her eyes glistened with tears, and she hesitated before retreating to her room. Sensing her daughter's quiet sorrow, Edith gently asked, why do you look so sad?

Magnolia paused, gathering her thoughts before she replied, "The last time you cooked so much, it was after Aunt Josie's death."

Edith moved closer to her daughter and wrapped her in a warm embrace. With a tender voice, she explained that in honor of Aunt Josie, they had decided that each Sunday, someone would prepare dinner, and she had gladly volunteered for the very first Sunday. The family collectively agreed on the importance of spending quality time with their cousins at least once a week.

As Edith shared these plans, Magnolia's face transformed with joy, and she brightened with a grateful smile as she walked away, thanking her mother for cherishing those precious family connections that Aunt Josie had so lovingly nurtured.

Magnolia dashed to her room, filled with excitement and anticipation for church. From her cozy space, she could hear what she fondly described as the sweet melody of Momma singing. While some folks might have thought her mother was off-key, to Magnolia, those unique notes were a warm embrace, a beautiful indication of her happiness. As she hurriedly got dressed, her stomach rumbled in response to the mouthwatering aroma wafting from the kitchen, calling her to come and share in the delicious feast. Magnolia could already feel that this Sunday was going to be something special.

When they arrived at church, a wave of joy washed over Magnolia. Reverend Provost spoke with such passion that his words seemed to resonate with a divine energy, and the choir's harmonies felt like they were straight from the heavens. That Sunday, an irresistible energy surged within her, and she found it impossible to stay in her seat. Usually, she would chuckle at those who were swept away by the Holy Ghost, but on this particular day, she couldn't contain herself. She joined in with joyful shouts and happy jumps, much to her mother's surprise. Edith reached out, grabbing Magnolia's hand, her eyes filled with concern, and asked, "Are you okay?" With a smile, Magnolia responded, "God loves me."

After the service, the children burst into laughter and play, while the adults gathered in cheerful conversations. However, as they made their way to Magnolia's home, a soft sadness settled over them. They all felt the absence of Aunt Josie, whose enchanting stories had once filled their gatherings with laughter and warmth. They realized that while they would slowly learn to navigate life without her, her absence left an unmistakable emptiness in their hearts.

After a year of trying to recapture the joy of their Sundays, the family determined it was time for a change, no one could ever take Aunt Josie's place. They decided to forge a new tradition; Saturdays would become their family day. They would explore new adventures together, whether at a park, a festival, or simply anywhere that brought them all together. This fresh approach revitalized the family spirit. The parents felt uplifted and the children forged deeper connections, marking Saturday as their special time for cozy family bonding, sharing laughter, and creating lasting memories.

With this new tradition, Magnolia found herself falling in love with gatherings again. It became a cherished time to revel in the warmth of family. Within the comforting walls of her home, Magnolia blossomed into a marvelous storyteller. She spun tales featuring a delightful character named Mrs. Ruth, a vibrant woman who traveled the world and experienced incredible adventures. Edith cherished listening to Magnolia's stories, especially the one where Mrs. Ruth ventured to Africa. There, she discovered the fascinating broom-jumping ceremonies. In order to prepare for this beautiful ritual, the man had to prove his worthiness, showing he was ready to care for a family. The entire village celebrated for seven joyful days, sharing wisdom through stories as the elders showed them the meaning of unity and family. The most daring among them were challenged to venture into the heart of the jungle. The quest? To return with a main dish, something that many attempted but few succeeded at. While some were hesitant to face the jungle's dangers alone, others returned, grateful to be alive but having forgotten the bravery that had motivated them. Magnolia described the jungle's sights, sounds, and the thrill of adventure so vividly that Edith could almost hear the roar of a lion just behind her, ready to leap.

Another adventurous story that Edith cherished was about how villagers chose their storytellers. In that vibrant community, storytellers played a critical role in uniting the past, present, and future. Everyone, including children, were encouraged to share a story, helping them discover their own narrative talent early on. This tradition fascinated

Edith, especially as she recalled many great storytellers from her own life. The thought that such a rich heritage began in Africa left her in awe, inspiring Magnolia to keep sharing her magic through storytelling.

Together, they found joy and strength through the power of stories, and Magnolia blossomed as a reminder that love, family, and creativity could always bring light, even on the days they missed Aunt Josie the most.

Magnolia's excitement for storytelling time gradually blossomed into something truly special. As word spread like wildfire among her family, they eagerly gathered around to listen to her enchanting tales. Her stories, rich with imagination and creativity, were distinct from Aunt Josie's older tales, they whisked listeners away to fictional worlds, often set in vibrant Africa.

At the heart of Magnolia's stories was Mrs. Ruth, a beloved character who took the family on countless thrilling adventures. However, one morning, Magnolia woke up with an inexplicable heaviness in her heart, as if she had lost a dear friend. The night before, she had experienced a poignant dream in which Mrs. Ruth revealed it was time for her to leave Magnolia's tales behind, because another little girl needs me, so ta ta, she said, just before Magnolia awoke, feeling a deep void.

As she opened her eyes, the absence of her friend weighed on her, making her realize it was time to create her own narratives. When she confided in her mother about her character Mrs. Ruth's departure, Edith embraced her with understanding and warmth. Throughout the years, Mrs.

Ruth had shared her wisdom with various family members, and they had all thrived after her departure. Though Edith had never met the fictional lady herself, she'd heard enchanting stories of her adventures and looked forward to reminiscing with Magnolia again, even as she noticed the sadness in her daughter.

As time went on, the nature of storytelling evolved within the family. As some of the older generations began to pass away, interest in the traditional tales began to wane, with younger relatives gravitating towards lively dances and the soulful rhythms of jazz. When Magnolia decided it was time to put an end to her storytelling, her mother understood and held a glimmer of hope that one day, she would spark this beloved tradition anew with her own children. Magnolia felt a lightness at letting go of the storytelling responsibility, even cherishing the thought that perhaps she would never have to share another tale again. But what she didn't anticipate was the quiet longing that would fill her heart. Those vivid characters had become her companions, and she soon realized just how much they mattered to her. Despite her attempts to conjure up a new story, it felt incomplete, leaving her to wonder if her wish had indeed come true.

After spending some delightful moments with friends, Magnolia found comfort in the connections around her. One enchanting evening, while sitting by the riverbank and letting the gentle waves soothe her, she suddenly felt a presence behind her. Turning around, she was greeted by a tall, dark, and handsome figure. Excitedly jumping to her feet, Magnolia's initial perception shifted as she saw he was indeed charming, though not as towering as she had imagined. It was the bag boy from the corner store.

"I'm sorry, I didn't mean to startle you. My name's Jack Jackson, but everyone calls me JJ," he introduced himself, a friendly smile illuminating his face.

Magnolia offered a cautious smile in return, joy bubbling inside her. "Oh, I know who you are. You're the one who bags the groceries," she replied, feeling a mix of nervousness and delight.

JJ's animated expression lit up, his confidence shining through. "So, you've noticed me? I thought I saw you looking." he exclaimed, standing a little taller.

With a playful grin, Magnolia teased back, "Of course. You're the only one at the store, so everyone has to pay attention to make sure no one's accidentally placing canned goods on top of the eggs." While she had long hoped he would initiate a conversation while she spotted him at the store, he had always seemed so focused on his work, occasionally glancing up just to grab the next item for the bag.

In that moment by the river, a new chapter began, filled with the promise of friendship and fresh stories waiting to be told. Magnolia's heart lifted, and amid the waves, she felt the beginnings of inspiration once more.

With a mix of determination and uncertainty, Magnolia turned and walked away. This wasn't quite what she had planned, but sometimes life takes unexpected turns, and she decided to embrace the moment, not wanting him to feel too special. Yet, deep down, she hoped he would call out to her or say something that might make her stay just a bit longer.

Unfortunately, he didn't say a word. When she glanced back, though, she saw him nodding, a pleased look on his face that brought a smile to hers. With a light heart, she continued on her way.

In the days following their fleeting encounter, Magnolia found herself asking her mother, if she needed anything from the store more often than usual. Edith began to notice her daughter's newfound enthusiasm, but it soon grew slightly weary from the constant inquiries. Eventually, she assigned Magnolia a simple task; go get a bag of sugar, something they always kept stocked, especially with lemons just ripe for the picking.

Excited at the chance to head back to the store, Magnolia rushed over, only to find that JJ had taken the day off. A wave of disappointment washed over her, and she left empty-handed. Once back home, Edith picked up on her daughter's unusual mood. With concern in her voice, she asked if everything was alright, and Magnolia could only shrug as she passed her by.

When she entered the living room, Magnolia was startled to find JJ standing there. He jumped up, and she instinctively jumped back, surprise written all over her face.

"Oh, I'm sorry I startled you. Seems like this is becoming a habit for me," he chuckled.

Magnolia couldn't help but giggle at the unexpected encounter as she stepped toward him, feeling butterflies in her stomach.

"I came by to see if you'd like to go to the river with me," he suggested, his intention clear in that warm smile.

With excitement bubbling over, Magnolia called out to her mother, letting her know she was heading to the river with JJ and would be back in a couple of hours. Edith beamed at the excitement in her daughter's voice, encouraging her to have a great time and be safe.

As they walked together, JJ shared stories about himself, weaving a picture of his life across the river. He told her how he had been named after his father and how his mother, a wonderfully vibrant Creole named Clementine, had instilled values in him. He was the youngest in his family, with sisters who had ventured off to school up north and a brother managing the store, where their family had built a legacy over two generations. In between, he worked diligently at the store after school and dreamed big, hoping to one day open his own chain of stores on both sides of the river. Magnolia listened closely, captivated by his ambitions, realizing just how inspiring he was. It made her think about her own dreams, something she hadn't really focused on before but now felt a spark to explore.

Before long, their friendship blossomed into something more special, they officially began courting. On their first date, he took her across the river on the ferry. To his surprise, she admitted she had never been on a ferry.

"If you love the sound of the river bubbling past, this will be a delightful treat." he promised.

He was absolutely right. As the boat set sail, she reveled in the gentle sway of the river beneath her. Closing her eyes, she let her imagination take flight, picturing herself as a graceful fish swimming through the dance of the water and the vibrant greens of the riverside. Suddenly, a tap on her shoulder jolted her back to reality, and they both erupted in laughter, the joy of the moment making it feel like they were in their own little world.

As they settled on the levee, gazing back at the stunning views of New Orleans, Magnolia was astounded by how different the city appeared from such a beautiful vantage point. She could almost spot her home and was fascinated by how the French Quarter and the French Market seemed to interweave. The boat ride back felt all too short, and as they disembarked, a small pang of disappointment hit her. She had hoped he would introduce her to his family, thinking that if a boy cared deeply, meeting his loved ones was a natural next step. But she remained hopeful, cherishing the wonderful moments they shared and looking forward to what tomorrow might bring.

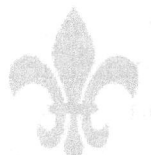

Seventeen

One bright morning, out of nowhere, JJ announced it was time for Magnolia to meet his family. This felt monumental to Magnolia; in her heart, it meant he was finally taking their relationship seriously. She had fallen deeply in love and was filled with dreams of a future family together. Edith, could see the excitement in her daughter's eyes but also sensed the delicate balance of emotions at play. Having watched this story unfold time and time again, she was all too aware of the common patterns; a young man would woo a woman, only to inadvertently lead her toward disappointment, leaving her feeling responsible for problems not her own. In many cases, this resulted in becoming emotionally invested in someone who ultimately wasn't ready to commit, hoping against hope that he would change his ways. Recognizing this cycle, Edith chose to stay close, providing unwavering support for Magnolia whenever the moment presented itself.

On this particular day, Magnolia's excitement was palpable as she prepared to join JJ for lunch, a meal that marked a meaningful step in their journey together. However, when the time came and he didn't arrive, her heart sank. She felt an ache of disappointment creeping in. Edith, ever the supportive mother, gently tried to lift her spirits by suggesting that something unexpected might have happened. But deep down, she understood that JJ's absence may be part of a larger pattern. As Magnolia's initial irritation transformed into genuine concern for JJ's safety, her mind raced with wild scenarios; had he fallen off his horse? Or perhaps he was caught up in some unexpected adventure? Each thought seemed more frantic than the last, escalating her anxiety. Realizing she needed a moment to breathe, she decided to take a walk and clear her head. Edith was fully aware of the truth, but felt Magnolia would need to discover it on her own.

Her first stop was the river, where she hoped to find people searching the waters, but it was desolate. She watched the ferry cross back and forth, fighting back the unease that was beginning to settle in her chest. Feeling a growing sense of urgency, Magnolia decided to head to the local store, hopeful that someone there might have news. Initially strolling slowly, her rising concerns for JJ quickened her steps, transforming her leisurely walk into a determined sprint. By the time she entered the store, her forehead was glistening with perspiration, and catching her breath felt challenging.

Seeing her frantic state, JJ's father quickly approached her, placing a comforting hand on her shoulder. "Dear child, are you alright?"

Magnolia attempted to answer, but it felt as though her throat was dry, preventing her from forming words. "I'm looking for JJ," she managed, desperation lacing her tone.

He paused, studying her. "Jack is off today. Are you sure you were set to meet him?"

"Yes. We confirmed it yesterday for lunch," she responded, trying to maintain her composure.

His sympathetic gaze told her everything she dreaded, he hadn't heard from JJ, and her heart dropped. Standing there, she battled an overwhelming urge to bolt, wanting to escape the moment without revealing just how vulnerable she felt. She forced a faint smile, mumbling, "Oh, I'll see him tomorrow," before turning to leave.

As she walked home, tears streamed down her cheeks, her mind swirling with disbelief. How could she have overlooked the signs? The idea that someone who professed to care for her could treat her this way left her heart aching. Yet somewhere, beneath the waves of disappointment, hope still lingered, a hope that she would find clarity and strength in this experience.

As Edith gazed out the window, a wave of relief washed over her; it was clear that Magnolia had seen through the deception. But just beneath that relief was a flicker of anger, knowing her child had to endure such disappointment. She waited eagerly for Magnolia to walk through the door, but when that didn't happen, curiosity got the better of her. She stepped outside and found Magnolia sitting alone on the porch, conversing animatedly as if someone was right there with her. In that moment, memories flooded back to Magnolia's childhood, when facing scary or upsetting situations, her daughter would have heartfelt chats with her imaginary friend. By the end of those conversations, her spirit would brighten. So, with a thoughtful smile, Edith decided to let Magnolia be.

She recognized that this moment was part of a larger transformation for Magnolia. Her daughter was grappling with her first real heartbreak and had decided to no longer see JJ. The situation took a turn for the worse days later when Magnolia found out JJ had gone on a double date with his sister. Despite trying to clarify the misunderstanding, Magnolia remained resolute, unwilling to listen. JJ reached out to friends for help, and when that failed, he turned to Edith, hoping she would convince Magnolia to talk to him. With a gentle assurance, Edith reminded him to offer Magnolia the time she needed, insisting that when she was ready, she would reach out. She also reassured her daughter that if JJ really loved her, he wouldn't have treated her that way and that someone wonderful would come along who would cherish her.

One afternoon, while Magnolia sat on the back porch talking to her old friend, she tried to make sense of the whirlwind of emotions swirling around her. Usually, clarity would come in just a day or two, but here they were weeks later. Edith often looked out to see her daughter quietly shedding tears; she ached to comfort her, yet instinctively trusted that Magnolia would ultimately find her own way.

Then, one bright morning, something shifted. Edith noticed that the cloud of sadness seemed to lift from Magnolia's spirit, replaced by a bright, hopeful energy. Magnolia eagerly asked if she could spend a couple of weeks at her cousins' house. Excited about rekindling those bonds, she asked for her mother's blessing. Edith agreed but reminded her gently to check in with her aunt. Magnolia beamed and rushed over to give her a heartfelt hug.

"Thank you, Mom. I love you." she chirped.

"Hold on just a second; we still need to make sure your aunt is okay with it." Edith chuckled.

I know, Magnolia laughed, her confidence radiating as she thought of her aunt, who always encouraged her to come spend time with her daughters. Being the eldest cousin, even by just thirty days, made her feel special and included.

After securing permission from her aunt, Magnolia quickly packed her things and set off the next morning. She even asked Edith to keep her departure a secret from JJ. Little did she know, Edith was eagerly looking forward to a conversation with JJ, ready to convey that her daughter was moving on.

Arriving at Aunt Josie's house stirred a wave of nostalgia for Magnolia. Memories of laughter and stories shared were woven into the fabric of that warm place. Aunt Josie had moved there out of necessity, keeping only her beloved rocking chair, a treasured companion through the years. Magnolia remembered spending countless afternoons on the porch, laughing and listening intently to Aunt Josie spin tales and sing songs that had a powerful history. After Aunt Josie passed, Magnolia found it difficult to revisit; that porch held bittersweet reminders. But this time felt uniquely promising. A positive energy surrounded her, pulling her toward the house, and in her heart, she sensed that she was meant to be there for a reason, ready to embrace what lay ahead.

One lovely evening, after the warmth of dinner had settled, Magnolia found herself cozily nestled in Aunt Josie's cherished rocking chair on the porch. As she rocked gently, a whirlwind of curious thoughts danced through her mind. Suddenly, she leapt upright and stared intently at the chair, as if it held a secret waiting to be uncovered. Just then, her aunt stepped outside, concerned by a noise that sounded something like a distant scream.

"Everything's fine, really. I just... when I sat in Aunt Josie's chair..." Magnolia's words trailed off as she continued to gaze at her aunt, her heart racing with excitement.

"What happened when you sat in her chair?" her aunt asked, stepping closer, intrigued by the mysterious turn of events.

Magnolia felt th e need to share something extraordinary, but first she wanted to establish trust. "Promise you won't laugh or think I'm losing my mind. You have to promise me that."

With a sincere nod, her aunt responded, "I promise."

Searching her aunt's eyes for understanding, Magnolia took a deep breath. "When I sat in the chair, I felt this incredible energy wash over me. It was as if Aunt Josie was there, telling me she had been waiting for me and wanted to share a story. Suddenly, the words began flooding my thoughts."

Her aunt's gaze was steadfast, encouraging Magnolia to go on. "What story?" she asked, genuinely intrigued.

"She wants to tell me a story," Magnolia replied, her heart pounding with anticipation.

A beautiful smile bloomed on her aunt's face. "Oh, I'd love to hear it. Please, can you share? I miss Aunt Josie's tales so much."

In a rush of emotions, Magnolia dashed inside, headed straight for her room to pack. Though thrilled by the energy she had felt, she insisted to her aunt, "I can't sit in that chair again; it belongs to Aunt Josie. Those stories are hers to tell."

Her aunt chuckled softly, a twinkle of understanding in her eyes. "You know, the wonderful thing about stories is that when they're shared, they can belong to anyone. Someday, someone else will carry those tales far and wide. If sitting in the chair doesn't feel right for you, that's absolutely okay."

As they both stepped back outside, her aunt took a seat in the rocking chair. Though she didn't hear a story, she sensed the powerful energy that surrounded the chair and began to grasp the sentiment that had stirred within Magnolia. Leaning over, she whispered gently, "Please, share the story. Remember, this isn't just your story, it's Aunt Josie's; she's sharing it through you."

Feeling torn, Magnolia hesitated, casting a thoughtful glance at the chair before looking back at her aunt. The expression on her aunt's face reminded her of the joyful anticipation of Christmas morning, and tears slipped down her cheeks as she felt an overwhelming wave of guilt wash over her for not being able to comply.

"I'm so sorry, Auntie. I really wish I could, but I just can't sit there," she confessed, her heart heavy.

Wrapping her arms around her, her aunt comforted her, saying, "You don't have to if it doesn't feel right. I should be the one apologizing, I didn't mean to upset you. I just wanted to spend some time with my favorite niece."

That brought a warm smile to Magnolia's face, and she hugged her aunt tightly, whispering back, "You're my favorite aunt too."

As they embraced, Magnolia's younger cousins tumbled toward the house and, spotting the two, rushed over for a group hug, their eyes glistening with emotion. One of the cousins explained, bearing concern that Magnolia might be bringing bad news since her visits had become so rare. Reassured by their mother that everything was indeed fine and that dinner would soon be served, the atmosphere lightened.

After a delightful dinner, Magnolia was eager to catch up with her cousins, curious about their lives since their older sister had moved in with their grandmother. They excitedly shared how school and church choir had kept them busy, despite missing out on a lot of fun.

Then the youngest cousin, eyes shining with hope, asked if Magnolia would share a bedtime story. Remembering how much joy her stories had once brought everyone, Magnolia's heart swelled with warmth. Even though her cousins were growing up, the thought of telling them a story was enticing.

Magnolia wondered if their mother had hinted at the idea, but the kids eagerly assured her it was their own wish. Looking into their eager faces, she could hardly resist. "Alright, I'll tell you a bedtime story tonight." she promised, feeling the familiar excitement return.

As she turned to leave, however, she noticed the joy on their faces quickly replaced by innocent anticipation as they turned to look at her, reminding her just how special these moments with family truly were.

After Magnolia left the room, their mother lingered in the doorway, her heart swelling with pride as the girls exchanged enthusiastic thumbs-ups. Although she hadn't suggested it, she felt a wave of warmth at their supportive gesture and returned their smiles before heading back to the kitchen. In the midst of tidying up, Magnolia strolled into the room with a bright smile on her face.

"Thank you," she said, her eyes sparkling with sincerity.

Her aunt looked up, pleasantly surprised. "Thank me for what, dear?"

Magnolia made her way over and took a seat at the table, clearly in a reflective mood. "Just for being my aunt."

As Magnolia stepped out of the kitchen, her aunt was left pondering the meaning behind that sweet expression of gratitude. Was Magnolia thanking her for hosting her for a couple of weeks? Did she feel especially close as the favorite niece? Or perhaps it was the joy of sharing bedtime stories that made her feel connected? Regardless of the reason, it filled her heart with gratitude to see Magnolia embracing family time with such joy.

Once the cousins had finished their baths, they excitedly called for Magnolia to join them in their room to share a story. With a big smile, she entered and launched into one of her all-time favorites;

The Little Girl That Couldn't Cry

Once upon a time, there was a little girl who mysteriously couldn't cry. Her mother had only heard her voice raise in tears once, at her birth. When the midwife gave the newborn a gentle slap, she let out a scream that echoed through the room, making everyone pause in awe. But as time went on, it became clear that this baby did not cry. Instead, she would gaze at those around her with expressive eyes whenever she needed something.

Her mother, curious and concerned, would occasionally poke her toes just to see if she'd react with a loud wail, but the little girl would merely scrunch her lips and furrow her brows, revealing her confusion.

One inquisitive cousin couldn't hold back and exclaimed, "Why couldn't she cry? What was wrong with her?"

Magnolia, ever patient, replied, "I thought you were excited for the story. Can I please tell it my way?"

Determined to figure out why her child wouldn't cry, the mother tried various tricks to evoke those tears. The most she achieved was a single tear trickling down her daughter's cheek. After multiple failed attempts, she realized that she was unintentionally causing discomfort and stress. This made her reflect on the fact that her attempts to provoke crying had led to unintentional harshness. So, she took her child to see a doctor, who proposed the possibility that the girl might not be able to speak, or even hear. The mother had never considered testing her daughter's hearing. The doctor kindly advised her to return in a couple of months to see if any progress had been made.

Another cousin chimed in excitedly, "Could she hear? I can't wait to find out. What's going on with her?"

"Please, let me finish the story." Magnolia responded with a smile.

Once home, the eager mother decided to put her child's hearing to the test. She placed the baby in front of the door and, standing behind her, yelled as loudly as she could. To her shock, the baby fell backward, bumping her head on the floor, yet she remained silent.

"Wait, so she could hear? But still, why can't she cry? Every baby cries." her cousin queried.

"I'm about to get there, I promise." Magnolia chuckled.

Relieved to learn her child could indeed hear, the mother was now puzzled about the deeper mystery; why couldn't her daughter cry? As the girl started to speak, the question of crying seemed to fade into the background. One sunny day, while her daughter played outside, a sound reached the mother's ears that was completely new. Rushing outside, she worried that her child must have hurt herself.

To her surprise, the girl wasn't crying at all; she was laughing joyfully. This was the first time she had laughed, and with happiness, tears streamed down her little cheeks. In that moment of realization, the mother understood that laughter was the true treasure of her daughter's heart. It was never about the crying; it was about encouraging joy and happiness. From that day forward, the little girl cried and laughed just like everyone else, filling their home with both emotions and making everything feel right in the world.

As Magnolia approached the conclusion of her cherished story, she couldn't help but notice how her cousin's eyes seemed to flutter shut in perfect harmony. Stepping out of the room, she spotted her aunt standing just outside the door, a warm, inviting smile on her face.

"That tale was my absolute favorite when I was a little girl. I believe Aunt Josie spun that one from her imagination," Magnolia fondly reflected.

They settled onto the porch, a cozy spot perfect for heart-to-heart conversations. Magnolia opened up to her aunt, expressing her frustration about being unable to conjure a story ever since she'd wished for those pesky thoughts to fade away. Surprisingly, sitting in Aunt Josie's chair had sparked something within her, bringing back the fondest memories of her childhood.

With a deep breath, she poured out her feelings about JJ and the uncertainty swirling in her mind about what steps to take next regarding him. Though Aunt Josie felt a strong urge to gently suggest that Magnolia distance herself from him, she wisely decided to give her niece the space she needed to come to her own conclusions.

In a reflective silence, Magnolia found herself lost in thought, her gaze drifting to the rocking chair nearby. It was clear she was yearning to sit there but felt a flicker of trepidation. Understanding and patient, her aunt remained silent, trusting that Magnolia would step into that comfort when she felt ready.

After a week filled with love and support, Magnolia finally felt the moment had come to venture out the front door and claim that rocking chair for herself. She held her breath, bracing for a rush of stories to spill forth, but at first, nothing emerged. Leaning back, she closed her eyes, and soon a wave of warmth washed over her as if she were lying in a sun-kissed meadow. When she opened her eyes, she was taken aback to see an older woman standing gracefully before a majestic tree. As Magnolia tried to rise, an unseen force gently held her in place, compelling her to keep her eyes focused skyward. Suddenly realizing she was still on the porch, alone and bewildered, her heart raced as she searched for her aunt. Overcome with confusion, she hurried into the house, nearly bumping into her aunt in her frantic state.

"Where were you? Why did you leave me out there all by myself?" Magnolia cried, tears streaming down her cheeks as vulnerability seeped through her voice.

She dashed into the bedroom, urgency propelling her to pack her bags. Her aunt, concerned and curious, asked why she had to leave so abruptly. Magnolia shared her unexpected experience while sitting in the rocking chair. A tidal wave of sadness had washed over her, and she was visited by that comforting old lady, whose presence usually brought solace, yet this time, fear had gripped her heart as if something dreadful loomed on the horizon. In that moment, an overwhelming desire to be with her mother surged within her, fueled by a deep-seated anxiety that something could happen to Edith, leaving her forever lost.

By the time Magnolia returned home, the panic had buildup within her. As soon as Edith caught sight of her daughter, she sensed the distress radiating from her and rushed to envelop her in a protective embrace, just as her body gave way in her arms. Struggling to gently place Magnolia on the sofa, Edith felt the warmth emanating from her daughter's forehead. Acting quickly, she retrieved a cool, damp towel. Just then, Magnolia began to tremble uncontrollably, sending a wave of fear through Edith. She recognized the symptoms all too well, a sickness known to take young lives too soon. Yet, deep down, she held onto hope, knowing that only time would tell the tale. As the fever eventually broke and Magnolia began to recover, she had an incredible story to share about her extraordinary experience, filled with lessons in strength and resilience.

One sunny Sunday, surrounded by loved ones celebrating her aunt's birthday, Magnolia felt a surge of excitement about a special moment she had been waiting to share. She gathered everyone on the porch, her heart racing with anticipation, eager to step into her role as the family storyteller. Magnolia had long recognized her unique gift a wonderful ability to weave tales that spark both wonder and reflection. Although some narratives might evoke a hint of fear, she knew that embracing her stories was an essential part of who she truly was. With a warm smile, she began to share her story;

"Let me take you back to my visit at Aunt Josie's house. I remember sitting in her cherished chair when suddenly, everything changed. As I closed my eyes, I sensed a gentle force holding my head back, almost like a friend guiding me. In an instant, the chair began to spin, followed by the porch, and then the whole house whirled around me. I felt myself being pulled into a deep, peaceful darkness. When the spinning finally ceased, I stood in a sunlit field, warmth radiating against my skin, almost like a comforting embrace.

Around me, people began to appear, their smiles bright and welcoming. They assured me that there was no need to fear; it was my time to assume my place within our family circle. One by one, the incredible women introduced themselves;

'I am Aye of Africa; my ancestors constructed magnificent pyramids.'
'I am Bezonya of Africa; my people created breathtaking sculptures and statues.'
'I am Phelana of Africa; I carry the legacy of great kings and queens.'

'I am Dmoena, who was taken from my homeland and given the name Lillian.'

As the introductions continued, a name caught my attention; 'I'm Viola of the Bedford plantation.' Soon after, came the name 'I'm Isza, who lead my sisters to freedom.' And I knew the next voice I would hear. 'I'm Aunt Josie, the spirit of storytelling.' With a twinkle in her eye, she reminded me how crucial it was to keep the storytelling tradition alive.

Each name brought with it a sense of belonging and pride. As they began to fade from view, Aunt Josie lingered, her pride radiating like sunlight. I noticed the smile on her face, beaming with joy as she acknowledged my growth. Just as she started to vanish, the comforting presence I had always known approached me, placing her hand gently on my shoulder.

In that moment, she reassured me, "Don't worry, my dear. Storytelling is a vital thread in the fabric of humanity. Knowing our history shapes our future; it helps us recognize what paths to take and what to avoid. History has a way of repeating itself, and there are lessons worth heeding. By sharing these stories, we can hope to prevent the missteps of the past and choose a brighter path forward."

Magnolia beamed with newfound confidence as she revealed to everyone that she was ready to share her tales without fear. They listened eagerly, captivated by her storytelling, including friends who would stop by just to hear her enchanting narratives. With each story she shared, she realized that being a storyteller was not just about her; it was about channeling the wisdom and experiences that flowed through her, connecting her to everyone who listened. The beauty of her journey was not just in the tales, but in the shared moments that enriched her family's legacy.

Eighteen

It's hard to believe that two months have flown by since Magnolia last saw JJ. On those warm, breezy days, she cherished the moments spent by the riverbank, where the gentle spray of water would kiss her face and the sound of the rushing river brought her a sense of peace. Lost in her thoughts, she was suddenly brought back to the moment by the sensation of a hand resting lightly on her shoulder. Recognizing it was JJ, she remained calm and didn't flinch.

"Mind if I join you?" he asked, his voice friendly and inviting. She kept her gaze on the flowing water and didn't reply, so he settled into a spot nearby, taking in the mesmerizing view of the river as well. The wind picked up that day, filling the air with the thrilling sounds of waves crashing against the rocks, and whitecaps danced playfully on the river's surface.

As Magnolia soaked in the atmosphere, she could sense JJ's intention to bridge the gap between them.

"That water sounds so relaxing, doesn't it?" he ventured, hoping to draw her out of her thoughts.

She didn't answer, nor did she even blink when a sudden gust of wind misted her face. Recognizing her need for space, he fell silent, waiting patiently until he noticed a slight movement of her head from side to side.

"I'm sorry," he offered gently.

Finally, she turned her head slightly to meet his eyes, but then returned her focus to the water.

"What more do you want from me? I said I was sorry," JJ pressed, a hint of frustration in his voice.

Magnolia stood up and walked briskly around him, feeling the weight of her thoughts.

"It's clear that you're sorry; I've seen that side of you. But honestly, a person can't enjoy their favorite spot with someone burdened by regret. There's nothing more disheartening than a person caught up in their own mistakes."

JJ wrestled with confusion, why couldn't she forgive him? It seemed harsh for a single misstep to overshadow all the cherished memories they shared, like their leisurely visits to the diner for root beer floats or delightful picnics by the river. What he failed to understand was that Magnolia felt their relationship had turned into a mere shadow of what it should be.

Hoping that giving her time would work in his favor, JJ waited, convinced she would ultimately return to him. When she walked into the store one day, radiating joy and laughter, he felt a flicker of hope. They resumed spending time together, and JJ believed it was only a matter of time before things would feel normal again. However, there was still an unvisited place between them that weighed heavily on Magnolia, symbolizing a relationship stuck in limbo. She knew many women were content with that reality, but deep down, she yearned for something more meaningful.

Sitting on the back porch one afternoon, contemplating how to distance herself from JJ for good, an insightful old woman appeared. Rumor had it that the stories we tell ourselves in nightmares are reflections of our real-life struggles, and Magnolia felt compelled to address her own. The woman offered a simple yet profound piece of wisdom; "Trust your inner feelings," before vanishing as mysteriously as she had come.

Reflecting on that encounter, Magnolia grasped that her life had been clouded by JJ's presence. Despite their friendship, it served as a constant reminder of her feelings of unworthiness regarding marriage. As long as he lingered in her life, true happiness would remain elusive. With renewed determination, she decided to end things once and for all.

It was a tough transition at first, but eventually, she found the strength to step back from their friendship. She began reclaiming her time, spending it with her family and nurturing her own interests.

This newfound freedom opened up a world of possibilities. Without JJ around, she found herself with plenty of leisure time, even if it sometimes felt lonely. The world was shifting; more people of color were venturing into various careers beyond traditional roles, breaking new ground in business and property ownership, and relishing the finer aspects of life. With such vibrant changes occurring in her community, she realized that stories were best shared among those who truly listened and connected, leading her to seek out new friendships that celebrated her voice and aspirations.

Magnolia eagerly began capturing her stories on paper, dreaming of the day she could send them to a publisher and see them beautifully bound in a book. Inspired by her vivid dreams, these stories emerged from her imagination, often infused with a sense of danger that mirrored the very fears that haunted her. For example, when she wrote about the soothing rain that rejuvenates the earth, her dreams would spiral into wild hurricanes, wreaking havoc and forcing families to battle the fury of nature. On similarly warm summer days, her tales of joy would twist into nightmares of fiery infernos consuming everything in their path. Despite the desire to stop writing altogether, Magnolia clung to the wise words of the elder women in her life, reminding her that storytelling was woven into the fabric of her legacy and her true calling.

One beautiful day, while resting on the riverbank, Magnolia felt a gentle tap on her shoulder. Assuming it was JJ, she remained seated, patiently awaiting his company. When he didn't sit down, her curiosity got the better of her, and she turned around, only to find herself face-to-face with a stranger. Startled, she jumped back, and so did he.

"Ma'am, I'm so sorry. I didn't mean to startle you," he exclaimed, his voice friendly and sincere. "My name is William Carl. I noticed you sitting here alone and thought you might like some company. Really, my apologies."

Feeling unnerved by the unexpected encounter, Magnolia quickly jumped to her feet and took a step back, her instinct to flee kicking in. Sensing her discomfort, William raised his hands in a calming gesture and said, "Please, I'm leaving now. Just... be careful. You're getting close to the river."

As he moved back, she cautiously kept her eyes on him, all while glancing warily at the water behind her. Once he reached the safety of the top of the riverbank, he settled onto a log, giving her the space she needed. Magnolia cautiously walked up the bank, her heart racing, before she turned to head home in a hurry. Just as she was leaving, she heard him call out, "Ma'am, my name is William Carl. It was great to meet you."

Though she didn't turn around to reply, a small smile crept onto her face as she walked down the road. Once home, she excitedly shared her encounter with her mother, wondering if she recognized him. She mentioned a new family had moved nearby, and they had a son around Magnolia's age. This revelation piqued her curiosity and made her realize how much time she had spent lost in her stories and with JJ, which might explain her lack of awareness regarding William.

The following day, she decided on a whim to walk in that direction, and there he was, sitting on the porch. Her heart skipped a beat.

"Good morning, ma'am. I'm William Carl. How are you?" he greeted enthusiastically.

Magnolia glanced up at him, then quickly looked down, feeling a rush of shyness. Unable to find her voice, she walked past without saying a word. Frustrated with herself when she got home, she realized she had missed a golden opportunity to engage with someone who seemed genuinely kind. Over the next few days, she spotted him on his porch frequently and felt a growing urge to introduce herself, yet her earlier embarrassment held her back. She didn't want him to think of her as immature or standoffish.

Then one day, she noticed him on the porch again, glancing her way and trying not to stare. Feeling adventurous, she decided to walk to the river in hopes that he might follow. With every step, she noticed him trailing behind. Arriving at her favorite spot along the river, she settled on a log nearby, and, unable to resist, called out, "Magnolia."

William's head snapped toward her. "Did you say something to me, ma'am?" he asked, genuine curiosity lighting his eyes.

With a small giggle escaping her lips, she replied, "Yes, I said Magnolia."

He looked momentarily puzzled, rubbing his chin as if deep in thought. "Magnolia, like the tree?"

Realizing he was teasing her, she playfully retorted, "No, my name is Magnolia."

His eyes widened in surprise, and with an outstretched hand, he said, "Oh, then I guess I should introduce myself."

"I know. You're William Carl, and you live down the road from me. How come we haven't crossed paths before? Your family has been living there for a while, and I feel like I have seen everyone but you."

"Oh, that's because I work on the riverboat," he explained, a gleam of excitement in his voice. "It only just returned to town, which is why our paths haven't crossed. I've spotted you plenty of times while the boat sails past here. Sometimes, you even wave to me."

Their laughter echoed along the river, filling the air with the promise of newfound friendship. Magnolia felt a wave of hope wash over her, believing that perhaps, just perhaps, her stories were about to find their way into a real-life narrative.

As she pondered, a familiar scene from the riverboat danced in her mind, where she often waved to someone from afar. Lost in her thoughts, she suddenly saw him waving enthusiastically back at her.

"Excuse me, ma'am. Do you remember me?" he called out, a bright smile lighting up his face.

She couldn't help but laugh. "Well, I must admit, you do look quite familiar when you wave your arms like that."

"Would it be alright if I joined you?" he asked, looking hopeful.

With no hesitation, he bounded over, full of joy like a child excited for their first fishing trip. As he settled beside her, he introduced himself again, "My name is William Carl. I know you have a beautiful name that comes from the Magnolia tree. My name is a legacy from my father, who got it from his father."

Her smile grew subtly, just enough to let him know she valued the conversation. Together, they gazed at the river as the water danced and played, seemingly telling stories of its own. Eventually, Magnolia stood up, glancing toward the horizon, sensing that her mother might be growing anxious for her return. As they strolled along, William asked if she'd like to tour the riverboat with him.

Magnolia had never experienced a riverboat journey before and felt a wave of excitement wash over her. Before she even knew it, she leaped into his arms, squealing with joy. Realizing how bold that was, she quickly pulled back and blushed, offering an apology.

William chuckled kindly, "Don't worry. Lots of girls are thrilled about going to the riverboat, too." However, he noticed her smile beginning to fade. It struck him that his choice of words might not have been the best.

With curiosity sharpening her tone, she placed a hand on her hip and asked, "So, how many girls have you brought to the riverboat?"

"Oh, no ma'am. I've never taken a girl there before. I see how they react when they hop on the boat with other guys, though. It's just never happened for me. Not even with my momma," he replied, his hands animatedly waving in front of him.

Magnolia raised an eyebrow, her playful demeanor returning. "Just because I'm going on the boat with you doesn't imply anything special."

William beamed, his eyes sparkling. "I was hoping it just meant we'd be friends. A friend would indeed invite another friend for a boat tour, right?"

Extending her hand with a grin, she replied, "That sounds fair. Friends it is."

As she arrived home, a wave of happiness enveloped her. She nearly walked past her mother, without a word, but just as her hand reached the doorknob of her bedroom, she heard Edith cough, a gentle reminder of her presence. Realizing she'd overlooked her, Magnolia understood she needed to make it right. She turned on her heels and walked back to the front door, remembering how, as a little girl, she would backtrack if she entered a room without greeting anyone. Visualizing her mother's gentle guidance, she stepped back with a smile that brightened her face.

"I'm sorry, Momma," she murmured, her tone sincere.

When she reached the door again, she declared, "Good evening. I'm back from the river."

Hands on her hips, Edith replied with playful authority, "I was just about to come look for you."

Excitedly, Magnolia recounted her day and how she had finally met William Carl. He seemed lovely, she noted, and she elaborated on their newfound friendship and his invitation for the riverboat tour. Edith's heart swelled with happiness as she watched her daughter's spirit shine brighter than it had in ages, even as a flicker of concern crossed her face about potential disappointments that might lie ahead.

During dinner, Magnolia animatedly shared every detail of her encounter, her enthusiasm spilling over as she spoke of how genuinely nice William Carl was and how eagerly she awaited their riverboat adventure. It was a delightful evening filled with warmth, laughter, and the promise of new beginnings.

The following morning, Magnolia woke up buzzing with excitement for the tour. Stepping onto the porch, she was met with an astonishing sight, the riverboat had vanished. She could hardly process it. Scanning the waterway, she searched for any trace of the grand vessel, but there was absolutely nothing. The river was perfectly still, not a ripple in sight. A wave of confusion washed over her, making her question if all of it had been nothing more than a vivid dream. Had she truly met William Carl by the riverbank? Did their conversation about the riverboat even happen?

Returning to the house, she settled at the kitchen table, feeling a heavy cloud of uncertainty. When Edith strolled in and noticed her daughter's lonely expression, concern filled her eyes. "What's troubling you, dear?" she asked gently. As Magnolia looked up, tears sparkled in her eyes, and she admitted her confusion. "I can't tell what's real anymore," she confessed, her voice trembling. Edith recognized the worry etched into her daughter's features; Magnolia's eyes always drooped at the corners when something was deeply troubling her. "Whenever you feel ready to share, I'm here to listen," she reassured tenderly.

Later that morning, as Magnolia perched on her bed, her mind swirled with questions about the mysterious house down the road. Did anyone truly live there, or had she conjured the entire story in her imagination? All morning, a tugging curiosity urged her to explore further, yet her feet felt anchored to the floor. She wrestled with uncertainty and fear, if it turned out the house and its inhabitants weren't real, would it shatter her fragile reality? Her reassuring words echoed in her mind, they insisted that everything was real and that William Carl existed. But self-doubt crept in, leaving Magnolia unsure about her own reality. What if she, too, was merely a figment of someone else's dreams? The thought was overwhelming, and part of her decided it would be easier to simply not know.

Then, around noon, a knock echoed through the house, making Magnolia's heart leap. The sudden thrill sent beads of sweat trickling down her face. This was it. Could it be him? Edith called from the other room, encouraging her to answer the door, but Magnolia stood frozen, heart racing. A second knock followed, and slowly, she gathered the courage to approach the door. Hope and anxiety swirled within her, and when she finally swung the door open, there he was, every bit as handsome as the first time she'd met him. Without missing a beat, she leaped into his arms.

"It's you. You're real. I can hardly believe it." she exclaimed, her heart soaring.

He spun her in delight, his smile radiant. "Of course I'm real. What's going on?"

Magnolia pulled back slightly; her voice tinged with confusion. "But where did the boat go? You didn't tell me it was leaving. I thought I might have imagined you. I'm so relieved you're real."

She noticed a quizzical look flicker across his face. "I thought we had a date to tour the riverboat," he replied, a hint of confusion in his tone.

In that moment, it struck her, she was still in her bedclothes. Embarrassed, she made a swift excuse and dashed into her room to change. As she breezed past her mother, she tossed her a playful wink, exuding newfound confidence. "I'm fine, Mom. Everything is going to be just great."

With a smile on her lips, Magnolia prepared for her day, ready to embrace whatever adventures awaited her.

Nineteen

Years after Aunt Josie had passed away, Magnolia decided to host a family reunion at her home. Over time, many friends and family members had reached out to express how much they remembered and missed Aunt Josie. She even received heartfelt letters from relatives she had only heard about through family stories. It felt like the perfect moment for her to bring everyone together and recreate that sense of belonging and connection. People made the journey from far and wide, with some discovering relatives they had never known existed. Everyone was eager to learn more about the beloved Aunt who had called New Orleans home.

Among the gathering were the family's great storytellers. Through the years, they had shared bits and pieces of their family history from different viewpoints, and this gathering presented a wonderful opportunity to weave together those diverse narratives. The storytellers were bursting with excitement to share the tales of their ancestors, stories that had been passed down through generations.

What surprised them all was the impressive size of their family and the many paths their relatives had taken in pursuit of freedom across the United States. They decided to organize themselves according to the eight branches of the family tree; Isza, May, Hilda, Viola, Clara, Teacee, Picola, and Baby. For those who were unfamiliar with the names, they were encouraged to gather in groups and listen to the shared memories, as any grandmother, grandfather, or great-grandparent could emerge in another's story. By the end of the reunion, nearly everyone discovered a connection to one of those original eight branches.

As discussions unfolded, relatives exchanged anecdotes and shared the few treasured documents and photographs they had. Magnolia noted something curious; no one seemed to have a direct connection to Aunt Josie, despite her being the inspiration for the event. Feeling a bit puzzled, she turned to Edith for answers about Aunt Josie's roots, learning that there might be a vague link to Paul's family, though details were scarce. The absence of a clear connection did not diminish the sense of familial love; after all, families often scatter far and wide. It is through the feelings and connections experienced in each other's company that people recognize true family. Aunt Josie undoubtedly belonged to this family.

Following the reunion, Edith found herself deep in thought about Magnolia's questions. Who was Aunt Josie, and what was her story? She recalled the enchanting tales Clara used to share from their childhood. Those memories opened her eyes to the fact that Aunt Josie hadn't always been present in their lives. During visits with her relatives, they would speak of the woman who had come to their aid at the cabin in the woods, and Edith began to wonder if that might have been Aunt Josie.

As she reminisced further, she remembered a time when she was just ten years old, and her mother fell gravely ill. Everyone feared the worst. Aunt Josie visited, and almost miraculously, Clara began to recover. It felt as though Aunt Josie had always been a part of their lives, and before long, she was sharing family stories, establishing a genuine bond with them all. In her lifetime, nobody questioned her role; it simply felt right.

Yet, despite this connection, Edith couldn't help but ponder Aunt Josie's true identity. The more she reflected, the more questions surfaced. Throughout her adult life, she had always been around Aunt Josie, yet she realized she hadn't delved into her background as deeply as she should have. Who was Aunt Josie, and where did she come from? This obsession with knowledge led Edith to speak with older relatives, but she found that no one knew significantly more about Aunt Josie than she did; she was simply there and utterly essential to their family unit.

For the entire year that followed, Aunt Josie's memory lingered in Edith's mind. It perplexed her that she didn't know more about her, and she wondered why she hadn't taken the time to share her origins, who her people were. Although she had shared a plethora of stories, this vital part of her life remained a mystery. She recalled Aunt Josie's emotional freedom day story, leading her to ponder whether perhaps Aunt Josie had no family of her own and how she had come to be part of theirs.

Strange occurrences began to unfold in Edith's life. She found herself dreaming of a cabin in the woods, reminiscent of the place Clara and Aunt Josie used to talk about. In her dreams, she felt as though she towered over the planet, gazing down upon it. From above, she could see the vast expanse of trees and water, echoing the vivid images her mother had relayed from her own stories.

With each passing day, Edith became more determined to uncover the truth about Aunt Josie's life. Little did she know that this exploration would not only reveal hidden family secrets but also deepen the bonds that tied them all together, drawing them closer as a family. Through this journey of discovery, she hoped to honor Aunt Josie's memory and the enduring legacy she had left behind.

In her dreams, Edith experienced a delightful blend of warmth from the sun, harmonized with the gentle coolness of a breeze wafting from the north. It felt as if the winds were lovingly embracing her, lifting her closer to the treetops, and she found immense joy in the sensation of floating. Nature had always held a special place in Edith's heart; to her, the trees represented a divine gift offering respite from the sweltering heat of summer days. There was nothing quite like the invigorating experience of strolling to town on a blistering day and feeling a refreshing gust of wind brush against her as she passed beneath a sprawling tree, prompting her to pause and appreciate the moment.

As the weeks unfolded, this enchanting dream began to recur nightly, each time starting with that same comforting warmth. Gradually, Edith felt herself drawn closer to the ground with every adventure in her dreams. One night, she found herself gazing down at a charming cabin and bustling figures. Initially, they seemed like tiny creatures, but in a moment of realization, she understood these were not mere figments but people. Upon waking, an exhilarating sense of anticipation washed over her; she was eager to uncover who they were and what stories awaited her. The excitement grew to the point where she could hardly wait to drift back into slumber.

Edith fondly remembered her mother, Clara, sharing her own childhood dreams of a place beyond the borders of the United States, where the melodic sounds of the French language echoed around her. Clara recounted how an elderly woman would guide her through the intricacies of that language in her dreams. It had been a wonderful revelation for Clara when she unexpectedly understood the words of French-speaking visitors at the plantation. This unique dream connection had proven invaluable, enabling her to communicate with the French-speaking plantation owners and facilitating her transition to life in New Orleans. Clara always urged Edith to honor her dreams, as she believed they carried significant messages.

Motivated by this encouragement, Edith began heading to bed early, eager to uncover the secrets her dreams held. However, mysteriously, the dreams faded away as if they were playing hide-and-seek with her.

One fateful morning, Edith awoke feeling utterly drained, unable to muster the energy to rise from her bed. After three worry-filled days, her loved ones grew increasingly concerned, noticing the fever that kept her from eating. Then, on a startling day, she found herself floating above a familiar landscape, gazing down. The sun blazed fiercely overhead, prompting her to seek refuge beneath a tree to escape its intensity. Fear gripped her heart as she realized that if she didn't wake up soon, she might succumb to the heat. In a frantic moment, her body flailed until, in a sudden burst of awareness, her eyes sprang open to find her family surrounding her. Someone exclaimed with relief, "You're back. You're back." Though she attempted to smile, her next memory was of being once again enveloped in that familiar warmth, hovering over the trees and longing to touch solid ground.

Over the following days, she remained in a semi-conscious state, grappling with her high fever. But once she regained her strength, flashes of memories returned, including Clara bringing her to that cabin during her childhood. Yet the precise details of how they arrived there eluded her. After days of contemplation, an epiphany struck, she remembered that they had taken the Desire streetcar to the Chef Menteur area. Filled with purpose, Edith realized she needed to embark on a journey to discover the truth of her dreams.

With excitement bubbling inside her, she packed a few essentials and set out. As she ventured towards the cabin, peculiar occurrences danced around her, whispers floated through the air even in the absence of anyone nearby. Initially unsettling, she remembered tales of similar experiences and allowed her determination to fuel her spirit.

Ignoring the tremors of fear, she pressed on with unwavering resolve.

Finally, after what felt like an eternity of walking, she arrived at a clear, familiar spot that resonated with memories from her dreams. Sunlight poured down upon her, and in that moment of clarity, Edith raised her arms to the sky, tilted her head back, and spun joyfully in pirouettes. It felt as though the trees warmly welcomed her back, and the waters around her danced to guide her path, as if anticipating her return. A deep sense of joy enveloped her heart, knowing she stood on the sacred ground where her mother and aunts had once savored their first taste of freedom.

As Edith twirled in joyful abandon, her spirit was momentarily interrupted by an unexpected sound. With curiosity piqued, she paused and scanned her surroundings, recalling Clara's stories about the sisters' time in the woods. Most of the time, the sounds they heard were merely the leaves dancing in the wind. Realizing she was alone, a sense of determination washed over her, compelling her to continue down the path. In her dreams, she had envisioned a charming cabin nestled just around a bend, and as she walked, she noted that the road ahead was straight. A flicker of doubt crept in, was she heading the wrong way? Yet, that inner voice urging her forward filled her with hope. Just when she felt she couldn't go on, there it was, the cabin she had longed to see.

As she turned to glance behind her, she took a moment to realize she had unwittingly rounded that elusive bend. With excitement bubbling within her, she rushed to the door. But as she reached for the knob, an unexpected force halted her in her tracks. She felt paralyzed, unable to move despite her desperate attempts to push through it. Fear momentarily enveloped her as she began to hear muffled conversations nearby. Though anxious to look around, her head wouldn't budge. What would happen when those approaching found her suspended in this strange moment?

In that suspended state, feeling increasingly lightheaded, she fought to keep her eyes open. When they finally fluttered back into focus, she was astonished to find herself looking down from above. Suddenly, it dawned on her, she was in a dream. This dream, it seemed, was reaching its conclusion just as she stood at the door. Why was this happening? Perhaps it simply wasn't her moment to enter the house.

Meanwhile, at her house, the doctor arrived to check on Edith. He informed the family that he hadn't found anything amiss and recommended she simply rest. Magnolia felt a surge of frustration; they all craved answers, why this was happening, when she would awaken, and what was wrong with her. All he could say was that she would awaken when she was ready. As he departed, Magnolia silently mused that the two dollars she had paid for the visit might have been better spent elsewhere.

Magnolia's heart ached with concern for her mother, memories flooding back of her Aunt Willa Mae. They had shared countless playful afternoons until one fateful day when Willa Mae sat in her rocking chair and simply wouldn't wake. When she finally opened her eyes, she spoke of having been with God, leaving Magnolia torn between disbelief and a comforting sense of faith. Then, one day, during a heartfelt conversation, Willa Mae closed her eyes for the last time.

That evening, Edith gently explained to Magnolia that Willa Mae had needed to rest.

Edith had been struggling with frequent bouts of sleep, and fear gripped Magnolia. She dreaded the thought of losing her mother, especially in the same way Aunt Willa Mae had departed. Determined to be by her side, Magnolia stayed close, praying with all her heart that her mother would wake and see her, understanding that recovery meant the world to them both. Eventually, exhaustion claimed her, and in her dreams, she encountered an old lady standing serenely in the corner. "It's not time for your mother to come home," the lady assured her. "Don't you worry your pretty little head."

A wave of relief washed over Magnolia, this apparition had never misled her before, and she felt buoyed by the conviction that her mother would be okay.

When Edith finally stirred, there was a noticeable change. She walked with a limp, and her words were muffled and difficult to comprehend. The community buzzed with concern and speculation; some whispered about a potential illness causing her symptoms. Magnolia poured her heart into helping her mother regain her strength, though the effort felt exhausting. Edith hoped that as her physical health improved, her memories would come rushing back.

The entire neighborhood rallied around them, embodying the essence of community support. Friends and neighbors dropped by, eager to engage with Edith, asking her to recall shared moments and testing her memory with anecdotes from the past. Although this outpouring of love was heartfelt, it began to overwhelm Edith. When multiple visitors appeared throughout the day, asking the same questions, frustration simmered beneath the surface until one day she exclaimed, "His name was McKinley, his shirt was red, and I saw him just two minutes ago."

In that moment, everyone recognized the spark of her spirit returning. Although her mind healed, the limp adhered to her as a reminder of her journey. Yet, there was an undeniable strength in her that shone through, a light that encouraged everyone around her. They knew with certainty that she would reclaim her place in their lives, and together they would embrace whatever came next with hope and resilience.

Edith gently told Magnolia that it was time for her to spread her wings and embrace life without the weight of constant babysitting. She encouraged her daughter to step out, reassuring her that staying cooped up at home all day was not the best way for a young person to grow. With newfound courage, Magnolia asked her mother for permission to go to a friend's party, promising to return straight home afterward. Expecting to hear a firm no, she was pleasantly surprised when Edith confidently replied, "Be back by nine." In that moment, a wave of love washed over Magnolia for her mother, more profound than ever before.

At the party, Magnolia experienced sheer joy. Her friends were thrilled to see her, as it had been a long time since Edith allowed such outings. This was a testament to the new Edith, one who recognized that Magnolia was growing up and deserved to feel the joy of being with friends.

One sunny morning, while Edith prepared breakfast, she found herself reflecting on her life before her illness and the dreams she once had of a charming cabin. Just then, a letter arrived, inquiring about Aunt Josie and her connection to the family. This letter opened a floodgate of memories and questions for Edith. Who was Aunt Josie? What was her story? Did she have family who was searching for her? In that moment, Edith felt a deep yearning to uncover the mysteries surrounding Aunt Josie. Remembering her dream of the little house in the woods, she felt it was the perfect starting point for her journey.

Edith wasn't sure if she had visited that house in reality or if it existed solely within her dreams, but she felt a profound connection to it, as though it was inviting her back. Even amidst the joys of spending time with Magnolia at the French Market, visiting friends, and nurturing her beloved garden, that feeling lingered. She recognized the need to embark on this journey in order to discover the truth.

Early one morning, when the world was still asleep, Edith quietly packed some belongings, leaving a reassuring note that she would return soon and that there was no need to worry.

Following the path she had seen in her dreams; Edith felt a mix of excitement and trepidation as the shadows enveloped her. It briefly crossed her mind that she should have waited for daylight, but deep down, she knew her family would have tried to dissuade her or even questioned her sanity if they discovered her plans. As the sun began to rise, she was mesmerized by the breathtaking colors shimmering through the woods, bouncing off treetops, reflecting in marshlands, and glistening in patches of water.

For a moment, the beauty felt surreal, prompting her to pinch herself. A sharp nip brought her back to reality, and she mused, "I'm not dreaming." As she continued her journey, she reached a stretch of land that sparkled with significance; the cabin was just around the corner.

As she rounded the bend, her heart soared, there it was. Just as she had envisioned in her dreams. Pinching herself again, this time with less force, she ventured inside the house, reassured that it was undeniably real since she had never been inside before. It felt as if someone had been living there, so she decided to stay and see if she might encounter someone or uncover the purpose of her visit.

While seated, memories of Aunt Josie's stories about the little house began to swirl in her mind. Standing up, Edith slowly turned around the room, sensing the presence of others. Tears streamed down her cheeks as she realized she was standing where the sisters had once savored their first taste of freedom. In that profound moment, she thought, "This is it. This is where my family, as I know it, began."

Edith was filled with a sense of hope and connection, fully embracing the journey that lay ahead.

As the darkness began to settle around her, Edith made the thoughtful decision to stay inside the little cabin for the night. She felt a sense of calm at the idea that if anyone came, she would have the chance to explain her presence. Lying there, she suddenly heard loud noises, horses galloping and distant screams that sent a chill down her spine. It struck her as strange and terrifying, for the outside world was enveloped in pitch darkness, vastly different from the bright lights of the city. The unsettling sounds made it seem as though there were distressing events unfolding just beyond her window, and despite her curiosity, fear held her in place.

Out of nowhere, the door creaked open, and her heart raced. A man, pale and unfamiliar, stood in the doorway holding a gun. His glance swept across the room, but it felt as though he didn't truly see her, he seemed to look right through her. When he finally closed the door, she instinctively pinched herself, but felt nothing. A wave of realization washed over her; she was dreaming again. That thought brought a flicker of relief, though she still couldn't bring herself to venture out and potentially discover otherwise.

Cocooned in her own embrace, Edith rested her head against the cabin wall, seeking comfort in its solidity. When she opened her eyes again, light had streamed in, brightening both the interior and the world outside. Stepping outside, she took in the trees and their rustling leaves, but when she turned around, there was no one there. In the distance, a figure seemed to stroll toward her, though oddly enough, it wasn't getting any closer. Another pinch confirmed her suspicions, she was awake. With curiosity piqued, she went back inside, anticipating a knock on the door. But when it didn't come, she ventured back outside, finding the silhouette still there, steadily advancing.

A spark of intrigue urged her to approach this mysterious figure; perhaps it had come to meet her. As she walked, it felt like the more she moved forward, the further it drifted away. Mulling over her options, she turned to head back to the cabin, only to find the figure had vanished. A whirlwind of emotions filled her, fear and excitement mingled as she felt both the urge to flee and the desire to chase after this shadow. Eventually, exhaustion took over and she paused on a rock to catch her breath, noticing that the shadow paused with her. This small connection gave her comfort, suggesting there was a reason for their encounter. Mustering her courage, she called out,

"Who are you, and where are you taking me?"

"You know who I am."

The voice resonated with a familiarity that sparked curiosity within her.

"Where do I know you from? Are you a ghost or someone from my past?"

"In time, you will remember me."

Intrigued, she pressed on, determined to uncover this enigmatic identity. As the image shifted, Edith felt compelled to follow, but a wave of apprehension washed over her. Was this really happening? She pinched herself once more but dismissed the idea of the pinch theory; this felt too real. Thoughts of death lingered at the edges of her mind, bringing sadness as she contemplated the possibility of not seeing her family again. With newfound resolve, she called out,

"Am I dead? Are we heading to heaven?"

"No," came the calm reply.

As they continued walking, she strained to see the shadow's face, yearning for recognition. Unfortunately, it remained a mystery, and doubt nagged at her. Perhaps the shadow had confused her for someone else. It reassured her,

"No, I know you are Edith, and you have nothing to fear."

"Do I know you?"

"Look into my eyes."

She focused intently on the shadow's eyes, hoping for a spark of familiarity to ignite her memory.

"I'm sorry, I don't remember you."

Pushing past her trepidation, she inquired,

"Aunt Josie, is that you?"

With a hearty laugh, the shadow confirmed,

"It's you. I've missed you so."

In that moment, the realization struck her, Aunt Josie had passed away. Was she truly conversing with a spirit? Confusion gripped her, and anxiety took hold. However, Aunt Josie wrapped her arm around Edith, spreading warmth and reassurance. The comfort was unlike anything she'd felt, sparking hope that maybe everything would be alright. Suddenly, a sound from behind stirred her, instilling fear of what lay beyond her view.

Aunt Josie gestured, and hesitantly, Edith turned to see a young girl approaching. To her surprise, the girl walked past them as if they were invisible, entering the cabin settling in a corner, tears spilling down her cheeks. Feeling the girl's sorrow profoundly, Edith's instincts kicked in, yearning to comfort her. Across the room, another figure caught her eye. Aunt Josie gently placed her hand on Edith's shoulder.

"See, she will be alright. She is not alone."

"Who is she?"

"Her name is Lillian; your great-granddaughter. She is a little girl who needs me now."

In that tender moment, Aunt Josie began to fade, leaving Edith in a whirlwind of questions.

"My great-granddaughter? What is she doing here? Who is her mother? Why am I here?"

These thoughts swirled in her mind, igniting a sense of purpose and a deep desire to understand her place in this unfolding story.

Twenty

Magnolia and William Carl had been happily together for two wonderful years when William decided it was time to take a big step in their relationship. He knew that proposing to Magnolia was a significant moment, and he wanted it to be special, but he was uncertain if his plan would be perfect. All he truly felt was the love that blossomed between them. After confiding in Edith about the trip, he felt encouraged to move forward with his proposal. To keep the excitement a surprise, Edith cleverly suggested to Magnolia that it wasn't the best idea to travel with a man while unmarried. This gentle nudge would keep Magnolia blissfully unaware of the surprise trip ahead, and she would think her mother had simply expressed some wisdom.

Once they had this plan in place, Edith eagerly sat down with Magnolia to discuss how she might approach the trip. Magnolia was filled with enthusiasm and admiration for her mother, and thought she was the best. With excitement bubbling inside her, Magnolia couldn't wait for the adventure that lay ahead. She was certain of her love for William Carl and believed this journey would be a thrilling experience, an opportunity to explore and create memories together, while also honoring her commitment to saving intimacy for marriage.

As the departure date approached, Magnolia began her packing a week in advance, buzzing with anticipation about leaving New Orleans. While the excitement was palpable, she also felt a hint of anxiety about traveling so far from home without her mother by her side. On the morning of the trip, a wave of uncertainty washed over her, causing her to hesitate as she got out of bed. A knot of fear tightened in her stomach; she couldn't shake thoughts about what might go wrong, like the boat capsizing.

When Edith passed by Magnolia's bedroom and noticed her sitting quietly on the bed, in her eyes she sensed something was amiss. Her eyes, reflected unshed tears, and the tousled bed that looked like it had seen a struggle.

"Momma, I can't do it," Magnolia exclaimed, jumping up to wrap her arms around her. As she leaned on her mother's shoulder, she broke down in tears.

Edith felt a pang in her heart; she had envisioned this day as one of the happiest in Magnolia's life. She gently pulled back, looking deep into her daughter's eyes, trying to grasp what had triggered this sudden fear.

"My sweet girl, I thought you were looking forward to this trip. What made you change your mind?"

With tears streaming down her cheeks, Magnolia said, "I'm terrified. What if the ship sinks, and we all drown? Momma, I can't swim very well, and even if I could, that's an awful lot of water."

Edith, filled with compassion, sought to comfort her daughter, reminding her of all the safety measures in place on the boat. But Magnolia shook her head, her fears palpable.

"He showed me the lifeboats available in case of an emergency, but do you really think they would let someone like me into one of those little boats? They don't even let me walk down the same street. I must have been crazy to agree to this. I need to tell him I can't go."

At that moment, Edith felt a profound concern for her daughter. Looking deeply into Magnolia's worried eyes, she searched for just the right words to ease her fears, but she knew this was a journey Magnolia needed to navigate on her own. While she wanted to support her, Edith couldn't shake the thought that if she pushed her daughter to go and anything went wrong, it would weigh heavily on them both.

Magnolia was given a few hours to reflect on her feelings. The journey ahead could be filled with joy and love, an adventure to embrace together. She just needed to understand whether her fears stemmed from the imagined dangers of sailing or from leaving behind the comfort of home. Encouragement and love surrounded her, and with some thoughtful reflection, she had the opportunity to discover her own bravery.

As Edith sat quietly, she couldn't help but bask in the beautiful memories of her childhood, particularly the powerful yearning she felt to visit her beloved aunt.

Her mother, Clara had mentioned they would embark on the trip in a couple of days, but Edith's excitement bubbled over, leading her to insist they go that very day. With a gentle smile and the sparkle of enthusiasm in her daughter's eyes, Clara eventually gave in to Edith's eagerness and agreed to set off at once.

On their journey to Auntie's house, Clara felt a flicker of unease creeping in, which made her quicken their pace. But the moment they arrived and spotted their aunt relaxing on the porch with a cool glass of lemonade, the worries melted away. Seeing Edith and Clara rushing towards her, Auntie jumped to her feet in alarm, fearing something was amiss. Once they caught their breath and settled down, Clara explained with warmth that Edith simply couldn't wait to see her. Auntie's eyes glinted with understanding as she welcomed them in, relieved to hear that all was well.

After a wonderful visit, the two excitedly headed home, but the atmosphere shifted when they spotted several law enforcement officers gathering in the woods nearby. Their home was surrounded. It turned out they had narrowly avoided danger; a notorious killer had been roaming those woods, only to be captured hiding right under their house. The shocking turn of events reinforced a lesson for young Edith; children often have a sense of intuition. If Magnolia ever expressed hesitation about going somewhere, she would respect her feelings completely.

Meanwhile, William Carl paid a friendly visit to check in on Magnolia. He fondly recalled the first time he had taken a boat out on the river, feeling nerves swirl in his stomach. Yet, he recognized this was a fantastic opportunity, especially for a Negro man, and found the courage to embrace it. By the time he reached Magnolia's house, all her previous fears seemed to wash away just at the sight of him. The comfort of his presence reassured her; in the event the boat capsized, she mused that there was no one better to share that experience with than the person she cherished most. In that moment, Magnolia truly understood that William Carl was the one for her.

When he left, Magnolia couldn't wait to let her mother know everything would be just fine. Excitement bubbled within her as she looked forward to their travels, each port promising new adventures. She even promised Edith a special gift from every stop along the way. Grateful for Magnolia's thoughtfulness, Edith reminded her daughter to also pamper herself with a treat, encouraging her not to spend all her money on her mother.

When departure time finally arrived, Edith walked with them to the river, her heart swelling with pride and a touch of bittersweet sadness. She had always dreamed of waving "bon voyage" to someone special but had never had the chance. As Edith watched her daughter on the upper deck, emotions welled up inside her; this moment would be the last she would see of her little girl for a while. The next time they met, Magnolia would be a grown woman and engaged to be married. Tears streamed down Edith's face as she waved goodbye, filled with love and hope.

Magnolia, standing tall on the boat's upper deck, caught one last glimpse of her mother as the vessel began to glide away. When the boat turned around a bend, the emotions of the moment filled her heart. As they passed a spot where people had begun to gather, Magnolia noticed two new bridges spanning the water, exciting landmarks she had heard whispers of but had never laid eyes on. As they journeyed through seemingly uncharted territory, a little blue house caught her attention, and to her delight, a Black woman stepped out onto the porch and waved, sharing a simple moment of connection.

Later, as Magnolia settled into her room in the belly of the boat, she began to feel a wave of nausea from the vessel's motion. Remembering earlier advice, William Carl suggested she press her thumb against the inside of her wrist. Skeptical yet willing to try anything to feel better, Magnolia followed his quirky suggestion, and much to her surprise, her discomfort lifted. Filled with gratitude, she realized that sometimes, unexpected wisdom can lead to the most pleasant moments. Every new adventure held the potential for delightful surprises.

During the first two days of her journey, Magnolia primarily saw William Carl when he brought her meals. She spent her days in the cabin, feeling a mix of uncertainty and loneliness about her new surroundings aboard the boat. Questions raced through her mind about what she could and couldn't do on this trip, leading her to wonder if taking this voyage had truly been the right choice. By the third day, the monotony became almost unbearable, and she found herself feeling as if she might pull out her hair out of sheer boredom.

But then came the fourth day, a turning point that filled her with hope. They finally left the Deep South, and with that change, her spirits lifted. She ventured to the main deck for breakfast and was met with an unexpected surprise. Much to her astonishment, the dining room buzzed with the vibrant presence of many Negro patrons, something she had never anticipated on this boat. As she entered the room, she felt a sudden wave of disbelief wash over her; White and Negro people were sharing tables, happily eating, chatting, and laughing together. It was such a stark contrast from what she had known, and for a moment, she thought she must have slipped into a dream or perhaps a place where societal barriers no longer existed.

Noticing the tears welling in her eyes, William Carl approached her with concern. "What's wrong?" he asked, puzzled by her emotional response.

"I'm going to miss my momma, that's all," she replied, trying to stifle her emotions.

He looked a bit confused but gently reassured her. "We're not in heaven; we've just left the South behind us. Things truly are different here in the North." This new information filled Magnolia with both relief and an undeniable sense of wonder about the world.

On the fifth day, something incredible happened after dinner. William Carl got down on one knee and proposed to her. Surprised but elated, she learned that the captain of the boat could officiate their wedding right there and then. He suggested they could have another ceremony when they returned home, but his urgency and hope to stand before the captain and share their vows in that moment moved her. For Magnolia, this was a life-changing decision. She loved him deeply and felt that her mother would surely understand her desire to make this commitment. Without hesitation, she accepted his proposal.

When she returned to her room, her heart raced with excitement as she discovered a beautiful white wedding dress draped elegantly across the bed. Holding it up before her, she admired its design, and when she glanced in the mirror, it took her breath away. The dress swayed around her as if it were casting a spell, making her feel like she was dancing in the arms of her prince. It truly was stunning, evoking a whirlwind of emotions within her. But as she sat on her bed and contemplated the significance of the day ahead, tears filled her eyes. This was one of the most important moments of her life, yet the absence of her mother weighed heavily on her heart.

Caught between the joy of her engagement and the sorrow of her mother's absence, doubt began to creep in. Seeking solace, she stepped out onto the deck to breathe in the fresh air. The sky was darker than she had ever seen before, filling her with a sudden unease. A fleeting thought about what could happen if she fell overboard sent her hurrying back inside. As she walked down the hallway, she spotted a woman who bore a striking resemblance to Edith, instantly igniting a spark of hope within her. Rushing to greet her, Magnolia smiled warmly and said, "Good evening," which helped ease the woman's evident surprise.

However, the notion of getting married on a boat, while charming, began to feel rushed. She knew Edith had envisioned this special moment for years, and she couldn't shake the feeling that it wouldn't be fair to deprive her of that dream. Even though they could plan a second ceremony after returning home, she felt a weighty significance in having her mother by her side on her wedding day. Determined to find the right words, Magnolia resolved to communicate her feelings to William Carl, hoping he would understand the depth of her desire for her mother's presence during such an important milestone in her life.

Thus, Magnolia found herself at a crossroads, a blend of excitement and reflection, her heart open to the joys yet to come while cherishing the connection to her family and dreams that anchored her.

All night long, Magnolia found herself caught in a whirlwind of thoughts, shifting restlessly as her mind raced. She couldn't shake the anxiety that gripped her, thoughts of being left behind in some unfamiliar city along the Mississippi River or fears that William Carl might decide he didn't want to see her anymore. A wave of apprehension enveloped her as she hesitated to tell him that she wanted to wait. She also dreaded the conversation she would have to have with her mother about getting married without her presence.

In moments of despair, she found herself sitting up in bed, covered in sweat. It was then she decided to turn to God, seeking guidance to find clarity in her heart. When she finally opened her eyes again, a wave of tranquility washed over her, illuminating the path she needed to take.

When William Carl entered the room, he immediately sensed something was wrong. Seeing Magnolia in such distress was a stark contrast to the joyful and carefree person he cherished. His heart ached, realizing that his actions had contributed to her sorrow. He approached her gently and asked what was wrong. Searching his eyes for comfort and understanding, she spoke with sincerity;

"I can't do it. I just can't. I need my mother here with me. William Carl, I'm so sorry, but I can't."

He placed his hand tenderly on her shoulder, genuinely concerned.

"What can't you do?" he asked softly.

"I can't get married without my mother by my side. I know you mentioned we could have another ceremony later, but that wouldn't feel right to me. If you decide you don't want to marry me anymore, I understand, truly."

With that, William Carl walked past her in silence. Magnolia reached out to hold his arm, yearning to express her love, but she realized he needed space to process her decision. As he left, she remained on the bed, grappling with a mix of emotions and reflecting on her choices. She believed in her heart that once William Carl contemplated her words, he would come back to her, so when he didn't, doubt crept in, and anxiety overwhelmed her once more. What if he had disembarked from the boat, or worse, decided to never see her again? Though she felt the urge to seek him out, she chose to stay put. That night, she enjoyed a peaceful sleep that confirmed she had made the right choice.

The following morning, a knock on the door shattered her reverie. When she opened it, there stood William Carl, impeccably dressed, arms outstretched. The sight left her momentarily speechless, but the joy was undeniable, could it really be that the wedding was still on? Hesitating, she stared at his open arms, welcoming and warm. Summoning her courage, she took his arm and stepped into the hallway. But the moment he turned, her knees felt weak; there stood her mother, beaming with pride.

"You didn't think I would miss this special day, did you?" her mother exclaimed.

Magnolia stood frozen, her mouth agape, completely taken aback.

"Come here and give your momma a hug." her mother called warmly.

Though she intended to move, her body felt as if it had forgotten how. In a moment of dizziness, she collapsed. The next thing she knew, she was lying in bed with the ship's doctor hovering over her.

"What happened?" she murmured, still dazed.

"You took quite a fall," he explained, "but you'll be fine."

Once he left, she tried to piece together what had occurred. It felt as if someone had knocked the wind out of her. Then, the door swung open, and there he was again, still impeccably dressed. The sight of him brought back the memory, and she exclaimed,

257

"Where is she? I want to see her."

"She's waiting in the hallway. I wanted to check on you first," he reassured her. "You took a pretty hard hit when you fell.

"Please, tell her to come in. I want to see her now."

Her heart raced with anticipation. It felt as if this day was about to become even more extraordinary.

When the door swung open, there stood Edith, her face radiant with pride even as joyful tears streamed down her cheeks.

"Momma, I'm okay," Magnolia reassured her, a touch of lightheartedness in her tone.

"I know, baby. These tears are just overflowing because my daughter is getting married," Edith replied, her heart brimming with emotion.

In her excitement, Edith hadn't realized just how impactful this moment would be until she spotted William Carl standing in the doorway.

"Magnolia, you want to marry me, don't you?" he asked, his voice filled with hope.

Magnolia beamed that carefree smile he adored, playfully asking him to step out for a moment while she got ready. Without missing a beat, Edith gently guided him outside, her heart swelling with anticipation. Turning to her mother, Magnolia's eyes sparkled with disbelief.

"Mom, you're here. How did you know?" she exclaimed.

"Sweetheart, I've been in on this for a while now. I boarded the boat a couple of days ago after William Carl shared his wonderful plans with me. I thought it'd be a delightful surprise, but I didn't expect it to be such a shock for you." Edith said, her voice warm and encouraging.

"I was even willing to set aside my feelings to have you by my side for this special day. I wouldn't want to do this without you," Magnolia confessed, her sincerity layered in every word.

"You adore him, and he cherishes you. I truly believe you both would have found a way to make this work, no matter what. And now, it feels like I'm stepping into a new chapter, one where I'm not your whole world anymore," Edith remarked, her heart full of bittersweet emotion.

They shared a heartfelt embrace, and as Magnolia began preparing for the ceremony, the beauty of the moment enveloped them both. The wedding dress fit her like a dream. As Edith watched her daughter transform into a bride, a wave of realization washed over her; Magnolia was no longer just her baby; she was becoming a woman in her own right. Edith walked over and wrapped her arms around her daughter once more, creating a bubble of warmth around them, and they settled in for a heart-to-heart talk.

"Sweetheart, this is a new beginning. Being married comes with new responsibilities, and it will change things," Edith shared thoughtfully.

"Mom, I get it. I understand all about love and relationships. I adore William Carl in a way I never thought possible. He occupies my thoughts when he's not around, and I'm absolutely certain he's the right choice for me," Magnolia asserted confidently.

Curious, she asked her mother when she had learned about their plans. Edith explained that they had initially discussed the engagement weeks before her journey, but the wedding was meant to occur after she returned.

"A couple of days ago, a telegram arrived, asking me to meet the boat in Perryville. I had just one day to get everything ready; the train departed the next morning. I feel so fortunate to be here for you," she said, her voice brimming with love.

Tears glistened in Edith's eyes as she met Magnolia's gaze.

"I love you too, Momma. You've been such an incredible mother," Magnolia responded, her heart full.

Following the wedding, Edith chose to take the train home rather than travel by boat, feeling more at ease on solid ground. Even during the short ferry ride across the river, she couldn't help but keep her head down, carefully avoiding gazing at the water. The river held painful memories for her, a tragic moment from her childhood that still left a mark on her heart. She had witnessed a heartbreaking incident where a young girl fell into the river, and several family members went in after her, causing a cascade of disaster for an entire family. The sorrow of that event echoed through their neighborhood, leaving its residents mourning, when the bodies were never recovered. The surviving children had to live with their grandmother in Mississippi.

Since that day, Edith had harbored a deep-rooted fear of the river. She took every precaution to ensure Magnolia learned to swim and understood how to escape safely should she ever find herself in danger. Despite her love for her daughter, she never felt capable of jumping into the river to rescue her, but she remained determined to protect her as best she could.

Twenty-One

Whe Magnolia and William Carl, affectionately known as WC, returned home from their joyful broom-jumping ceremony, they settled in a cozy little house nestled at the back of his family's property. This new chapter in their lives was exciting, but Magnolia soon found herself facing a significant challenge. Used to having Edith take care of things, she realized with a shock that she didn't know how to cook. Standing in front of the stove, staring uncertainly at a raw egg in a buttered pan, she knew this had to change. She knew well that a delicious meal is the heart of a thriving family, and she was determined to master the art of cooking. After all, it was important that WC come home to something wonderful, rather than feeling the need to seek meals elsewhere after a long day's work.

In those early days of marriage, WC often found himself stopping by Grandma Reatha's house, drawn by the comfort of her cooking whenever he knew she had prepared one of his favorites. Although Edith generously brought over home-cooked meals, Magnolia was resolute; she believed it was vital for her to learn to create meals for her family. Recognizing her determination, Edith began visiting more often to guide her through the process of cooking. At times, she would invite Magnolia to her home, allowing her to watch and join in the preparation of special meals. Before long, WC realized the delightful truth; his wife was becoming a capable cook.

One day, as WC stepped through the door, something felt off. The inviting aromas of dinner were absent, a clear sign that something was amiss. One of the highlights of his day was entering their home, closing his eyes, inhaling deeply, and trying to guess the evening's meal, he loved that delightful anticipation. When he walked into the kitchen and saw an empty stove, anxiety began to seep in.

"Magnolia." he called out, and a faint sound from the bedroom caught his attention. As he approached, he found Magnolia still in bed, clad in her nightgown. Concern washed over him as he observed her stillness, and he rushed to her side, wrapping her in his arms and feeling the heat emanating from her body. In a flash, he grabbed a cloth and a pot, filled it with water, and returned to the bedroom. Gently, he placed the damp cloth on her forehead and wiped her down, relieved to feel her temperature beginning to cool. Magnolia had been trying to call for help, struggling to get out of bed, but her voice was muffled. She felt trapped, knowing rest was essential but feeling a strong pull to engage with her responsibilities.

After that incident, family members became more attentive, checking in on her frequently. A couple of months later, the joyous news emerged, Magnolia and WC were expecting their first child. However, the pregnancy presented its own set of challenges. Morning sickness was a constant battle, leaving her exhausted and uneasy at the mere sight of food; her body ached from the strain of it all. The doctor advised her to keep off her feet as much as possible, causing Edith to nearly move in. Yet, despite following medical advice, Magnolia found herself in the hospital a few times because staying still proved to be a struggle. Lying down was uncomfortable for her back, sitting up brought discomfort to her hips, and even walking felt torturous on her feet. This led her to realize that action was essential, both for herself and the well-being of her little one.

One of the toughest aspects of pregnancy for Magnolia was the dizziness. Standing often made the world spin, and she found herself grasping for support. Eventually, she discovered the trick of focusing on a stationary object, which helped ground her when bouts of dizziness struck. One sunny morning, feeling invigorated, she decided to spend time in her beloved flower garden. With a child on the way, she was eager to add some vegetables to the mix. However, as she bent down, the world around her suddenly shifted, leaving her momentarily disoriented. Before she knew it, she was lying on the ground, gazing up at the brilliant sun.

"Are you okay?" a concerned voice rang out from above.

Startled, Magnolia struggled to see who was speaking; the sun's brightness made it difficult. Just then, a sharp pain pierced her back.

"Don't move; someone will be here soon."

As her eyes began to drift shut, she fought against the urge to give in to sleep.

"It's okay; you will be alright," the voice reassured her, filling her with hope and comfort.

The next time Magnolia opened her eyes, she found herself in the familiarity of her own bed. As she tried to get up, a sharp pain shot through her head, feeling as though she had been struck. Instinctively, she called out for help, and WC, Edith, and Reatha hurried into the room. Cradling her stomach with anxious concern, Magnolia asked, "Is the baby okay?"

WC quickly reassured her, explaining that she had fallen in the backyard and sustained a cut on her head. This news left Magnolia wide-eyed with alarm. "Did I hurt the baby?" she asked, her heart racing.

With a calm demeanor, WC explained that if she hadn't quickly packed her wound with dirt and leaves, she could have been in real danger. Reflecting on his words, Magnolia recalled a reassuring voice that had comforted her during her ordeal. "Where is the old woman? She was right here, helping me," she questioned, pointing toward the spot where she remembered seeing her. However, as they all turned to look, they realized no one recognized who she was talking about.

It seemed that Magnolia had been alone on the ground, potentially in distress without anyone realizing the extent of her situation. WC had found her in the garden after returning home from work, and from that moment on, she was never left alone again.

Fast forward seven months into her pregnancy, Magnolia's world shifted once again when labor began in the early hours of the morning. With urgency, she was rushed to Charity Hospital, where the midwife had recommended delivery, anticipating possible complications. The doctor, recognizing the gravity of her situation, advised that she remain in the hospital for two weeks, emphasizing the importance of her health. There were concerns about her strength to safely give birth, and although a C-section was considered, the procedure posed significant risks. The doctor noted the high mortality rate associated with it and wanted to avoid unnecessary alarms.

Thankfully, on the first day of her ninth month, Magnolia managed to give birth naturally to a beautiful, healthy baby girl. However, she soon found herself battling severe illness. For a brief moment, her condition was critical, requiring an extended hospital stay as her body fluctuated through fevers and chills. Lacking the strength to stand, she struggled to hold or feed her newborn. In those moments, feelings of resentment occasionally washed over her, almost as if she were attributing her suffering to the baby's presence. Despite the doctors' efforts, they were at a loss for the cause of her illness, suggesting that time would help her recover.

When Magnolia finally returned home, she felt a disconnect from those around her, especially from her baby. The infant's cries seemed overwhelming, making her feel more burdened than bonded.

One day, as Edith prepared lunch in the kitchen, she heard the baby wailing and instinctively paused, hoping Magnolia would respond. When it became evident that she wouldn't, Edith put aside her tasks to tend to the baby. In that moment, it dawned on Edith that the support they had offered Magnolia might have been counterproductive. Therefore, she decided it was time to step back, allowing Magnolia the space to embrace her new role as a mother.

Before leaving, Edith gently explained to Magnolia that she needed to take a step back, to give her the necessary room to bond with her child. Magnolia sat quietly, gazing out the window, her silence speaking volumes. Just as Edith was about to leave, Magnolia asked her to visit Reatha and bring her to the house for the baby. While Edith agreed to this request, her true intention was to invite Reatha to stay with her, hoping to encourage Magnolia to take on more responsibility.

Reatha, however, was concerned about the baby's well-being if Magnolia was left unattended. Nonetheless, Edith felt confident that Magnolia would rise to the occasion and take charge as a mother. They had been supportive long enough, and now it was time for her to step up. With a sense of hope, they believed that by the time WC returned in a few weeks, everything would be better, and Magnolia would flourish in her new role.

After Edith left, Magnolia eagerly anticipated Reatha's arrival to lend a hand. When the baby began to cry, she felt a surge of uncertainty. She lovingly lifted her up, rocked her gently, changed her diaper, and fed her, yet nothing seemed to soothe her little one. Overwhelmed by the situation,

Magnolia laid the baby down with determination to seek help. She knocked on Reatha's door but received no response, so she confidently decided to walk down the road to find her mother.

As she walked, a wave of fatigue washed over her, prompting her to pause and sit under the comforting shade of a tree. Sweat trickled down her face on what was undoubtedly one of the hottest days in recent memory. Sitting beneath the magnolia tree, she raised her head toward the sky, closed her eyes, and took a deep breath. The warm air, filled with the sweet aroma of magnolia flowers, transported her back to the carefree days of her childhood. Suddenly, a vital realization struck her; the baby was home alone in the heat.

With urgency igniting her spirit, Magnolia quickened her pace, the echo of her baby's cries resonating in her thoughts. As she began to run, her mother's house came into view, and she took a moment to remind herself, "I don't live here anymore; I need to go home and care for my baby."

She spun around, nearly losing her balance, and sprinted back home with determination. It felt like the more she ran, the farther away her house appeared. Exhausted but resolute, she silently prayed for the strength to reach her precious baby girl. The sound of the baby's cries filled the woods around her, fueling her resolve. With her head down, she pumped her arms and ran with all her might.

Finally reaching her house, she kicked open the door and rushed into the room where her baby lay in the bed, still crying. Magnolia hurried over, lifted her child into her arms, and cradled her close, gently rocking her while whispering promises of love and protection. "I'll always be here for you," she vowed, making a heartfelt commitment to be the best mother she could be.

As she sat there, tears of joy clouding her vision, rocking her sweet baby, Magnolia recognized just how precious her child was and how special the opportunity of motherhood truly was, nurturing one of God's little angels. As she gazed at her little one, a thought struck her, this beautiful baby needed a name.

With a smile, she declared, "I'm going to name you Caroline."

In that transformative moment, a wave of maternal love filled Magnolia's heart, a love so profound that she hadn't experienced it from anyone else. Tears of joy continued to flow as she held her baby, feeling a deep sense of connection. Instinctively, the baby relaxed, sensing the warmth and unconditional love encircling her.

The following day, Magnolia decided to visit her mother and was delighted to find Reatha there as well. Although she didn't need to say thank you, she felt grateful for their support every step of the way. Picking up her baby, she turned to the two women and joyfully announced, "I present to you your granddaughter and your great-granddaughter, Caroline."

Their faces lit up with delight upon hearing the name. Edith prepared some refreshing iced tea, and the three of them settled on the porch, engaging in heartfelt conversations. Magnolia had always yearned to partake in the adults' discussions, and now she embraced her new role, she was one of them.

When WC's boat finally docked, he was pleasantly surprised to see his wife and daughter waiting for him. Magnolia couldn't help but chuckle as she watched him nearly leap off the boat before it fully stopped, enthusiastically pointing at them and sharing his excitement with everyone around. His reaction warmed her heart; he had often advised her to stay away from the docks, explaining that sometimes boats ran late, leading to long, anxious waits. He had seen the worry etched on the faces of women waiting, fearing that something terrible might have happened.

This time, however, Magnolia felt it was important to share the joyous news of her and the baby's well-being as soon as possible. It was a moment worth celebrating, and she was excited to show him just how wonderful their new life together was.

As he stepped off the boat, he sprinted towards them with such excitement that she couldn't help but worry about him knocking them over if he didn't slow down. As he drew closer, she closed her eyes, bracing herself for the impact. When nothing happened, she cracked open one eye, only to discover that he had sidestepped to stand proudly behind them. She turned her head, searching for him until he gently tapped her on the shoulder. When she turned around, she found him beaming with joy, like a proud father witnessing his child for the very first time. He leaned in to plant a big kiss on her and then showered the baby with affection. With joyous enthusiasm, he lifted their little one high toward the sky and proclaimed,

"This is my baby girl, her name is..."

He paused, looking at Magnolia, who sweetly whispered,

"Caroline."

"Her name is Caroline. Isn't she the most beautiful thing you've ever seen?"

The excitement was infectious, and soon, everyone who had been on the boat came rushing over to catch a glimpse of the precious baby. In that moment, it was crystal clear, he was the proudest father in the world.

When WC wasn't busy on the boat, you could find him seated under a magnolia tree, sipping on refreshing lemonade, with his daughter playing nearby. They often set up a delightful tea party, complete with a charming table and chairs, where they dressed up and enjoyed each other's company.

WC adored fatherhood. So, when Magnolia shared the wonderful news that she was expecting their second child, his joy was boundless. Whenever people asked what he hoped for, he would casually say that it didn't matter. But deep down, he cherished the dream of having a son. What father wouldn't want a little companion to share in the joys of fishing, baseball, and building amazing things together? These dreams filled his heart. Having a son would allow him to relive cherished moments from his own childhood, play the games he loved, and teach him lessons learned through experience, guiding him towards manhood.

The journey of the second pregnancy felt so much smoother than the first. Magnolia experienced very little morning sickness and managed to keep her weight gain in check compared to her experience with Caroline. Her happiness radiated this time around. She truly cherished her visits to her mother. Over the years, they had grown so close that they felt more like sisters. Edith couldn't have been prouder of her daughter and instantly declared Caroline the most beautiful child she had ever seen. When Edith learned that Magnolia was pregnant again, a flood of memories from the first pregnancy washed over her. Yet she quickly found reassurance in the knowledge that Magnolia was stronger this time. It was evident that she already loved the baby before its arrival, a profound feeling that was different from her first experience.

One sunny day, on her way to Edith's house, Magnolia felt a powerful kick from the baby. She paused for a moment, hoping for another reassuring movement. When it didn't come, she continued on her path. Midway there, a sharp pain struck her side, urging her to pick up the pace. Then, another jolt hit, and she found herself dropping to her knees, glancing at Caroline's worried face. With a warm smile, she asked,

"Sweetheart, do you know where Grandma lives?"

Caroline pointed eagerly up the road.

"Do you think you could go get Grandma all by yourself?"

Caroline nodded vigorously.

"Alright, darling, go get Grandma, quick."

After Caroline dashed off, Magnolia crawled over to a nearby tree to wait until help arrived. When another wave of pain surged through her, she couldn't help but cry out, musing an old saying; If a tree falls in the woods and no one hears it, does it make a sound? If not, what happens to that sound?

As she lost herself in thought, another powerful wave hit, pulling a shout from her lips. She heard footsteps approaching and called out,

"I'm over here; I need help."

When she spotted her mother, relief flooded over her. But then, a twinge of concern struck her when she noticed that Caroline wasn't with Edith.

"Where is my baby? I sent her to find you. Where is she?"

Magnolia's heart raced with concern as her mother attempted to comfort her.

"Where is my baby? You need to go find Caroline." she urged, full of urgency.

Just then, another wave of pain surged through her, forcing her to sit down and take a deep breath.

"Caroline is safe; she's at my house," her mother reassured her, gently calming her frantic spirit.

With those words, a cry of relief escaped Magnolia's lips. Edith smiled softly, letting her know the midwife was on her way. She had anticipated this moment and knew that her instinct was right.

Settling beneath the comforting shade of the tree, Magnolia managed to embrace the pain while waiting with her mother. As they spotted the midwife approaching, a surge of relief washed over both women.

Magnolia welcomed a beautiful baby boy into the world, naming him William. Her heart swelled with anticipation as she thought of WC returning home, knowing he would be overjoyed. When the boat's arrival drew near, Magnolia, Caroline, and the newborn made their way to the docks to greet him. In the distance, they could see the boat, as Caroline playfully explored the rocky shore while they waited.

As the boat sailed closer, Magnolia called out to Caroline, urging her to join her. Facing the approaching vessel, Caroline turned back, her eyes sparkling with excitement. When she spotted WC, she couldn't contain her joy, bouncing up and down and tugging at her mother's dress as she shouted,

"Daddy, Daddy."

Magnolia stood firm, a mixture of emotions brewing within her. Caroline's exuberance only grew as she continued to jump in delight.

"Momma, it's Daddy. He's back."

Magnolia remained focused, but the anticipation was palpable. As WC stood on the boat's deck, he noticed her reaction and instinctively felt a surge of hope and excitement.

"Honey. Honey."

When she still didn't look his way, a wave of worry hit him, making him race towards the gate, fearing the worst. But then, the moment Magnolia turned, he was swept away by a rush of joyous relief as he saw his beloved family together. His heart brimmed with happiness, tears of joy rolling down his cheeks and a smile radiant enough to light up the distance between them.

"Is it a boy or a girl?" he inquired eagerly.

When she didn't respond right away, the realization dawned on him.

"It's a boy, isn't it? I have a son."

Magnolia's expression spoke volumes, confirming his every hope.

"I knew it. I just knew we were having a boy. he exclaimed jubilantly.

Caroline dashed into her father's arms, who twirled her around in glee. He then approached Magnolia, gently pulling back the blanket to catch a glimpse of their son before kissing her tenderly. On their journey home, Magnolia excitedly recounted the details of the birth and beamed with pride for Caroline, who had stepped up to help in such a meaningful way.

TheirStory

Twenty-Two

Magnolia and her family had been one of the families who reap the rewards from being free and industrious Negros during the time when most was in bondage. It wasn't uncommon to pass by her home, and see neighbors sitting on her porch resting a spell, or drinking a cold drink, or sometimes even eating a meal. Things began to change; a lot of people were out of work, but she was one of the fortunate ones because WC still had a little work. These were hard times for everyone in the country.

After Caroline was born, Magnolia planted a vegetable garden and when the joblessness and homelessness started getting severe, she enlarged the garden. On the weekends, Magnolia loved carrying some of her prize vegetables to the French Market to sell. People always made a commotion over her produce, trying to get the techniques she used to grow such a beautiful and plentiful harvest. Her tomatoes were redder and juicier than everyone's, the onions were sweeter and most people had never seen red, orange and yellow bell peppers before. All of the produce would be sold almost before she finished setting up.

By the time the great depression was in full force, they had two children. WC was not working as steady as he once did and money was short. Because of Magnolia's garden, she had enough food to eat with left overs that she could trade. People quietly made trades. Within the community, commodities had become the new money and Magnolia's family seemed to be doing ok under that system. It was said that in some towns during the night people were so desperate they would ravish the farms, steal the livestock, and vegetables, and then destroy the land. Magnolia was worried because in some cases the mob would be so intense the people would kill and everything in sight would be burned. People from other places started coming to their town looking for work on the docks. The docks had always been a good place for a Negro to find back breaking, honest work, but times were hard for everyone, and white men began taking those jobs that at one time they would not have given a second thought.

Not only were Negros being forced out of work, but they also were being forced out of the area. If you didn't own your home, and you lived near the dock, it was a sure bet that you would be forced to move because the new workers needed to live nearby. The Negros were forced to move to backatown. The land wasn't owned by anyone and most of it was swamp. It was thought to be dead land because nothing would grow on it, not even grass. Fortunately, Magnolia and her family owned their land, and it didn't seem to bother her new neighbors that they lived there, mainly because the man who hired most of the people that worked on the docks was their friend, and he often visited them. Magnolia found out that he was a Negro that was passing. His granddaddy was a mulatto who married a white woman. He was not raised to be ashamed of his heritage, but he understood what he needed to do. As often as he could, he would bring WC into work. If people started complaining, he would let him go, and when things would calm, he would bring him back.

The depression was in full swing; everyone was out of work. It seemed like the government couldn't do anything but feed you. There was no work for anyone, Negros, Whites, Frenchmen, no one. Farms were being attacked all around them. Because of it, Magnolia had stopped growing vegetables to sell, only enough for the family. They had very little livestock, so they figured everything would be ok, and the bandits wouldn't think of attacking their little piece of land.

When this type of behavior began getting close to their home, Magnolia decided to stop gardening all together, and let it be known. The bandits were stealing anything they could get to trade, and if they thought you had food they would come in the darkness. On Saturday's she would go to the market to purchase potatoes, people were surprised to see her there. She explained that her land was no good for vegetables anymore. She planted stuff but nothing came up. People knew if all you were buying was potatoes then there was nothing at your house to steal.

Later that year the bandits hit their area, their home was spared, but others lost livestock, and their gardens were destroyed. The people in the neighborhood got together to see what could be done to protect their land and families. At the meeting, they were surprised to see the white families participating. That put the Negros on edge. People were afraid to speak because they didn't know if the bandits were sitting in the room with them. All that Whites had put Negros through, they were not willing to trust them, not yet. Some got up and left, but WC wanted to see what it was all about. They talked about arming themselves, some wanted to get the law involved, a couple heard that there was work up north and thought it was time for them to leave the area. WC thought it was strange to hear a white man say that things were better up north because to him, north meant freedom and that the white man always had freedom, so why run north. What would he gain? Later that night, a couple of people that were at the meeting were targeted. It was obvious that at least one of the bandits lived among them, so everyone knew they had to be careful of what they did and said.

There was almost no food to be bought, and even if there was food no one was making money. WC, who had loved going hunting with his father, started hunting again. Every day he went out, he came back with plenty of meat. Most of the time it would be small squirrels, possums, raccoons or nutria rats, but on a rare occasion, he would drag home a wild boar, which meant a feast for everyone.

Magnolia remembered the first time WC came home with a boar. He had been gone all day, and it was beginning to get dark. She was worried about him, and using her wild imagination she thought that perhaps the bandits had killed him, taken his catch, and she didn't know what to do. Then she heard something moving around outback but was too afraid to go to the window; she grabbed the children and went to the room that was below the floor. WC had dug the hole and created the room when the white people began running all the Negros out of the area. The room was about six feet by six feet, with a tunnel that you had to slide on your belly, which lead you to safety. She and her children sat in the room listening for the signal. They had signals to do certain things. If you heard a whistle, it meant to leave through the tunnel, a knock on the wall meant that everything was ok, and if she didn't hear anything stay put.

Magnolia sat listening, then heard it, someone was tapping on the house. She told the children to be quiet, she would return, and if she didn't, she wanted them to go through the tunnel. When looking out of the window, she saw him standing outside. She ran out and jumped into his arms.

You're back; I thought something had happened to you. Where have you been?

Before he could answer, she jumped into his arms once again.

I was so afraid.

Magnolia remembered the children were in the room, and that she told them if she didn't return to leave through the tunnel. She ran back into the house and down to the room just in time to see Caroline's feet hanging out of the tunnel and yelled for them to come back. When she went back up, WC was still standing outside. She asked him why he wasn't in the house. He pointed to the ground. She hadn't noticed the large boar that was at his feet. He told her that he would have to skin and clean it before morning. She was happy and scared because if the word got out that they had that much meat they were sure to be in trouble. WC knew that he had to have a plan by morning. He gutted, cleaned and portioned the meat. By morning he had a plan of how he was going to quietly distribute the extra meat to the rest of his neighbors because the last thing he wanted was the bandits to know about his catch. From time to time, some of the neighbors would go hunting with him and they would have a neighborhood party if the catch was plentiful. They invited everyone, that way the bandits would think that there was nothing left to steal.

Things slowly began getting better for people as they adjusted their lives for the depression. Magnolia was able to start her garden again, and people were once again selling their harvest at the French Market. The steamboats began cruising the Mississippi again, so WC was able to get more hours. When he got home, he talked about all the places he had visited and that up north things were getting back to normal. There was a lot of building going on, and those jobs were paying more money. He thought that he should go and earn some of that money then come back home. Magnolia thought it wasn't a good idea because they were doing fine. He explained to her that they needed to have money saved to protect themselves and their children. He was going to go and find some work and come home on weekends. There was nothing Magnolia could do or say to stop him.

When WC first started working for a construction company, he was happy. When he first saw a professional drawing, he knew he would be able to do that job. He hadn't realized that he was a great carpenter; when his work was compared to others, he knew he was among the best. He had been drawing structures for as long as he could remember, never thinking that someday he would be able to make money doing it. He became very valuable to the company in a short time. His layouts and designs of buildings were unique, and no other carpenter of his day even came close to his expertise. All of his buildings were designed with hidden vaults. In the beginning, he would put them under the building like he had in his home, a room that no one knew about, and then he thought of creative ways of putting them on different floors. A cabinet might become the doorway to a secret room or maybe a bookcase would have a tunnel leading to outside. In one case, the entrance to the secret room was under a desk.

On a particular Saturday, Magnolia was very upset with WC because he hadn't been home in two weekends. She was very worried about him and had no way of knowing how to find him. It wasn't uncommon for men to leave for a better job and never be seen again. When he finally returned, she got up early to cook breakfast. Trying to wake him from what appeared to be a deep sleep, she slammed doors and banged pots; while hoping he would come to see what was going on, but he didn't. Magnolia was convinced that she had reasons to be upset. And he was hoping that she let off some steam before he went out there. Her vivid imagination was in full force, and she was determined to stay mad until they talked face to face because if he wanted to be with his new family she was going to find out that morning.

When she turned around, Caroline and WC Junior were standing in the doorway rubbing their eyes. Magnolia told them to go and wash up because breakfast would be ready soon. Just seeing them standing there calmed her. She realized that in order to get this resolved she would have to talk to WC. When she returned to the bedroom, he was sitting on the bed with his head hung between his knees. She knew that something was wrong, and that he had chosen the other family to be with. All of a sudden, she could feel the sadness overcoming her. She looked at him with tears running down her face.

How could you, how could you do this to your family? I love you and your children love you. Why are you doing this to us?

He snapped his head up to face her.

Woman, what are you talking about?

He got down on one knee in front of her, with his hand behind his back.

Happy anniversary, I love you.

She stood there staring at him but not reacting. It was as if her brain was confused and didn't hear a word he was saying because she was expecting something else. When her eyes focused, he had four tickets in his hand.

Honey, happy anniversary, you and the children are coming to Chicago with me. I have a week off, so I can show you all around the town.

She dropped to one knee and he gently placed his hand behind her head.

I love you.

She heard the children scurrying about the house, so she gave him a kiss and returned to the kitchen. He followed tapping her on the behind all the way there. When they all sat down to eat, she told them that their father had some very good news. When he told them about the trip, they jumped out of their seats and ran over to him and gave him big hugs and kisses. They were yelling,

When are we going, when are we going to the big city? Will we ride the train or take the boat to the big city?

Magnolia stared at WC to hear the answer to the questions. When he said the train will be leaving at the end of the week, the children started yelling,

We're taking the train.

WC Jr. yelled, we're taking the train; I love the train.

All week long, the children were running around excited about this new adventure. They were playing all types of train related games. Lawmen and robber seemed to be their favorite. WC Jr. loved being the robber. Caroline would run him down, catch him, tie him up, and take him to jail. He would be fussing all the way as she laughed at the mess he'd gotten himself in. Living near the train they heard it coming every day but this time was different because soon they would be passengers. All week when the train was coming, Caroline and WC Jr. would jump, scream, and hug each other. By the day of the trip, they were so exhausted from anticipation that they almost slept through it all.

Magnolia was amazed by the city, so many big buildings and so much noise. People were everywhere, one of the things she liked doing was people watching. Magnolia knew if she lived there, she would not be able to get anything done. That evening he took her and the children to a fancy large one room restaurant. When they walked in, they were surprised that all the people who were working were dressed in what looked like their Sunday best. If she would have known, she would have dressed her and the children differently.

The owner of the restaurant name was Viola. Magnolia told her that her grandmother had a sister named Viola. The women asked where her people were from. Magnolia told her that the family started out in Mississippi but through the years, they traveled throughout the United States. Viola said that as far as she knew, her people had only lived in South Carolina. Magnolia enjoyed the meal, and the children acted as if they hadn't eaten in weeks. Viola told her about a big park that was nearby for the children to play, and that her daughter could show them where the park was.

When they first got to the park, the children didn't know what to do. Caroline asked her mother where the colored section was. She was old enough to know before you even thought about playing in a park you needed to know your boundaries. Magnolia had to explain to Caroline that in Chicago she could run and play all over the park. She would never forget the smile on her daughter's face. As she ran away, Caroline yelled to her brother.

We're free to play anywhere, we're free.

She had not realized how Jim Crow had affected her children. They had to sit in the back of the streetcar, watch white folks let their dogs drink from the water fountain labeled Colored Only, not able to try on their clothes or shoes in the department stores, or sit in a restaurant that white folks attended was out of the question, even if it was owned by someone who was colored. Magnolia felt a tear running down her face; she thought that it must have been the way Negros felt when they got the word that they were free and wondered how many of her generations will have to be set free.

When they returned home, she told everyone about Chicago. How there were no colored only signs, children could play in the entire park, and you didn't have to get on and off the bus. She hadn't realized what kind of bondage people in the Deep South was forced to live under, and for a moment wanted to live in Chicago, but realized she loved her city, and hoped that someday things would be better there.

Nine months after the trip to Chicago, Magnolia gave birth to a baby girl who they named Charity. Magnolia was happy because things were going great for the family once again. WC was still working in Chicago, but not as much. There were less and less jobs there. There were new jobs that were popping up all over the south for colored men, like work offshore. WC decided to come back home to find work. Magnolia was not happy because people were talking about the lack of safety and all of the accidents that occurred off shore. He explained that he needed the work, and they needed the money, so he took the job. He wasn't on the job three months when he fell and broke his back. If you had an accident like that, you were put in God's hands because there was nothing, they could do for you. Sometime people fully recovered and other times they didn't, all you could do was pray and wait to see where you fit in.

It took him a year to be able to move around without anyone's help. He was one of the lucky ones, he recovered physically, but he was hooked on the medications. When the doctor stopped prescribing the medicine, he turned to alcohol. Magnolia watched her loving husband become an alcoholic, and there was nothing she could do about it. When she got pregnant with their fourth child, he stopped drinking and went back to work on the boat. She named her Lillian; every one called her Baby Lillian for a long time. Baby Lillian was different from all the other children; she loved being under Magnolia. When all the children were out having fun, running through the wooded area, swimming in the pond, you could find her hanging on to her mother's dress tail. Magnolia tried everything to separate, to get her to be with her brother and sisters, but nothing worked she loved being with her mother.

Twenty-Three

During Edith's illness, she made the heartfelt decision to move in with her daughter, which brought them all together during a tough time. With WC back at work on the Queen Mary, he often found himself away for weeks at a stretch, but he always returned with vibrant stories of his journeys. He would share exciting tales of incredible places and how people of color were shaping the ever-evolving landscape of America. Magnolia adored listening to him spin stories, as they sparked fond memories of her own storytelling days, moments she hadn't revisited in quite some time. As WC described the sights, smells, and sounds of his adventures, Magnolia would close her eyes and let her imagination take flight. Sometimes, he would suggest she consider moving up north, and while she found some of those place's fascinating, her heart was firmly rooted in New Orleans.

When WC returned home, it was always for a fleeting couple of weeks before the call of the river beckoned him away again. However, tragedy struck when his grandmother, Reatha, fell gravely ill and passed away unexpectedly. Unfortunately, he was unreachable during this difficult time. Once the ship docked, spotting Magnolia standing with the children made his heart sink, something was clearly amiss. At first, worry washed over him; he instinctively counted the children to ensure they were all present. As a river worker, he understood the haunting fear of losing a child, a heartbreaking reality that was far too common. He took a deep breath, and once he counted the children, a dreadful realization struck him; his pain was related to his beloved grandmother. Covering his mouth in shock, he closed his eyes, briefly feeling her comforting spirit nearby. She had gone to rest, a comforting place she often spoke of with warmth.

Once he disembarked, he quickly noticed Magnolia looked unwell, barely able to stand. Rushing to her side, he caught her as she nearly crumbled into his arms, feeling her frail frame against him. Concerned, he sought to understand the situation, and the children informed him of their great-grandma Reatha's passing and how their mother had been caring for Grandma Edith. Though they had done their best, it hadn't been enough, so WC gently carried Magnolia home, determined to nurture her back to health.

After a week of rest, Magnolia was slowly regaining her strength and was excited to care for her family once again. WC, full of love and commitment, declared he would no longer leave; his family needed him nearby. Yet, Magnolia, wise and understanding, insisted that he still had to work to provide for them, especially since her small vegetable garden couldn't fully support their needs.

When the time came for him to return to the river, WC found himself unable to leave; the situation at home had become too precarious. Feeling a heavy burden of protection resting on his shoulders, he knew it was vital for him to remain close, especially with the doctor delivering heartbreaking news about Magnolia's mother. The diagnosis of cancer, with no treatment options available, weighed heavily on them all. All they could do was provide tenderness, support, and hopeful prayers that Edith would not suffer.

Undeterred by her circumstances, Edith resolved to take action and began cultivating her own garden, growing an impressive array of beautiful vegetables. She nurtured everything from the simplest crops to vibrant produce and generously shared whatever she couldn't use. Despite the pain that sometimes radiated through her as she tended to the garden, she never let it extinguish her spirit. With fierce determination, she would shake her fists toward the heavens, defiantly declaring, "Not yet; I'm not finished, not yet."

In this challenging time, their family came together with unwavering strength, love, and resilience, nurturing hope for brighter days ahead. They were bound by their commitment to one another, determined to face whatever came next as a united front. In the light of adversity, their shared hope and love illuminated even the darkest moments, reminding them all that life, despite its challenges, is filled with beautiful possibilities.

After taking a six-month break from work, WC felt a strong urge to return, especially with the boat scheduled to come back into town. He was pleasantly surprised to discover that his job had been saved. While he was grateful to be welcomed back, he learned that his salary would be halved. Though perplexed by the cut, he chose not to question it; he was just thankful for the opportunity to get back to work.

This recent journey had been particularly challenging for WC. He witnessed the crew, predominantly Black men, facing harsh treatment that felt reminiscent of past injustices, with some even forced to engage in fights for the amusement of white gamblers. With alcohol flowing freely and gambling prevalent, WC found himself stuck in an atmosphere he found troubling. Despite the negative circumstances, he did take solace in his skill as a gambler, a talent that gave him a slight edge. Magnolia, was unaware of the pay cut but could sense a change in him, and she found it difficult to accept this new version of him.

Meanwhile, Magnolia could see her mother, Edith, showing signs of slowing down during her doctor visits. Each time, the doctor assured Edith that she was on the right track, yet Magnolia observed a decline in her mother's energy and vitality. When they worked together in the garden, a cherished activity for both, Edith shared her heartfelt wish that Magnolia would teach the children how to cultivate their food, expressing a belief that self-sufficiency in nourishment was paramount. After offering this wisdom, Edith mentioned feeling tired and decided to take a nap, wrapping Magnolia in a warm hug before retreating into the house.

Left alone in the garden, Magnolia felt a knot of anxiety tighten in her chest. She feared that if she went inside, she might discover the worst, that Edith had passed away. In an effort to keep her mother close, Magnolia busied herself outside, tilling the soil and nurturing the plants. Suddenly, a loud commotion erupted from the house, a cacophony that sounded alarmingly like her children crying. Heart racing, she sprinted inside, her mind spiraling with worry. She envisioned worst-case scenarios; her mother on the floor, her life fading away, or possibly injured and in pain, her face twisted in anguish.

Yet, as she burst through the door, she was met with a sight that filled her heart with warmth and relief. There was Edith, sitting on the floor, joyfully tickling the children, their cries not those of distress but bursts of laughter! One child giggled and asked, "Momma, what's wrong with you? Why are you crying?" The absurdity of the moment struck Magnolia, and she couldn't help but join in, laughter bubbling up from deep within her. She settled on the floor beside her mother and the children, sharing an unexpectedly joyful moment of unity and love.

Later, Magnolia confided in Edith about her fears. She had interpreted their earlier gardening discussion as her mother's way of imparting final wisdom, convinced that Edith would soon pass. She had braced herself for the heart-wrenching reality of losing her mother.

Conversely, Edith had harbored similar thoughts, expecting to retreat inside to her final moments. Yet, as she opened her eyes to find the children playing, she felt an irresistible pull to join their joyful chaos. Regardless of how much time she had left, she recognized the value of sharing those precious moments with her daughter and grandchildren. Together, they often engaged in games that brought laughter and camaraderie, reminding them all of the beauty of life. Magnolia delighted in witnessing her mother, once again a source of joyous energy, playing those classic childhood games and hearing delights like, "Tic-tag, you're it!" as Edith joyously ran around the house.

Through this season of uncertainty, Magnolia and Edith discovered the importance of cherishing the precious present and celebrating the love that bound them together. Embracing each day, they found strength and joy in one another's company, transforming fear into laughter and despair into moments of pure happiness.

Her mother, astounded everyone by living two years longer than the doctors had initially expected. In her final days, she shared with Magnolia that the happiest moment in her life was the day Magnolia was born. She beamed with pride about her daughter and the entire family. Edith's love was profound; she cherished her own parents, relatives, and husband deeply, but nothing compared to the overwhelming affection she felt for her grandchildren.

When Edith passed away on a rainy day, a day she always treasured, it felt like a poignant farewell. She often said there was nothing quite as soothing as lying in bed, listening to the gentle patter of rain on the tin roof, those moments brought her such peace. For Magnolia, this was an incredibly challenging time as she had to prepare for a funeral while her husband, WC, was away. As he arrived at the dock and caught sight of Magnolia and the children, he immediately understood the gravity of the situation without needing to count heads. Magnolia bravely shared with him how her mother had been during her last months. Although the thought of losing her mom was heartbreaking, she felt a sense of tranquility. Edith had once told Magnolia that she had made her reservation for the afterlife years ago, so it was merely a matter of time before she would be called.

During this period, Magnolia noticed some changes in her husband, WC. She reached out to him, hoping to understand what he was feeling, but he remained distant. Instead, he began volunteering to work on his days off, and when he was home, he often spent his time at the docks. Then one day, a light seemed to return to his eyes. He excitedly shared that he had decided to leave his job on the boat, explaining that he felt the work environment was becoming toxic for men of color. WC had been hired as a foreman for a crew doing repairs on docked boats. Magnolia loved this change. Knowing he would be home regularly for dinner made her heart feel lighter. Unfortunately, like before, that job didn't last.

Determined to support her family, Magnolia resumed selling extra vegetables at the French Market. Thankfully, things at home appeared to be improving. WC started working at the shipyard with reliable hours, enjoying a steady eight-hour workday and weekends off. Every evening, he made it home in time for family dinners. There were moments when Magnolia would indulge in a bit of extra rest, especially knowing that her daughter, Caroline, loved to cook. However, one morning, Magnolia woke up feeling unwell. That day, Caroline took the reins and prepared breakfast for everyone. After the family meal, the children went off to school, WC left for work, and Lillian snuggled beside Magnolia for a bit more comfort. WC felt a sliver of concern but suspected it was that time of year when sickness was prevalent, so he encouraged Magnolia to rest, confident she would feel better by evening.

As the day dragged on, Magnolia felt too weak to even rise from her bed. Each hour stretched on, feeling like an eternity. By the time the children returned home, Magnolia knew she needed to seek help and urgently called them to fetch assistance to go to the hospital. When WC arrived home, he found the house eerily quiet with no one around. Assuming Magnolia had dashed out to the store, he settled in to wait. But after about half an hour, a wave of panic washed over him. Where could his family be? Venturing outside, he spotted the children returning home, and as soon as they saw him, they rushed toward him in tears. His heart sank when he heard one of them cry out, "Momma is in the hospital!"

The weight of those words sent his heart plummeting.

"Is she okay? What did the doctor say?" he asked urgently.

"She was asleep when we left. The doctor told us to go home and tell you to get to the hospital as soon as possible."

Rushing to reassure his children, he instructed them to head inside before setting off towards the hospital at a frantic pace. Unable to wait for the bus, he ran the entire way, fear gripping him that he might be too late. Once he reached the hospital, he hurriedly inquired about Magnolia's condition. The doctor, although serious, soon delivered unexpected news.

"Your wife is very ill, I'm sorry to say," the doctor began, before pausing to look at WC with a smile, "but congratulations. She's pregnant."

WC stared in shock, confusion washing over him. He couldn't comprehend why the doctor was smiling when Magnolia was so sick. But seeing the doctor's genuine joy, he felt a of hope mixed with disbelief. "Congratulations! Your wife is having a baby!" the doctor reiterated, shaking WC's hand.

In that moment, amidst the fear and uncertainty, a flicker of hope ignited in his heart. Life was ready to bring them another gift amidst the trials they were facing, and he would be there for his family, no matter what lay ahead.

WC stood in disbelief; his expression frozen as the doctor delivered the remarkable news. Moments later, he felt his grip on reality loosening, and a surge of joy swept over him. Suddenly, a broad smile illuminated his face, and he exclaimed with pure excitement,

"My wife is going to have a baby! Can you believe it? My wife is going to have a baby!"

In an overwhelming display of joy, he scooped the doctor up into a surprise twirl.

"Is my wife going to be alright?"

With a touch of humor, the doctor replied, "Could you please put me down? Your wife will be perfectly fine; we're just going to keep her for a couple of days for observations."

Anxious to see her, WC quickly asked where she was, and the doctor pointed towards her room. With eagerness in his heart, WC dashed down the hallway. When he entered, he found her sitting up, glowing in her own beautiful way. In that moment, she radiated the youthful spirit that had initially captured his heart.

"The doctor told you, didn't he?" she asked, her face lighting up.

"Yes! We're going to have a baby?" he replied, still in awe.

"Is this alright at our age?" she asked, a hint of concern in her voice.

"You're hardly over thirty-five! My mom had me when she was forty! What are you worried about?" he responded, grinning.

"I thought I was done having children," she confessed.

"You're going to be great; I know you will!"

After spending a few tender moments together, WC began to make his way home, as the children were eager for his return. He shared the exciting news with them, and they erupted in joy, jumping around and singing a catchy tune Caroline had crafted. Their lively celebration paused momentarily when they asked whether they were having a boy or a girl. Before he could even respond, WC Jr. confidently declared they should have a boy since they already had two lovely girls. WC gently explained that the gender of the baby didn't depend on how many siblings there were, and that they wouldn't know anything until the baby arrived. He reminded them that when their mother came home, they should be extra helpful, as she would surely need their love and support.

When Magnolia finally returned home from the hospital, she felt as though she had stepped into a new world. Their children had taken the initiative to clean the house from top to bottom, and though everything was perfectly in place, she couldn't ignore the turbulence her pregnancy was causing. She reminisced about her first pregnancy, which now felt like a delightful stroll compared to the challenges she faced with this one. That little one inside her seemed to be full of energy from the start, and as she reached five months, reality struck and she had to go on bed rest. Fear crept in as she worried for both her own health and that of her baby.

WC became her unwavering support system, doing everything in his power to keep her spirits high, although it never felt quite enough. He often reminded the kids to be patient and understanding, explaining that their mother's unusual moods were simply the result of her pregnancy. He encouraged them to think about how it would feel to be instructed to stay in bed for an entire day. Initially, the children's expressions suggested they thought it would be a dream come true, until he explained that it meant no playing outside with friends or attending school. With those thoughts in mind, they quickly understood just how tough it could be.

Magnolia longed for the end of her pregnancy. As the ninth month rolled around, she buzzed with excitement, knowing the baby could arrive at any moment. She had her heart set on welcoming the little one at the very start of the month. The first day came and went, then the second, and two weeks later, patience was wearing thin. By the third week, she was so eager she almost imagined cutting the baby out herself at this point. Concerned, she decided to visit the doctor to ensure everything was alright. Her vivid imagination led her to believe that the doctor might possess a magical method to force the little one out.

When she expressed her worries to the doctor, he glanced at WC, who stood attentively beside her. With a knowing look, WC silently communicated, "What can I do?" But deep down, they both felt the excitement of what was to come.

As the doctor brought Magnolia into the examination room, he knew this was an important moment for her and her family. After a thorough examination, he sat down with WC to discuss Magnolia's current situation. WC expressed his concern, saying that if Magnolia didn't give birth soon, she would become increasingly distressed. The doctor listened attentively and advised that the best course of action would be to keep her in the hospital overnight for monitoring and tests to ensure everything was proceeding smoothly.

That night, as the house settled into a tranquil quiet, the family couldn't quite grasp how deeply Magnolia's condition had impacted their everyday lives. The next day, when she returned home from the hospital, emotions ran high as Magnolia was understandably irritable. It was a challenging atmosphere, and her anger made it difficult for everyone to engage positively. Caroline and WC Jr. found themselves staying after school to tackle their homework, knowing that finding peace at home was a hurdle during this time.

On the last day of the month, a beautiful moment arrived; Magnolia gave birth to a precious baby girl. However, as soon as the doctor placed the baby on her chest, a wave of worry washed over Magnolia. She could hear the baby's struggle to breathe, and when she looked up to the doctor and the nurses, their solemn faces confirmed her deepest fears; this little one was fighting for survival. In that profound moment, looking down at her newborn, Magnolia felt an overwhelming understanding that her family, including her mother and grandmother, was eagerly waiting to embrace this innocent life. As the baby took her last breath, Magnolia experienced a transformative realization that she would cope and be okay.

Life moved on, and Magnolia embraced her role as a loving mother, always encouraging her children as they blossomed into independent adults. She cheered them on as they ventured off to college, entered into marriages, and started families of their own. The family's recent heartbreak came when Lillian's daughter disappeared, which ignited a deep desire in Magnolia to become a more loving and engaged grandmother, cherishing every moment with her family.

In her role as a grandmother, she thrived as a storyteller, bringing joy to her grandchildren through her enchanting tales. The pure delight on their faces as she spun stories, both from her past and those woven from her imagination, filled her with a deep sense of fulfillment.

One night, Magnolia was in a dream like state, she finds herself sitting peacefully on her porch. She noticed an elderly woman making her way up the street. Although she didn't recognize her, an inexplicable feeling told Magnolia that this visitor had come to connect with her. Upon introducing herself as Isza, the woman's name triggered memories in Magnolia, who welcomed her with warmth and kindness. By this point, Magnolia had become accustomed to the visits from old friends sharing TheirStory before moving on to their next destination.

Isza shared that she had traveled a significant distance to recount her own story. After enjoying some refreshing lemonade together, she remembered her last visit to the cabin, expressing her surprise that it still stood. Recalling her feelings of exhaustion and confusion from her earlier visit, Isza reminisced about lying down in the corner by the window, just as she had done in years past. Suddenly, a knock echoed through the house and startled her. Answering the door, she was thrilled to see Viola and Paul standing there. Though Isza felt a bit faint, she welcomed them in warmly, eager to hear their stories of what transpired after they were sold. They shared how, tragically, they had passed away just days apart in 1860, and assured Isza that she was never alone. Their pride in her resilience and their joy in knowing their children had found freedom radiated from their words.

Then came another knock, this time it was Clara, Magnolia's grandmother whom Isza hadn't seen since Teacee's wedding. Clara expressed her bewilderment at not being able to locate the house after everyone had left, as if it had vanished. Isza comforted her, reassuring Clara that if she needed the home, it would reveal itself when the time was right.

Before long, the rhythmic knock echoed again, signaling the arrival of Teacee and Baby. Teacee shared joyous updates about her life, mentioning how she successfully raised Baby in Atlanta, where they enjoyed a sense of freedom. They had worked on a plantation but had the liberty to leave at will. When circumstances shifted, they proudly moved into their own home and built a happy life together. Baby chimed in, sharing exciting news about her family; after relocating to New York, she welcomed a son and a daughter into the world. Isza beamed with pride as Baby revealed that her son went on to become a doctor, while her daughter embraced a new life in Africa, raising a remarkable family of eight girls.

Through these heartfelt exchanges, a sense of connection and continuity filled the air, weaving together the lives and stories of past and present, underscoring the strength and love within Magnolia's spirited family.

The next gentle knock at the door was from Picola. With a warm smile, she shared how Isza had impacted her life, enabling her to raise two vibrant boys who blossomed into incredible fathers. It was a beautiful moment of gratitude, reflecting on a life filled with fulfillment and joy.

Soon after, another knock echoed from the sisters Isza had dearly missed; Viola, May, and Hilda. Their spirits were bright, radiating happiness just to be reunited, bringing warmth to Isza's heart.

Then, a final knock startled Isza, and she instinctively knew it was Mae. There was a comforting thought that Mae would reassure her that the search for understanding was over, that everything was well, and it was time to rest peacefully.

With a mix of anticipation and excitement, Isza opened the door, only to be surprised by a lovely old woman standing before her. Glancing around for Mae, she stepped back to invite the woman inside, curiosity swirling in her mind. As they settled in, Isza found herself drawn to the old woman's eyes, feeling an unexplainable connection that made it hard to look away.

"Momma, it's me! It's really me!" the woman exclaimed.

"Momma? What do you mean?" Isza replied, confusion and wonder mingling in her voice.

"Look closely; you know me."

"Mae, is that truly you?" Isza asked, incredulous.

"How is this even possible? You've aged so beautifully!" she exclaimed in disbelief.

"I've embraced a long, healthy life, and I've been eagerly awaiting your return home," Mae said with warmth.

In an instant, they embraced, a heartfelt reunion filled with love, before they stepped out together, hand in hand, ready to embark on a new journey.

Suddenly, Magnolia found herself wandering down a winding dirt road. Disoriented, she pondered how she had arrived there and where it might lead. It felt almost dreamlike. As she walked, the faint cries of a baby broke through the tranquility. Peering around, she saw no one and continued her path, curiosity guiding her.

Before long, a quaint little house appeared, and through the window, she spotted a child sitting quietly in the corner. Instantly, recognition flooded her heart; it was her long-lost little one.

"Momma, I've been waiting for you!" the child called out.

"I'm here, my baby! I'm finally here!" Magnolia responded joyfully.

As she turned around, everyone she cherished stood there, arms outstretched and hearts open, welcoming her home with unconditional love.

www.ingramcontent.com/pod-product-compliance
Lightning Source LLC
Chambersburg PA
CBHW060532180626
46817CB00002B/529